CLEARWATER

CLEARWATER

KIM McCULLOUGH

COTEAU BOOKS

Edited by Kathryn Cole
Designed by Tania Craan
Typeset by Susan Buck
Printed and bound in Canada by Imprimerie Gauvin

Library and Archives Canada Cataloguing in Publication

McCullough, Kim, 1971-, author
        Clearwater / Kim McCullough.

Issued in print and electronic formats.
ISBN 978-1-55050-565-8 (pbk.).--ISBN 978-1-55050-566-5 (pdf).--
ISBN 978-1-55050-750-8 (epub).--ISBN 978-1-55050-751-5 (mobi)

I. Title.

PS8625.C865C54 2013   C813'.6   C2013-904962-2
                                                C2013-904963-0

2517 Victoria Avenue
Regina, Saskatchewan
Canada S4P 0T2
www.coteaubooks.com

Available in Canada from:
Publishers Group Canada
2440 Viking Way
Richmond, British Columbia
Canada   V6V 1N2

10 9 8 7 6 5 4 3 2 1

Coteau Books gratefully acknowledges the financial support of its publishing program by: the Saskatchewan Arts Board, The Canada Council for the Arts, the Government of Canada through the Canada Book Fund and the Government of Saskatchewan through the Creative Industry Growth and Sustainability program of the Ministry of Parks, Culture and Sport.

For

Brothers and Sisters –
Caelan & Delaney
and
Kelley & Dustin

with love

THRUST

ONE

Northern Manitoba
May, 1983

Framed by the window of my sister Leah's tiny Chevette, the sky is an ink-dark canvas held in place at its bottom edge by the pointed tops of even blacker spruce trees.

Halfway between our old life in Regina, and our new home at an airport community on the shores of Clearwater Lake, the emptiness framed by my window is a perfect picture of how I feel about our move. I search above the jagged treeline for the moon or a star, the flashing lights of an airplane or a satellite, anything to anchor me. Nothing.

I stretch my legs out as far as I can, grateful to take my turn up front and be free of the cramped back seat that has held me prisoner since we left. Beside me, Leah sits hunched over the steering wheel, her hands firm at ten-and-two. The lights from the dash highlight the anger on her face.

Leah's twin, Daniel, is crammed in the seat behind her, his long legs bent at awkward angles. Stacked next to him are the clothes that Leah laid out from her closet, not trusting the movers with her wardrobe. I look back to see my brother shove the teetering pile of sweaters, jeans, blouses and jackets away from him. He slips on his headphones and turns on his portable cassette player. There really isn't room for him back there, as Leah well knew when she pulled over and kicked him into the back seat after their last argument.

Leah dragged out our departure so long that we now drive this deserted northern highway in the dark. The twins have sniped at each other and argued off and on the whole way: Leah sending her venomous comments flying at my brother; Daniel lobbing single-word answers back at her. She's still pissed at him for agreeing to this move. In the fall, the twins will start their last year of high school, and Leah is furious at losing the best year of her life by moving to the last outpost of hell, as she calls it.

I turn back to my window and wish again that I'd travelled with Mom. She left yesterday to get the house ready and to meet the movers when they showed up. She went ahead to make sure the furniture, especially Daniel's piano, arrived in good condition. However, she was in one of her I-need-my-space moods and made it pretty clear that she'd rather I travel with Leah and Daniel.

Not that they wanted me. Leah didn't even wait for me to leave the room before she lit into Mom, making it clear that she didn't want to babysit me. I'll be sixteen on my next birthday – only two years behind the twins, but they treat me like I'm twelve. But Mom wasn't having any of it. She wanted time to herself, whatever the cost to the rest of us, and so Leah's pleas fell on deaf ears.

My mom was excited about the government job in northern Manitoba as soon as she heard about it. Good pay, a cheap place to live and a fast-track chance for a government posting once the two-year term is up. A promising move not just for her, she claimed, but for us, as well. Her descriptions of the clear, blue lake and wilderness made it sound pretty inviting. Canoeing and fishing and swimming within walking distance.

Leah refused to go.

Finally worn down, my mom worked it out with my grandparents that my brother and sister would stay behind, and only I would make the move to the small community a half-hour outside of The Pas.

Then Mom asked Daniel to come with her when she went up to scout the place out. He came home and announced that he, too, would be moving.

Never before had Daniel made a decision without consulting Leah. Disagreement is rare between the twins.

Now, for the third time since leaving Regina, Leah picks up the argument that landed my brother in the back seat. "If it weren't for Daniel wanting to get in touch with his inner lumberjack, we wouldn't even consider this."

The *we* doesn't really include me. It never does.

"He's ruining my life."

"I can still hear you, Leah." Daniel scowls at me. "What are you looking at?"

Leah goes on, but Daniel turns up the volume on the cassette player so loud, even I can hear it. Mozart, I think.

When I look again, his head is back and his eyes are closed. His fingers flash pale against the dark seat as they tap out the complicated notes of the piece.

Once Daniel made it clear he wanted to move, Leah had no choice but to agree. She wouldn't stay behind without him. Those two are inseparable.

I'm just relieved I'm not going alone. Unfortunately, it's only one year before the two of them will be off to university, leaving me on my own with my mother. Petra Sullivan is notorious for not being around when she's needed.

We drive in silence for a while.

When she finally speaks again, Leah sounds like she wants to cry. "All that stuff about camping and fishing and hiking. Give me a break. All he cares about is playing the damn piano, and he can do that anywhere."

I stay out of it. I've learned the hard way not to take sides. Anyway, it's done. We're all moving. There's nothing left to say.

I do understand why Leah is upset, though. The truth is that our new home isn't even a real place. It's so unofficial, it can't be found on a map. Mom says everyone there works for the government – meteorologists, air traffic controllers, maintenance workers. And the water quality researcher she'll be replacing.

I tilt my head back toward the window. Still black, still empty. Still.

The headlights illuminate a desolate corridor split by a pitted line of yellow paint. The trees next to the pavement seem to sidle close enough to grab me, should I dare to reach a hand out my window. Far ahead, the road disappears into the dark forest at the tip of the narrowing triangle of asphalt.

My eyes are drawn to a glowing sign on the right side of the highway. I squint as I read the words out loud.

"Sixty seconds to Orbit. What does that mean?"

My brother and sister ignore me.

A sign every two hundred metres or so counts down. Fifty seconds. Forty seconds.

Before we reach the next sign, a snowy owl enters the sweep of our headlights. I recognize it right away: majestic white wings spread wide in flight; dark banding; large eyes in a rounded head.

Leah slams on the brakes and wrenches the steering wheel to the right. I brace myself on the dashboard in front of me, my fingernails digging into hard plastic. Leah's arm shoots out and nails me in the chest as the great bird hits the front of the car with a thump.

From the corner of my eye, I see Daniel throw his hands up.

Too late.

His face smacks into the back of Leah's headrest. His headphones fall to the floor as he clutches his nose.

"What the hell?" Dark blood seeps through his fingers, covers his wrist and drips onto his white T-shirt. "Kleenex?" Daniel's voice is muffled.

Leah hands him the whole box. "Everyone okay?" Her voice quavers.

"Not the owl," I say.

With shaking hands, Leah reaches past my knees and grabs a flashlight from the glove compartment. She steps out onto the empty highway and slams her door. She checks the front of the car first, then walks along the ditch looking for the bird. My eyes track the beam of the flashlight as it picks out the owl about ten metres back, lying along the edge of the road. I move onto my knees and watch Leah bend over the owl. I barely glance at Daniel as he fumbles one-handed for the latch that will release the seat in front of him. The tissues he has pressed to his face do little good.

The owl is much bigger than I thought. The grand bird lies still in the weak spotlight, feathers ruffled, head turned toward the car. Its golden eyes gleam, even as Leah turns back toward us. Though the glow from the tail lights washes the owl in red, the blood on its feathers is as black as oil.

Daniel pushes the seatback forward with his elbow and gets out Leah's door. I can't see their faces, but I can see Daniel's hand on his twin's shoulder.

"You okay?" His voice is muffled and nasal.

"It's dead," Leah says.

"I'm driving." Daniel leans in. "Get in the back, Claire."

I clamber between the two seats as my brother settles behind the wheel.

Leah walks around the front of the car and takes my place. Her pale face reflects the dim greenish light from the dashboard as she clicks the seat belt into place.

"Let's just get home, okay?" says Daniel. He tosses his bloody tissues on the dashboard and reaches for more as he pulls back onto the highway.

"Right. Home." Leah laughs, a shrill, shaky sound, and runs her fingers through her tangled hair. "That scared the hell out of me."

All the anger has slipped from Daniel's voice. "Well, the car's okay. We're fine, Leah."

In the wake of the accident, the twins are friends again.

I lean against my sister's clothes, the faint scent of Leah's perfume in my nose. I curl my legs underneath me and rest my cheek, wet with tears, on my arm.

Any thoughts of entering orbit have flown, and I close my eyes against what I've seen.

I'm certain that as Leah walked away, that dead owl blinked.

 Jeff stands in his room in front of his easel, glad to be free of the tension downstairs. Now that all the moving in next door is done, the other side of the duplex is quiet, and he can hear his father bitching at his mom as they watch TV.

He slouches to dab a final bit of seagull grey on the canvas in front of him. His mom bought him the easel for his eleventh birthday, five years ago, and it's too short for him. His dad says he won't waste the money on another, and Jeff can't see spending his own savings on a new one. Two more years and he'll be gone to art school. He can't wait to get out of this place.

Earlier that day, he'd watched the movers as he helped his mom in her garden. He wondered why anyone would ever choose to come here, especially teenagers, if the rumours around the airport were true.

It had been a good afternoon. It isn't often Jeff can spend time with his mother without his dad haranguing them. But with school letting out for summer at noon, Jeff had her to himself until his father was done work.

Jeff unloaded the bags of manure-rich soil his dad had picked up in town, then helped his mom spread it around the tiny green shoots that struggle to grow in the rock-hard dirt patch in the backyard. *A month in the ground, and all that thrives are the potato plants and the lettuce. But somehow she'll bring it around.* It took a lot of work to grow anything in this place, but Jeff figured his mom liked it that way. *Keeps her mind off living with the old man.*

Jeff worked on the far side of the garden, away from where Rita's long, black braid swung from side to side with her efforts. She stopped often to wipe the sweat out of her dark, shadowed eyes. As he shovelled, he kept an eye on the four movers next door. They shuttled furniture down the ramp attached to the back of the moving truck to the other side of the duplex. Every so often, a blonde woman came out of the house to check on their progress, then disappeared back inside.

It was late afternoon when they rolled a piano to the edge of the truck. Jeff and Rita stopped working to watch.

"Good afternoon, Rita!"

Jeff forced the blade of his shovel into the hard-packed earth a little harder than he needed to. He'd recognize that voice anywhere. Janet Vronsky, out for her daily walk. Never once had she invited his mother to join her, but she sure didn't mind stopping to spew gossip.

It pissed him off how Rita kept her head down as she greeted Janet.

"So you're getting a new neighbour. Her name's Petra, whatever kind of name that is. You better watch your man, Rita. I hear she's single. Though with three teenagers as part of the deal, I don't know who'd be interested."

His mom didn't even pretend to laugh.

Next door, the movers eased the old upright piano down the ramp, its wheels sticking and groaning. Two men moved in front of the piano to slow its descent, and then the other two took over and pushed it up the pitted walk beside the driveway. It took all four men to transfer it to a skid to get it up the three steps at the back door.

"No one's ever moved a piano in there before," Rita said. His mom would know. She'd seen a lot of people come and go over the years.

Janet stepped away from the fence, ready to carry on. "Well, we could do with a musician around here. Jazz up the Christmas and spring concerts."

"Yes," said Rita. "Wouldn't that be nice?"

Now, Jeff switches to a narrower brush and searches through his box of paints. With the sun gone from the sky, the overhead light in his room casts odd shadows on the canvas, but he paints anyway. He mixes colours – Prussian and cobalt blues, some brilliant white and a touch of manganese violet – and listens to the sound of the CBC news downstairs in the living room.

Although Janet had pretty much summed up the gossip going around the airport about the new family, Jeff's dad put it more bluntly when he came home for supper.

"Three teenagers and no husband. Crazy bitch." Jake Carlson shook his head and pointed his fork at Jeff's mom. "Take it from me, Rita, you're lucky you have me. You could never make it as a single mother."

Angry words of protest welled up in Jeff, but knowing better, he pushed them down.

He'd rather see his mom destitute and on the street than watch her stick around here while his father sucked every drop of life out of her.

His father's fork took aim at him. "I bet those kids are assholes, with no father to tell them how to behave. You watch yourself, boy."

It was always easier to agree than argue.

But his dad wasn't done. "I've got it all settled at work. Jeff's going to work with me on the morning shift," Jake said. "There's going to be no lazing around at the lake this summer. Monday morning, boy. First thing."

His mom tried to lighten the mood. "Jeff did quite well on his report card. Would you like to see it?"

"I'm eating, Rita. I'll look later."

Jeff was glad his dad let it go.

His mom doesn't understand why he hates school so much. Jeff's tried to explain it to her, but she just doesn't get how much effort it takes. It's not the actual school work, as much as the balancing act. He has to keep his marks up high enough that his dad stays off his back, but not so high that the teachers think he's some kind of prodigy. In elementary school and junior high, no one really cared that he got good marks, but after six weeks at the high school, the teachers all had some kind of meeting and called his parents in. It pissed him off. Much easier to be average. He never wants to hear another infuriating lecture on his so-called potential. The teachers wouldn't make such a big deal of it if he weren't half native. The white kids are expected to do well. Teachers only seem surprised when it's the kids with browner skin who succeed.

Even his own father was shocked by how well Jeff did that first term. "You must get those smarts from me, boy."

Yeah, right.

So now, Jeff just works on his art and on flying under the radar until he can finish school and get out of this place.

Jeff steps back to assess his painting. *Not bad, but it's too dark in here. I'll have to quit soon.*

Downstairs, Knowlton Nash's newsman voice is drowned out by the sound of Jake harping on Rita, but as soon as the TV is turned off, Jeff will have less than a minute to hit his light switch and make it to bed in time to pretend to be sleeping.

If his dad sees his light on, he might come in and want to have another of his so-called man-to-man talks; those endless sermons that usually consist of his dad's drunken, rehashed remembrances of their past hunting and fishing trips if he's in a good mood, or complaints about the length of Jeff's hair if he's not.

Three different shades of blue stain Jeff's fingers. He's painting the lake across the highway again, still trying to get the colour just right. So far it's been an impossible task. The lake has too many moods: bright blue and practically glowing on sunny days; menacing and dark on cloudy days. Close to shore, the water is as clear as glass; farther out, lake and sky meet in a collision of indigo.

Downstairs, the TV is turned off. Jeff makes the circuit from easel to light switch to bed in record time. Footsteps hesitate outside his room, but they are soft. His mom. Then, the purposeful stomp of his dad climbing the stairs. He hears his mom move on up the hall. Jeff's thankful when his father goes into the bathroom and slams the door shut.

The wet paint on Jeff's fingers sticks to the sheets. His mom won't be mad, though. She won't say anything. She pretends, like he does, that everything is just fine.

TWO

I kick at the broken lower rungs of the red iron railing on the back step as I wait for Daniel and Leah. With all of us helping Mom, the house was unpacked and set up in no time. She released us from our chores, and now the three of us have all morning to check the place out.

Our new house is a duplex, the last building on what could loosely be called a block. The back step where I wait isn't even a true back step, because the door is actually on the side of the house. It opens onto a wide concrete platform with stairs on both ends. One set of steps leads to the driveway and main road, the other points toward the front of the house. I've already taken a look out there and discovered a deserted gravel road that runs in front of all the homes. It loops around just past the empty clearing next to our yard and joins up with the main asphalt road out back.

Past the curve is a section of chain-link fence. That must be the runway. My mom told me jets land here twice a day, but it's quiet now.

No matter which way I look, my sightline ends with trees. Everywhere, trees.

The morning sun barely warms the air, and I wish I'd worn something warmer than shorts and a T-shirt. A quick stab of homesickness for the hot, yellow summer mornings back in Regina pierces me.

The screen door bangs open and the twins come out. Daniel doesn't say a word, just walks by like he doesn't see me. I follow Leah to the car, but my sister stops before she opens the driver's door.

"We're going to go on our own." Leah's voice is soft, but it doesn't blunt the message.

"Sure." I step back. "Okay."

Leah hesitates. "We'll come back for you, Claire. We just want to go check the place out. We want to be on our own for a bit."

Of course they do.

I drop my gaze to the front of the car. Caught in the grille is a long, white feather. I reach out and pull it, but it sticks to the mess of bug guts and owl blood, and only half of it comes away. I close my fist around it.

Leah gets into the driver's seat. She brakes as she's backing out and waves. Daniel doesn't even bother.

I walk down to the end of the driveway and watch them go. They turn left off the street, then make another quick left onto the highway. Gone.

I look at the faded rainbow of houses that line our side of the street. They're twelve to a side, with no pattern to the colours, just a motley jumble of pale blues, yellows and greens. Our house is a squat Pepto-Bismol-hued duplex. The rest of the houses on this side are tall and thin. Directly opposite, there is a treed-in lot followed by a row of smaller, white, cottage-style homes that stand firm in the face of the pastel assault from across the way. Every yard is surrounded by a chain-link fence. I'm struck again by the fact that it is the plain backs of the houses that face each other across the paved road.

I walk a little way up the street to take a closer look at the lot across the way. It's the only one screened by spruce and poplar trees. I stand at the bottom of the cracked driveway. Other than this apron of asphalt slowly being reclaimed by long grass, there is nothing there. No house, no chain-link. Just emptiness.

"That was the Bug Man's place."

I spin around. A tall, lanky teenager stands there, a little older than I am, sixteen, maybe seventeen. He has collar-length, nearly black hair and blue, blue eyes. He wears dark jeans and a navy hooded sweatshirt. He's not smiling.

"I'm Jeff Carlson. I live in the other side of your duplex." He gestures behind him.

My voice shakes a bit as I introduce myself. "Claire Sullivan." I tuck the owl feather in my pocket and wipe my hand on my shorts before I hold it out for him to shake.

"We just moved in." Stupid, so stupid. I wish I could take it back. "I mean, obviously." I swallow. "My mom is here to do water testing at the lake."

He nods. "I know. Everyone knows. Word gets around." He turns to walk back to his house. "They left you behind, hey?"

"They usually do." I stifle a sigh and fall in behind him.

In his driveway, a red dirt bike rests on its kickstand, engine exposed. Parts and tools and bolts are scattered beside it. The manual lies open on the step. I glance at it.

"Changing the plug?"

He looks over at me. "Yeah. It's stuck, though." He picks up a socket wrench, crouches down and fits it over the spark plug. He leans on it, but it doesn't budge. "Help me out?"

I stand behind him and put my hands over his. His head is right below mine; I can smell his hair, sweaty and a little sweet. On his count of three, I push down, and with the added force, the plug comes loose with a bump. I bang my chin on his head.

He swears.

"Sorry."

Jeff rubs his head. "It's okay. Thanks."

I tip the new plug from its box into my hand. "Do you have a gapper?"

He digs in his tool box until he finds the right tool. He hands it to me and watches as I check the manual for the specifications. I slide out the proper size gauge and measure the gap. Once I have it adjusted, I hand the spark plug back to him. He raises his eyebrows.

"I took mechanics at school this year. I had to get special permission because I'm a girl." I shrug and put my hands into my pockets. "I'm not really the home ec type."

A quick smile, just a flash of white teeth. "Let's get this thing put back together. If it runs, I'll take you for a ride. You don't need a car to get to the cool places around here, anyway."

The bike starts on the third try. I get on behind Jeff and loop my arms around his waist. I sit back on the seat and try not to let my legs touch him. As soon as he puts the bike in gear and takes off, though, I have to grab on tight. I settle against him, his back warm against my chest. His jeans chafe my bare legs.

We drive out past my place, skirt the edge of my yard, then cross the gravel road that runs in front of the houses and enter a large field. Jeff opens the throttle, and we jounce and bump along past a green shack toward a small group of grey houses. Jeff slows down and raises his voice to be heard over the engine.

"Three families live over here, too. That apartment building over there houses some of the single guys who work with my dad in maintenance." He speeds up and drives through a ditch and up onto the main road. "The airport was a US Forces base a long time ago, and there used to be a hospital across from the hall."

In the distance I can see the yellow-orange tail of a plane above a narrow, cube-like building. I grasp his shirt tight in one hand and point with the other.

"Water bomber, for putting out forest fires. You'll see a lot of it this summer, probably."

I read the signs on the buildings as we pass: Aerofuel, Airport Terminal, Northwood Hall. It's like a little town. Off-road again, we head toward a tall water tower and a long, low building. Curling rink.

"Do you curl?" I ask.

Jeff brings the bike to a stop. "All the airport kids curl at least once a year. There's a big junior bonspiel in February." He motions behind us. "Back there at the hall, we have a Christmas concert every year, and a spring concert, too. The little kids like it. Some dance, some play piano, some do drama."

"What do you do?"

"I watch."

Jeff twists the throttle and speeds up a trail next to the curling rink. Up and down trails, pale dust flying, he shows me the layout of the airport, my new home.

We cross the highway and head along a power line. I grip Jeff's waist as we bump across a worn path into a field littered with chunks of cement. Straight ahead stands a ruined red-brick building covered with black spray paint accented in Day-Glo pink and orange. *Keep out. Clayton was here. Class of '81.* Every window is smashed and the front doors hang from bent hinges. Jeff brings the bike to a stop at the base of the chipped concrete steps.

"What is this place?" I get off the bike.

"The old residential school. They used to round up Indians and make them come to school here."

I have a picture in my head of men on horseback with guns, harrying children, herding them as though they were cattle or sheep, forcing them into trucks and onto train cars. When I tell Jeff this, he nods, his face grave.

"I think you're not too far off."

"Let's go in," I say.

Jeff takes his time setting the kickstand on the bike. He follows me up the cracked, grey front steps.

Before us lies a large, open room. A sea of green trees can be seen through the missing windows on the far wall. The filthy carpet has been torn up in places, exposing the bare wood beneath. The walls have yellowed, but above the door, there is a pale patch of paint in the shape of a cross where a crucifix once hung. The third leg on a three-legged table in the corner is bent, and the table tips forward, as though forced to kneel. A cardboard Peace on Earth sign, similar to the one my grandma hangs over her TV every year at Christmas, is pinned to the wall above the table. Instead of glossy blue and silver foil letters that reflect light, the sign is dull, covered in dust.

I shiver. Whatever bravado brought me in here has disappeared. It's cold out of the sun. Beneath the scent of musty carpet and urine, lurks something darker. I force myself to follow Jeff down a long hall. Frail wooden doors open to the right and left. I peek into the rooms as we walk to the far end. Old mattresses and bed frames are propped against walls; papers and broken glass are strewn all over the floor.

We come to stand side by side in the doorway of the last room before the staircase. Inside, a dead duck lies on the floor, the illusion of life created by thousands of writhing maggots. I gag at the stench of death and hurry down the hall to the front door. I sit on the top step with my head on my knees and wait for Jeff to come out.

Jeff is quiet as he sits next to me. I lift my head and gaze out at the field.

"It's creepy."

Jeff takes a deep breath. "My mom says unhappy spirits gather in this place." He looks at me. "I'm actually not supposed to come here."

"It's not like I'm going to tell."

"I know."

I gesture to the field. "Were there other buildings there?"

"Yeah, those are foundations of the homes of the powers that be." Jeff stands. "People moved some of those old buildings to the lake to use as cabins."

I think about this. I can't imagine a time that this place would have been welcoming. Homey.

Then I think about the duck, and touch the owl feather in my pocket. It's my second dead bird in twenty-four hours. I tell Jeff about the owl, as we descend the stairs back to the curved front drive.

"My mom would say that's a sign." He doesn't say if it's a good sign or bad sign, and I don't ask. Jeff gets on the bike and starts it. He motions for me to get on. He seems impatient and a little annoyed. "Come on."

As we take off, I tighten my arms around him and close my eyes. I rest my forehead against his back, out of the wind. The engine whines in my ears and lulls me into a feeling of calm. It's the first time I've felt settled since leaving Regina.

When I open my eyes and peek around his shoulder, I see that we've returned to our street at the opposite end from where we live. People are out now, but Jeff doesn't stop to introduce me to anyone. Men doing yardwork look up as we pass. Children playing do not.

Jeff drives up to his house and kills the engine.

"Thanks for the tour," I say, as I get off the bike.

Jeff sets the kickstand and bends down to pick up the tools we left on the step. "Sure."

We both look up at the sound of the creaking spring on his back door. A thin man comes out and stands on the step, hands on his hips. His face is all angles, sharp and lean. His fair hair is shot through with strands of grey, but the blue of his eyes is an exact match to the colour of Jeff's.

He glares at Jeff. "You left a goddamn mess." His tone is icy. "Next time you clean your shit up before you go running around."

"Okay." Jeff's voice is tight, closed. His cheeks redden. He doesn't look at his father. Or at me.

"Okay, what?"

"Okay, I will, Dad." No inflection, no hint of emotion. The air around us has soured and thickened with tension.

Jeff's father turns his gaze my way, and I feel pinned in place. I wait for a reaction, a sign from Jeff, but there's nothing. He just stares at the ground.

"Claire."

I jump, startled, but I've never been so relieved to hear Leah's voice. She stands at the edge of our overgrown garden, her slender arms resting on the chain-link fence that divides the lot in two. Her straight, pale hair blows in the breeze. Her blue eyes are narrowed, her jaw set as she glares at Jeff's dad. In a brave move, my sister raises her hand and waves at him.

His mouth puckers like he's tasted something sour. He turns and goes back into the house, the door snapping closed behind him.

Leah says a polite hello to Jeff, then nods at me. "It's almost lunch-time."

I can't believe I've been gone so long.

I start to walk away, then stop. I want to tell Jeff I'm sorry he got into trouble, but he's still not looking at me. "Hey. Do you want to come eat with us?"

Jeff glances up at his kitchen window. A woman stands there in shadow, arms crossed. His mother, I guess.

"Better not," he says in a soft voice. He hesitates. "I could meet you after, for a bit." He looks up at the house again. "Which is your room?"

I point to the large window on the left. "I share with my sister."

Jeff nods.

"Our house is a mirror of yours. That's my room." He gestures to the window right next to mine. A ghost of a smile touches his lips. "One-thirty, then? We can meet at the Bug Man's place."

After lunch, Jeff decides to leave the bike behind, so they walk. Since it's warmer out now, he's changed into shorts and a T-shirt.

He leads Claire down a faint path between the Bug Man's lot and the first white house. They cross the deserted highway and descend into a grove of aspen. Soft green tamarack and prickly black spruce tower over them.

Jeff walks, sure-footed, down a twisting trail with Claire following close behind. As the trees fall away at the edge of the lake, she stumbles to a stop.

"Oh my God."

Jeff looks out at the view, knowing what she's taking in: the impossible range of colour that lies before them. From water so crystal clear at his feet that he can see every tiny black-and-white stone on the pale, sandy bottom; to where it blazes into a luminous turquoise blue, then deepens into a dark indigo strip where the lake meets the pale sky on the horizon. The lake is empty, not a boat in sight; just a wide, liquid expanse of crystalline beauty. He never tires of it, and he never tires of seeing people's first reactions to it. The look of shock on Claire's face doesn't disappoint.

"I know, hey?" They stand close enough to each other that his arm brushes against hers, but she doesn't seem to notice. "You're lucky to see it for the first time on a sunny day. But it's still beautiful when it's cloudy. You'll see."

"Lakes are green and thick where I come from. This is something else."

He points out a jetty off to their right. "That's the pumphouse – the water for the airport comes from there – and the boat launch. Some people go fishing down there."

"But you don't?"

"My mom says not to."

She looks up at him. "Bad spirits?"

Jeff can't tell if she's making fun of him. He shrugs and gestures the other way. "Back toward the turnoff to town there's the Cove, and a bunch of cabins. You can kind of see them from those rocks."

They make their way along the shore to where huge silver-black outcroppings of rock lie.

"They look like they were stacked there by a giant," Claire says.

"A giant glacier." Jeff hops up on a slab and reaches down to her. She brushes his hand aside and climbs up on her own. They sit next to one another and gaze out at the water. A loon swims into view.

"My mom went to a residential school. Not that one, though." Jeff has never told anyone this.

She's quiet and he can tell she's studying him.

"Does she ever tell you what it was like?"

"No. And I know better than to ask. She's from Churchill though, and has lots of stories about polar bears."

The loon's plaintive call breaks into the quiet awkwardness.

Claire clears her throat. "Do you go to the high school in town?"

He nods. "Grade eleven in the fall, thank God. What about you?"

"Yeah. Going into grade ten. I'm a little nervous." She rests her hand on his arm. It's warm. "You'll be there in the fall, then?"

"I'll be there." His words are sharper than he means them to be. He shifts and looks out at the lake.

"What's it like?"

"It's school," he says, like it's something that must be borne. "I'm glad I don't have to think about it for two months." He hopes she takes the hint.

Claire nods. "Yeah, well, I think school is pretty fun."

"Especially when they let you take auto mech?" He nudges her with his elbow.

"And science. Hey, maybe you can answer this for me. Last night on the way here, I saw a sign about 'orbit.' What does that mean?"

Jeff bursts out laughing. "They're garbage cans at the rest stops. There's one on Highway 10 at the 287 turnoff."

The loon, startled by the sudden noise of Jeff's laugh, flaps its way to an ungainly takeoff.

Claire shakes her head. "Graceful."

Jeff looks down at her. "Grace doesn't figure into it. A loon is built for diving, not flight. Sometimes I watch them and wonder how they ever get off the water when nature works so hard against them."

They watch as the loon flies overhead and disappears in the direction of the airport.

"Do you want to swim?" He pulls off his shirt. He slips off his runners and socks and slides into the lake without a flinch.

Claire reaches down and begins untying her shoes. "I'll put my feet in."

"Be careful. You might freeze them. The ice has been off the lake for less than a month. It doesn't really warm up until mid-July."

She peels off her socks and sticks them into her shoes and jumps into the water, sucking in her breath at the cold. The water is past her knees. "It's deeper than it looks."

"This isn't some warm Saskatchewan slough. It can be dangerous here." He's in to his waist now.

"What about you? Aren't you cold?"

He looks back. She leans against the rock, watching him.

"Nah. I'm used to it. I'm usually in a week after the ice is off. I grew up here, Claire."

It's kind of a lie. It's cold, all right, and as always, his first dive under seems to freeze the breath in his lungs and turn his heart into stone. But he never lets this stop him, and he pushes through, his arms and legs propelling him to the first of three sandbars, where the water barely reaches his thighs. He turns and calls to her. "Come on out!"

Claire laughs and shakes her head. "You come back here!"

He races his way out to the third sandbar, then makes his way back to where she now sits on the rock.

He pulls himself up beside her, and she gasps as he drips icy water on her arm. "You're crazy."

He wipes his face with his T-shirt before putting it on, and scoops up their socks and shoes. "Let's go." He walks barefoot toward the path.

Behind him, Claire wades in the shallows, following him in her own time, back to the shore. When she catches up, she takes her shoes with one hand, and reaches the other out. She drops three stones onto his palm. One is black with a thin white stripe, one is flat and pure white and one is the colour of Silly Putty.

Jeff tucks the stones in the pocket of his shorts and gestures at her legs. "Nice." From the knees down, it looks like she has a bad sunburn. "Admit it, it was cold."

"It's not so bad." Claire looks up, a smug look on her face. "It was refreshing."

For the second time, he laughs. He shakes his head. She may be a year younger than him, but she's brave and more than a little stubborn. Summer looks like it might be a lot better than he thought it would be.

Time would tell.

THREE

I can't believe that the sun can get so hot so far north, even in August. I meet Jeff by the Bug Man's driveway, and we retreat to the cool green shade of the rock he took me to, back on my first weekend here. Nestled in a small copse of trees at the north end of the runway, the boulder is taller than I am, taller even than Jeff. The sun through the trees speckles light across the rough surface of the rock. Green moss covers the places the sun never touches, and spots of yellow lichen dot the rest of the surface.

I clamber to the top of the rock, my fingers slipping into the now-familiar crevices to gain enough purchase to pull myself up. I reach down the nearly sheer back side of the rock and stretch my hand down to the thick piece of moss that covers a deep, secret shelf. I pull out a silver plastic container the size of a tackle box.

A gift sent from my grandmother, it arrived filled with cinnamon hearts and foil-wrapped chocolates. Jeff and I made short work of the candy, and now use the empty box to hold the trinkets and bits and pieces we find while exploring the thicket of trees that divides the airport from the highway.

I open it to check that everything is still there: a small, speckled rock that looks like a petrified bird's egg; a bolt Jeff says he's sure fell off an airplane on approach; an adjustable gold ring with a blue stone we found near the site of the old hospital. There is a collection of palm-sized, smooth, flat stones from the lakeshore. On each, we've written words that catch our interest in some way.

Jeff settles in beside me and takes the box. He pulls a thin felt pen and a pure white stone from his pocket. He writes on it and hands it to me. A French word today. *Voler.*

"It means 'to fly.'"

I know this. "It also means 'to steal.'" I drop the stone into the box and reach back to replace it on its hidden shelf.

Jeff lies, back flat on the rock and eyes on the canopy of green above, arms behind his head. I sit cross-legged beside him.

"I had a bad dream last night. It freaked me out, but I don't know why." I pick at a patch of rough lichen in front of me.

"What happened?" Jeff's eyes are closed now.

"I dreamed I was walking by the lake and I met up with Leah. She was wearing a white dress, an old-fashioned one, with lots of ruffles and bows and stuff. She didn't even stop, just kept walking. The weirdest thing was her shoes."

"Why?"

"They were orange. Shiny orange dress shoes with straps. And white frilly socks."

"Like a Creamsicle." Jeff's voice is slow and soft. He sounds like he's about to fall asleep. He often does when we come out here. When I look down at him, though, he's watching me, his blue eyes shining. "Why does that scare you?"

"Oh. That part doesn't, really. It's just weird. But she had no eyes. Just black holes. That scared me."

Jeff is quiet. I lie down beside him and look up, trying to keep track of the patches of blue sky that appear when the trees move in the wind.

"Okay, that would be kind of freaky. Freakier than orange shoes." He reaches for my hand and I let him take it.

He holds it in front of him. He uncaps the felt pen with his teeth and presses its tip to the back of my hand. "What else?"

"That's it." That's not it, but I really don't want to analyze the dreams I'm having. I've had a few about Jeff, too. Those ones are definitely not nightmares. I close my eyes. Jeff's hands are warm, and the pen tickles my skin. "That guy my mom's been seeing? Colin?"

My mom met Colin at the first community dance of the summer at the hall. He runs a fishing lodge at the lake. They're dating as much as a person can date in a place with nowhere but the beach to go. And as usual, when my mom has a boyfriend, he's all she can think of.

We've been through this more than once.

"Yeah, I know Colin."

"Well, tonight he and Daniel are wallpapering the room they built in the basement for Leah. She moved her bed and dresser in last week. Couldn't wait for the finishing touches. She's pretty thrilled that she doesn't have to share with me any more."

"So? You get your own room, Claire."

"I guess so." I'm not so sure it is a good thing. I've shared a room with Leah since I was born. First in the duplex in Gladmer Park where we lived with our dad. Then, after he left, we shared the den at our grandparents' house while Mom went back to school, and finally, a room in the townhouse we rented before we moved here. Excited as I am for my own space, I like having my sister near at night. It's really the only time I get her to myself.

Last night when I woke from my nightmare, I was alone. In the past, I always could go over and crawl in with her. Now I have no one.

Jeff caps the pen and I look down at the twisting tree he's created on my hand. The gnarled trunk reaches just past the bones of my wrist. My fingers, skinny as they are, have become bare branches blown by the wind every time I wiggle them. I smile, but he's already closed his eyes.

We lie there, side by side on the rock. Above the sound of the wind in the trees, I hear waves rushing toward the shore down at the lake. The runway is silent. The morning flight has already gone out, and it'll be hours until the scheduled evening flight arrives.

Jeff dozes. I know he doesn't sleep well at home. He says it has something to do with his uncomfortable bed, but that he can sleep anywhere else: the rock, the school bus, on the rough shore of the lake.

I turn on my side, my back already getting sore. I rest my head on my arm and gaze down at my best friend. His dark hair fans out underneath his head. It hasn't been cut in a while. His skin has darkened since the beginning of summer, his cheekbones tinted by the sun. Still, I can see the shadows under his eyes.

We've become closer with each passing week since the beginning of summer. Mom got Leah and Daniel jobs working for Colin at his fishing lodge down at Pioneer Bay. Leah cleans cabins, and Daniel works as a dock boy and general gofer. On busy weekends, I help

Leah with the cabins, but during the week, I babysit for the airport manager's wife in the mornings. This leaves my afternoons free for hanging out with Jeff, who finishes his shift in maintenance with his dad by lunch.

Some afternoons we get on his dirt bike and drive down winding paths out to the lodge, where we walk along the shore to the public beach. When we tire of the whiny kids, bitchy moms and drunken teenagers, we wander back and take one of the lodge's canoes out. I'm getting better at paddling – still, I'd rather look down over the edge as we go, trying to catch the exact moment the water becomes too deep to see the bottom.

Beautiful as the lake is, I prefer to stay around the airport. As soon as we go near the lake, Jeff wants to swim, and I'm still not comfortable going out over my head. He's tried to convince me, and sometimes I'll go in partway, but more often I sit on the shore and watch Jeff's arms churn through the water as he strokes toward a sandbar. He's strong and he's fast.

Last week, we hiked out near the curling rink where he showed me an enormous snakepit. It still turns my stomach to think of it. Peeking over the edge, I felt dizzy, but I really wanted to see. Jeff kept my arm in a tight hold, and, knees on the ground, I leaned way in. Below me, the snakes crawled over each other in a writhing, pulsating mass. It was impossible to tell one from the rest. They seemed to form one huge creature moving in a million different directions at once. It was thrilling and disgusting, and even now I shiver at the memory.

Jeff shifts next to me. I want him to wake up, to talk to me, but he doesn't. Soon, my mom will be off work and will want to head for the lodge so we can eat dinner with Colin. Then we'll all come back so Daniel and Colin can work on Leah's room until eleven or so. My mom and Colin will head back to his place. Colin can't be away from the lodge overnight. He needs to be there in case his guests need something. And I guess my mom thinks she needs to be there for him, because she spends a lot of her time there.

I poke Jeff in the shoulder. "Let's go. I'm hungry."

He sits up. "Didn't you eat lunch?"

"I was busy."

I don't want Jeff to feel sorry for me, so I don't tell him there isn't much to eat at home. With most of the family practically living at the lodge, my mom hasn't done a good grocery shop in weeks. I pretty much live on Cheerios and bananas; Cheez Whiz and Wonder Bread only go so far.

Jeff's invited me a few times to eat lunch at his place, but his mom is always there. Rita is kind to me, but she's too quiet. She rarely meets my eyes when she does speak to me. Rita dotes on Jeff, but he seems oblivious to the way she hovers, anxious to please. The one time I asked him about it, he scoffed.

"There's more to being a mom than feeding someone, Claire." He spoke in the same dismissive tone he uses when speaking of school.

I let it go.

Sure enough, as we slide down the rock, Jeff invites me to dinner. "Then you won't have to go to the lodge."

Worse than his mom, I can't bear to be around his dad. He always quizzes me on what Jeff and I have been doing, and it makes me nervous. I never know if what I say is going to get Jeff in trouble.

And so I decline. Our time together runs out, and we make our way up the trail back to the airport, Jeff in the lead, me following.

Jeff says goodbye to Claire at the foot of his driveway and goes into his house. Rita is inside the back door, pulling on her gardening gloves. Beside her is the big steel bowl she uses to hold the vegetables she plucks from the soil. It's empty now, but it won't be for long. Jeff wouldn't have believed that nasty patch of dirt could support the mass of green pea vines and hills of potatoes that are ready to be harvested, but it's the same every year. His mom works some kind of magic and produces an actual crop.

"Why don't you come out?" Rita asks. "You can tell me about your day while we gather some food for supper."

"Just let me grab a quick drink and I'll be right there." With his help, his mom will be done before his dad gets home from work, and she won't have to listen to the old man tell her how the way she digs up carrots is wrong.

She looks up and studies him as he comes out.

"What?"

"Sometimes I can't believe how much you remind me of my brother."

His mom doesn't speak of her brother, Gabriel, often. Since she left Churchill, she has only seen him a few times, and those were back when Jeff was too small to remember. He's happy to let her talk.

"He wears his hair in a long braid, and of course his eyes aren't blue like yours, but when he was a boy, he was thin like you. His T-shirts looked just the same on him."

Over the next half-hour, he listens as she tells him about living in Churchill, how even though they were poor, they tried hard to be a family.

When she's like this, he feels close to her, with none of the anger he feels when she's placating his father.

They're almost finished when Leah pulls into the Sullivan drive-way to pick up Claire and her mom. She comes walking over. *Shit.* Jeff's stomach knots up. His dad will be home soon.

Leah greets Jeff and Rita and starts yanking out the few weeds that haven't been choked out by the massive plants.

Rita asks her how she's doing.

"I moved into my new bedroom last week. I'm having a great time decorating. I picked out the wallpaper and the quilt. Navy blue. It's really nice, Rita." Leah's voice is bright, but Jeff doesn't trust her. Whenever Leah shows up, which is more and more often, he feels like she has an ulterior motive.

"We're pretty much done, here, Leah, so you don't really need to help." Jeff tries to make his voice cheery like hers, but he ends up sounding like an asshole. Rita gives him a strange look. He bows his head and rubs soil from a bunch of thin carrots before dumping them into the bowl.

"Yeah, so, I wanted to tell you, Rita. I can kind of hear your TV and stuff. It comes through really clear in the basement." Leah stares at Rita. "You know?"

Rita pretends not to know what Leah's talking about, but Jeff knows. His dad went off again last night, upset about something Rita forgot to do. He didn't hit her or anything, but he yelled a lot. Jeff is used to it. He's not even sure what the fight was about. He's pretty good at judging the ones where Jake will get physical, and last night wasn't one of those times, so Jeff let him rant without stepping in.

Still, he didn't get much sleep. Instead, he lay awake making elaborate escape plans.

He expects Leah to say more, but she doesn't. Rita continues to work like nothing has been said. Jeff is used to this, too. Sometimes his mom seems to live in an entirely different world, one where nothing can reach her.

"Well, look who's here. Hello, Leah." Jake must have parked in the front tonight. Jeff didn't hear him drive up. He nods at Jeff and comes to kiss Rita on the cheek. Jeff can feel his expression twist into one of disgust, but he quickly lets it go when he sees Leah looking at him.

Rita clears her throat. "Leah was just saying that she can hear our TV really good in her new room."

Leah stands and brushes the dirt from her hands onto the butt of her jeans. Jake's eyes follow the movement. "Really?"

"Yeah, I can hear pretty much everything."

Holy shit, thinks Jeff. *She's baiting him.*

Jake takes a step closer to Leah, but she holds her ground. "Well, princess, we don't want to disturb your sleep, do we? I guess I'll have to be more careful." He takes another step toward her. Leah still doesn't budge.

Jeff feels anxiety pulsing through his whole body. Leah can't know what that tone of voice means. "Dad."

Jake's gaze swings to him. His eyes remind Jeff of a wolf, or a snake. "Did you have something to say?"

Jeff shakes his head. If Leah wants to play this game, let her. His mom, too, for that matter. It exhausts Jeff, always to be watching out for her.

Jake reaches down and picks up the bowl. "Rita, let's get this stuff inside." He nods at Leah, a sneer on his face. "Thanks for coming by, sweetie." He heads inside, Rita at his heels.

Leah rolls her eyes at Jeff. "Jesus, Jeff. How do you put up with that?"

"Well, first of all, I try not to egg him on." Jeff leans the shovel against the fence. "He's not someone to mess with, Leah."

"I've told your mom she needs to put some money aside. One day she's going to need to get away from that asshole."

The ball of anxiety in Jeff's stomach contracts. If his mom goes, he'll be on his own with the old bastard.

"Just stay away. You'll just get her in more trouble, Leah."

Leah starts for home. "Right, Jeff. I'll just keep my mouth shut when I see something wrong. Just like you and everyone else around this fucked-up place."

FOUR

When school first starts, there is a lot of fighting about Leah driving us to school, but once my mom's arguments about safety fall on deaf ears, she plays her trump card and tells Leah she'll be paying for her own gas. Leah parks the car and only takes it out when she has to. She's determined to save her money for university. She is not sticking around here, and she makes sure we all know it.

This morning, though, it seems like all the arguing is over. Leah is already up. I can hear her and Mom talking while Daniel plays his scales on the piano.

I get ready and go down for breakfast. Leah is settled into the big chair by the piano, math textbook in hand. Petra has spread out page after page of water-testing reports across the end of the table. Now that the summer vacationers have left the lodge, Colin is busy guiding fall hunting trips, so Mom's been home a lot more. Things seem normal today.

Daniel plays, his eyes closed, his body loose and swaying as his fingers stretch to reach the keys.

The piano needs to be tuned, I notice as I head to the kitchen to make a piece of toast.

Daniel's interpretations of Bach and Beethoven and Abba and Billy Joel flow throughout the house. I hum along as I eat, content in the familiar routine. Then it's time to go.

The bus trip from the airport to town is a kind of time travel. Once we bounce our way out of the bus loop, it's as though we leave the safe little bubble of our community, and time starts again. Airport kids talk to lake kids that we don't see after school or on weekends, and then once at school, the whole lot of us integrates with the town kids as though we don't live a twenty-mile bus ride away from each other. Then at the end of the day, the bus gets quieter the farther we get from town, especially after the three stops for the lake kids. Once we get off, only five or six kids remain to be dropped off, down near the lodge at Pioneer Bay.

Sometimes I wonder who Jeff sat with before I came along, but I never ask. Instead, we talk about math and French and his art class.

I know he's a good artist, but not because he lets me see what's in his sketchbook. At the end of the science hallway at school, a massive, multicoloured mural covers the wall. He's never said anything, but when I saw the initials J.C. in the bottom right-hand corner, I asked one of the girls in my English class.

"Oh yeah, it's Jeff," she told me. "He's fantastic. He'll paint something for the school fundraiser, too. It always fetches the highest bids."

I knew he liked to sketch, but the painting on the wall is stunning. It's a kaleidoscope of fish and lake and sky and buildings in town, and a train and airplanes. When I told him how good it was, he shrugged it off.

"I did that my first year. I don't paint like that any more."

The time-travel thing seems to work on us, too. Jeff and I don't often run into each other at school.

I saw him outside at lunch one day the first week. He pretended not to see me. He stood on the fringes of a crowd of guys wearing jean jackets and high-tops. I walked up behind him and gave him a little shove to say hello. He stumbled forward, to the amusement of the group. Right away I knew it was a mistake.

"Sorry."

"It's okay." He gave me a tight smile before turning back to his friends. He made no introductions. I haven't seen him around much since.

Today, on the bus, we're doing math when I ask him where he goes.

"What do you mean?"

"Jeff, I'm not stupid. I know you leave the school."

He shoves his books into his backpack. "Sometimes I just need to get out of there." He watches me work on my math for a minute. "God, you're smart, Claire."

"It's because I don't skip."

He laughs and turns to look out the window.

"Don't change the subject, Jeff."

"Why do you care?"

"Because school is important. Because you'll fail. Or they'll call your parents."

"I won't fail, Claire. I get all the work done. And as long as they call my mom and not my dad, I'm fine. She won't do anything."

"Your dad would be mad at you."

"So? What else is new?"

He's like this sometimes, at the start of the day.

"No big deal, Jeff. I was just curious." I put my books away, too. We ride in silence the rest of the way to town.

 Jeff scuffs his Nikes into the gravel and wishes again he had a watch. He slipped the note into the crack of Claire's locker just before the break. *Meet me by the bins out back.* But he's not sure she's coming.

Jeff is weary of her constant questions about why he misses so much school, and where he goes. He wonders if she'll be brave enough to skip class.

The heavy metal door at the back of the school hits the brick wall with a bang. Jeff looks around the Dumpster, but it's not her. He doesn't even have to see the faces on the two guys who come out. He can tell it's the McClintock brothers by their white-blond hair and those stupid lumberjack shirts they always wear.

Jeff sighs as they spot him. He's not their usual target, but he tenses up anyway.

Sean reaches him first. "Jeff."

Jeff takes his hands out of his pockets and raises his chin in greeting.

"Hey, halfbreed," says Patrick. "Where you headed today?"

Jeff shrugs and turns away from the school. He hopes Claire doesn't come through the doors now.

"Want to come down to the tracks?" Sean makes a motion like he's drinking from a bottle.

"No, thanks."

The brothers don't say goodbye, they just move on, both walking with that loose, jangling gait that has fooled more than one person into thinking they're easy targets. It's not until they disappear up the alley that Jeff takes a full breath.

The scent of yesterday's rotting french-fry grease from the cafeteria rises from the bins. Jeff paces, giving a flattened pop can a kick at every pass. The movement's the only thing that seems to calm his nerves. She's taking too long.

Claire won't rat him out — if she gets caught leaving, she'll just get sent back to class. Jeff knows no one will be looking for him. Only certain kids, the white kids whose parents live along La Rose Avenue, are worth the time and effort it takes to phone home. Most of the kids on the reserve don't have phones, and the half-white kids, like him, look enough like Indians not to warrant a second glance. Not when it comes to skipping school, anyway. Walking down the aisles at the Bay is a different story. There are second and third glances to spare, then.

The door to the school squeaks.

It's her.

The slanted September sunlight sparks red in her dark curls. She practically glows as she runs toward him.

"Hey."

He points her toward the back alley across the street. The McClintocks are long gone. "Let's get away from here."

Once out of sight of the school, they stop. She doesn't ask where they're going, but then she never did in the summer, either.

"I don't want to get in trouble, Jeff."

He shrugs. "Then you should go back."

"No, I want to come." She chews on her bottom lip as she thinks it over. "How do we get back on the bus at the end of the day?"

"Just come back. No one cares." Jeff looks at her, with her pale skin. Someone might care about her. "Or we can get on over at the junior high."

"Maybe you can get away with that, but if my mom finds out, she'll kill me."

Jeff doubts that Claire's mom ever worries about anyone but herself.

"You make the call, Claire. Come, or don't. I'm going."

Jeff starts down the alley. After a moment, she falls in with him.

"I'll come until lunch, then I'm going back. I'll tell them I was sick or something." They continue on, dodging main streets and open parking lots.

Claire chatters on a bit about the class she's missing – biology with Selinger. Such a fun teacher, she says. Jeff listens in silence. Selinger's a dick. He had him last year. Jeff drove him crazy by getting superstar marks without even showing up. The teacher took issue with how often Jeff fell asleep during those boring Darwin DNA videos. Jeff can't count the times he woke to the sound of chalk shattering on the desk in front of him. And then he'd yawn through endless lectures after class about his *potential*.

It's getting warmer out, so they decide to get a couple of slushes and head down to the river. The Dairy Queen at the mall is open by the time they get there. Afraid someone will see her, Claire waits outside while Jeff goes in.

When he comes out with a blue raspberry slush for him and a cherry for her, she is backed against the wall talking to those two blond idiots. They must be dying in those shirts in this heat.

Jeff can tell the guys are giving her a hard time. Claire's smiling, but her jaw is tense, the way it is when Daniel and Leah get on her case about something.

Sean reaches out and grabs Claire's wrist. She tries to pull it back, but he holds on.

Jeff grips the paper cups so tight that blue ice drips down his hand. "Let's go, Claire."

Sean looks back at Jeff. "Look at you two, on a date. No wonder you didn't want to come to the tracks." He lets her hand drop.

Patrick laughs. "Maybe we should join them."

There's a tight knot in between Jeff's shoulders. He feels like a fool holding on to the two cups. He shifts his weight forward. If they come at him, he's ready.

Claire clears her throat. "We're going back to school." Jeff is disappointed, but not surprised. "You're welcome to join us there, if you like."

Jeff can't help it. He laughs, a quick, sharp laugh that he hopes doesn't sound as nervous to them as it does to him.

They stare at Jeff for a second, then push past, both bumping into him. Black fury fires up in Jeff's chest, but he keeps it in. A fight'll just end up getting him in trouble, and Claire's already nervous about skipping school. Plus there are two of them.

Claire and Jeff watch them walk away.

"Those two are such creeps." Claire's voice shakes.

"Yeah. I've known them a long time. I beat Patrick up once in grade three, so they kind of stay away from me." Jeff passes her drink over. "They set the boys' change room on fire back in grade nine. Four hundred students evacuated. They were heroes for a few days, until the guys at school realized they'd have to put their gym clothes on in the bathroom until the change room was redone. Those guys are total morons." Jeff's almost afraid to ask. "So back to school for you?"

She gives him a long look while she takes a sip of her drink. "No, I just said that."

They cut over by the hospital and cross Fischer, Claire looking behind her the whole time.

"They're gone, Claire."

"I'm not worried. Just making sure no one from school sees me." She looks back again. "They won't tell, will they?"

"Those assholes? No, Claire, they won't tell."

They toss their empty cups into the garbage can outside the Catholic church. Jeff leads her down the riverbank toward the wide-but-sleepy, brown Saskatchewan River. They pass underneath the bridge that they cross every day on the way to school, then follow the curve of the bank around the rickety railroad bridge.

They push through a snarl of willow and rushes. Ahead lies a rock, similar only in its level flatness to the slabs of stone at the lake. This rock, instead of the pale gold dolomite found near the airport, is white and chalky as death.

Claire hesitates, then hops up on it and sits. Jeff settles next to her.

The river passes by in front of them, silent and silty. A red-winged blackbird flashes a bright swatch of colour as it flies by. Behind them, two magpies squawk in the tangle of trees that separate them from the road that skirts the valley edge.

A train approaches, then passes overhead, wheels grinding on the rails. Along the bank nearby is a long metal fence, its links rusty and unravelling. Barbed wire is haphazardly strung across the top, a deterrent to no one.

It feels good to be together again. It's one thing to be summer friends, confidantes, but Jeff knew things would change once school started. A year younger, she runs with a group that's more interested in lip gloss and movie stars than lakes and trees. He misses the Claire he knew in the summer.

Once the noise of the train passes, she elbows him.

"You think you could swim all the way across?"

Jeff scans the murky water where it lazes in slow eddies along the shore. He shrugs. "Probably."

"You wouldn't catch me dead in that dirty mess." Claire gathers her heavy hair and holds it away from her neck. "It's so warm. I wish we were at the lake."

Jeff leans back on his elbows and closes his eyes. He'd rather be there, too.

He thinks back to one hot day in August when they made their way across the sizzling asphalt of the narrow, single-lane highway and raced down through the trees to the lake.

As he did on the first day they met, Jeff stripped off his T-shirt and plowed into the waves, swimming way over his head, then farther, until his hands brushed up against the third narrow sandbar from shore. He stood in waist-deep water looking back to where a doll-sized Claire sat on their rock watching him.

And just like that, it changed for him. His breath heaved in and out from the effort of his swim, the familiar feeling of sun and breeze drying the water on his chest and arms, drop by drop. But it was the anxious tightness in his belly that he had never felt before that made him realize that he liked her. A lot.

Even now, looking at her as her eyes follow the caboose on the train, his words stick somewhere in between his throat and his stomach. She looks over at him and grins. He looks away.

Her voice is quiet as she stretches her legs out beside him.

"Is this where you come every day?"

"One of the places."

"Why?"

"Because it makes me happy. I can draw. I can think."

A car passes on the road at the top of the valley.

Claire's eyes follow it as it drives away. "You should be at school."

"Yeah, okay, Mom."

"We both should be."

"Claire. Relax."

He points to a tall hydro pole off to their right. "See that bird up there?" Impossible to see the markings from here, but he's sure it's the right one.

She sits up and looks. "Yeah."

"Just watch it."

They sit in silence, eyes turned up, but the only movements are the small jerks of the bird's head. Then suddenly, it swoops, down, down into the long grass near the shore. It flies up, a wriggling mouse in its beak.

"Oh, no."

Jeff likes that she doesn't scream. "Just watch."

The grey-and-white, black-masked bird speeds toward the barbed wire and impales its prey on the rusty spike. Claire groans.

The bird leaves the mouse twitching on the fence and returns to its perch.

"God," she says. "I've never seen a bird like that before."

"I asked my mom about it. She says it sounds like some kind of shrike, but that it's out of its range. Either too far north or too far south, depending on the type."

"It's dead, Jeff."

She's right. The mouse is still.

"That's disgusting." There are tears in her eyes.

"The bird has no talons, Claire. It has to hold its prey somehow."

"Still. It's barbaric."

In the time they stay, they see the shrike attack twice more, but it comes up empty each time, its prey no doubt aided by the rocks Claire throws into the grass before the bird strikes.

She gets up to go first. "We should get back, Jeff." She puts out her hand.

He takes it and pulls himself up.

They climb the bank back up to the road. The sun is as high as it's going to get in the clear September sky. It lights the yellow leaves of the ash trees in the yards they pass. The needles on the tamaracks are yellow and sparse, most having already dropped to the ground.

As they walk, Jeff looks down the cross streets and every so often catches a glimpse of the McClintocks as they walk parallel to them. A feeling of dread settles into his stomach.

Jeff motions with his head.

"Let's go back this way, then go up the back alleys. Try to avoid them."

Claire slips her arm through his as they cut across an empty lot to Third Avenue. From up ahead he can hear yelling and laughing. Swearing.

As they round the corner, Jeff sees the two hoods punching a person who's lying on the ground. He can tell by the dress that it's a woman. Her hands are over her head.

Jeff calls out.

"Oh shit, oh shit, oh shit." He can hear Claire chanting beside him, but he doesn't look over. All of a sudden, the two brothers are running at them, one of them digging in the woman's purse. He pulls out her wallet and cheers. As they pass by, he tosses the purse at Jeff.

Jeff doesn't watch them go, just moves toward the woman. There is blood on the sidewalk, trailing from somewhere beneath her head. She hasn't moved.

Jeff glances at Claire where she stands, half a block back, by the mouth of the alley. She is as motionless as the woman next to him. He kneels.

There are sirens in the distance.

"Claire." She just looks at him. Her eyes are wide with fright. "Claire, I need your help."

He's afraid to touch the woman, so he asks her if she's okay. No answer.

A long screech fills the air as an RCMP cruiser barely makes the corner and comes to a stop.

Jeff drops the purse to the ground beside him.

"Get your hands where we can see them."

Jeff looks over toward Claire, but she's gone.

Something at the very centre of him sinks.

His hands do little to break his fall as the officer pushes him face down on the ground.

They keep him there long after the ambulance takes the woman away. The cops harass him, ask him what he knows, but he sticks to his story. He saw two guys, has no idea who they are. No, he doesn't know the girl who ran away, either. He just happened upon the beating.

They let him go when one of the Mounties comes back from the hospital. The woman's description of the attackers matches his story, so the cop that kicked him down takes him back to school, where he spends the afternoon in the office.

He's already on the bus when Claire gets on. She pushes to the back and stands next to his seat.

"I'm sorry, Jeff."

"Me too, Claire."

Her eyes are red and puffy. "I was so afraid of getting in trouble."

He knows.

He moves his backpack off the seat to make room for her.

Jeff didn't think things could get worse, but when he arrives home to find his dad already there, he knows what's coming.

He doesn't even have a chance to take his shoes off when Jake jerks him by the arm into the kitchen. His father grips the front of his jacket and shoves him up against the fridge.

"You little bastard."

"Dad, I didn't do anything." From the corner of his eye, he can see his mom, silent at the entrance to the dining room.

"Why the hell weren't you in school?" He pushes his fists hard into Jeff's chest. Behind him, the bottles and jars rattle inside the fridge as it rocks. "Do you know how embarrassing it is to have the cops call me at work? Do you know how that makes me look?"

Jeff isn't going to apologize or make excuses.

As usual, though, his mom does.

"Jake, it's actually lucky Jeff was there. If he hadn't been, those boys would have –"

Jeff doesn't know why he's always surprised at how fast his dad can move. He turns, and in two steps is in front of Rita, jabbing his finger in her face.

"You be quiet. You're always sticking up for the kid. You're as bad as he is. I thought I made it clear that the girl from next door is to stay away from here."

Jeff looks at Rita, confused for a second. He is very careful not to let Claire come over when his dad is around. Then he realizes who his father means.

Leah.

Jake continues. "Janet Vronsky told her husband, who told me, that she's been doing more than helping you in the garden."

"Leah stopped in for tea once, yes."

Jeff is both relieved that he's not the target any more, and afraid for his mom, because if not him, then it's her.

He hears the door slam closed on the Sullivan side of the duplex. In a few seconds, Claire will be waiting for him at the end of his driveway so they can head out to their rock. He'd already be out there if it weren't for his dad.

Jeff aches to go, but he can't leave his mom. Her misery hangs from her like a drab housecoat. It protects her.

"Jeff's the one who should be helping you in the garden, not some stranger."

Jeff knows that any effort to redirect his anger will bring his father's scorn down on them both. Still, he has to try.

"Dad, I do help."

Rita steps away from Jake and picks up her teacup from the dining-room table. "She's just a girl, Jake. I think she's a little lonely. Her mom's busy. She likes to talk."

Jake slams his hand against the wall. Jeff doesn't even jump, he's so used to his dad's temper. Rita starts, though, and spills her tea. Jeff turns to grab a towel.

"Where are you going?"

Jeff holds up the towel. "Just cleaning up, Dad." He tries hard to keep the sarcasm out of his voice, but can't quite hold it in.

"Don't you talk to me that way." Jake's voice is dead calm.

Rita takes the towel. "You better get going, Jeff." She nods toward the window. "Claire's waiting."

Jeff meets his father's gaze. He swears this time he won't look away first. He stares at his father, until with a wave of his hand, Jake looks away and tells him to get moving.

"And you goddamn well better stay in school tomorrow." He stalks off, into the living room.

By the time Jeff gets outside, he feels powerful with the knowledge that his dad balked first. But he's furious, too. He doesn't say a word to Claire, just takes off at a fast clip through the field to the trees that shelter their rock. Fuck that asshole. One day he's going to punch his father right in his angry face.

Claire follows and she doesn't press him. In the silence he can almost hear his heartbeat slowing.

At the rock, Jeff closes his eyes and turns his face toward the tepid warmth of the sun and takes a deep, steadying breath. He feels Claire's fingers tuck into his hand. He quashes the urge to squeeze them, hard.

"Jeff. Are we still friends?"

He swallows it all: his father; his mother; the cops and their assumptions.

Claire running off, saving her own ass.

"Of course. Always."

FIVE

By Halloween, I've attended enough socials at the hall to know what to expect. Jeff and I usually stay until ten or so, until the other teens clear out in a mass exodus, either on their way to another party, or to the clearing down by the lake to drink. Jeff likes to keep his own company, though, and considering my brother and sister are always with the group, I have no problem avoiding the after-parties. Jeff and I like to wander the airport roads in the dark, or go to my place, leaving the adults to their drinking and dancing and displays of affection that grow sloppier as the night wears on.

Tonight, Jeff's even quieter than usual. Earlier, when I asked him what was wrong, he just shrugged. Now, we sit and sip pop as we watch the adults get drunk. A few seats down from us, Leah and Daniel and their friends spike their drinks from mickeys the girls keep hidden in their purses.

They really don't need to hide, though. The adults are already drunk. My mom flits around, dancing with the airport manager, the guy who releases the weather balloons every morning and the baggage handler at the terminal. Colin's already had a few turns with my mom, and now sits against the wall at the end of a table next to Rita. Their chairs are turned so the two of them sit side by side. Every so often, Colin leans in and says something to her. She either nods or looks over at Jeff's dad, who stands over by the bar, drinking shot after shot of rye. I glance sideways at Jeff. He's watching his dad, too.

"Will you dance with me, Jeff?"

He pulls his eyes from his father to give me an incredulous look. "No."

I figured. But I had to try.

Daniel leans over to ask Jeff to come with them to a party at a cabin at the cove. Lately it seems it's not enough he gets my sister to himself, he wants to hang around Jeff, too.

"Sure," Jeff says. "If Claire comes."

"Forget it," says Daniel.

Leah stands and hands Daniel his jacket. "Time to go."

I watch the twins leave, then ask Jeff to take me to the party.

"Claire, it's just a bunch of people getting drunk or stoned, having sex, puking in a corner."

"You would have gone with them if I weren't here."

"Maybe. But probably not."

"I want to go. Can't we, just for once, do what I want to do?" I'm angry.

"Claire, we always do what you want to do." He couldn't sound more bored if he tried.

"Well, I'm going. I know I can get a ride with someone."

When Jeff doesn't respond, I walk over to where three girls are getting ready to go. I know only one of them from the airport. The other two I recognize from school. I secure a ride and come back to the table for my jacket.

I grab my coat. "Have fun by yourself. See you."

"Later." Jeff puts his coat on, too, and heads out the side door.

The late October wind takes small, nasty nips at my face as I follow the girls out front to the parking lot. I climb into the back seat of the tiny Honda, and the two girls from town crowd in after me. A guy I don't recognize comes running out of the hall clutching a six-pack to his chest.

"Look what I scored! There was a bunch of booze just sitting on the floor by the washrooms."

He gets into the passenger seat and hands everyone a beer. Then as the car lurches on its way, the opener is passed around. When it comes to me, I give it back to him.

"I'll save mine for later."

Everyone laughs. I wish I'd stayed with Jeff.

Music blasts from the tape deck. Nazareth. I know this song. Daniel has the same album.

We speed up the road away from the hall, and peel around the corner onto the highway. At this speed, it's a short drive to the cove. We pull in behind a pack of cars parked behind a large A-frame cabin.

Once out of the car, I trail behind, slow enough that the others are long gone before I reach the door. A man in his early twenties stands guard, taking the alcohol the guests bring. He has to raise his voice to make himself heard over the pounding of the music.

"Give me your booze and I'll give you a ticket. One ticket per beer, one ticket per ounce of alcohol. When you want a drink, you go to the bar in the loft and get it." He raises his eyebrows. "Whatcha got, sweetie?"

My cheeks grow warm. "Just this."

He laughs and takes it from me. He pulls an opener from his pocket and pops it open. "Go crazy."

I step inside and wander into the living room. I don't see Leah or Daniel, but I do see a group of kids from school standing together near the window. I don't know them well, but head over anyway.

I drink a few sips of beer as I listen to them brag about how much they've already had to drink. I have nothing to contribute to the conversation. I've never had more than one beer at a time in my life. Jeff refuses to drink, and I spend most of my time outside of school with him.

My classmates all came in one car with someone's older brother. Joey Bignell comes up and hands me another beer and stands way too close as I finish the first one. He puts his arm around me and tries to kiss me in that friendly, goofy way he has. The same way he does in the cafeteria every day at school.

At school it's a game, but he's drunk tonight, and more persistent. I turn my face from him and pull away. He holds my arm a moment too long, then lets go so abruptly, I stumble.

It was a mistake to come here.

I move on, looking for Leah and Daniel. I follow a group of people to the loft. Most people here, I don't know. Many of them are in their twenties, or even older.

Upstairs, another guy I've never seen before leans in and yells in my face. "You're Daniel's sister, right?"

"Yeah."

"He wants to see you. He's over there." The guy nods toward the small bar where Daniel is passing out drinks. Relieved, I go over and sit on one of the bar stools.

My relief doesn't last long.

"You stupid idiot." Daniel raises his voice to be heard above the music.

I don't say anything. I just spin the stool away and face the room. The motion makes my stomach churn, and I realize I've nearly finished two beers. Daniel says something about getting me home, but I ignore him.

Looking out at the room, I catch sight of Leah. She slow dances with a tall, dark-haired man. She looks weightless, boneless in his arms. Eyes closed, Leah rests her head on his shoulder.

I've wished Jeff was with me since I left the hall, but watching my sister being held like that turns my wish to an ache that fills my chest.

"Who's that guy?" I ask Daniel.

"Shane Fowler. He's been hanging around her for a while." Daniel leans on the bar beside me. "He's a loser. Graduated last year, works at the mill. He sells pot on the side. His dad was a Mountie, some kind of local hero. The cops let Fowler do whatever he wants." He reaches over and plucks the near-empty beer bottle from my hand and changes the subject. "You're in big shit, Claire. You need to go."

I can't take my eyes off my sister. "That's weird. I would have thought she'd find someone more like her."

Daniel's voice is bitter. "Well, she does whatever he wants, so I guess they have something in common."

In silence we watch as Shane and Leah kiss. My stomach flips. I've never watched anyone kiss like that before, not even in the movies. Leah seems submissive, face turned up to Shane's, waiting for more, pulling him to her, clutching him close. I'm used to Leah running the show.

My mouth tastes rancid from the beer and my chest hurts. Leah and Shane are on the couch now. Shane pulls out a thin white cigarette and lights up.

"Daniel? Is that a joint?"

"Yeah. Jesus, you're stupid."

I watch Shane pass the joint to Leah. She takes a long drag.

"Stay here." Daniel slips from behind the bar and walks over. I can't hear what they say, but from the look on Leah's face, I can guess. Leah stands and straightens her clothes. Her steps are careful as she makes her way over to me. Daniel follows close behind.

"You need to go home, Claire." Leah struggles to focus on me.

"Oh, this is about me," I say.

"You shouldn't be here." She sways a little on her feet. Long blinks.

"Neither should you." I slide off the bar stool. "Come on, Daniel will drive us home." I look into my sister's eyes, but they're empty. It seems there's more than pot smoking going on. She stands, half turned away, head cocked as though listening to a far-off conversation.

"Shane will drive me."

I feel a lump of panic in my throat. "Leah, he can't drive."

"Don't be a baby. Go home." Leah starts to walk away. I grab her hand.

"Please. Mom won't be there." I'm suddenly desperate to convince her.

Leah yanks her hand away. "And you wonder why we don't want you around. Don't do this, Claire. Daniel, take her home, for God's sake."

Daniel shakes his head. "She's not my responsibility." He crosses his arms. I see what he's doing. He's using me as the excuse to get her out of here so he doesn't have to be the bad guy.

Leah pushes at him with both hands. "Fuck! She's not mine either! Why does everyone think I should take care of her? I am so sick of this." She walks a few steps away, then turns back, her finger jabbing clumsily at the air. "I'm staying with Shane tonight. Handle it, Daniel."

I sink back against the bar, the soreness in my chest blossoming as Leah rejoins Shane on the couch.

"Claire, I'll meet you at the door. I just have to grab my coat."

"That's okay, Daniel." My voice is small. "I can get home. I know some people downstairs. I'll come get you if I can't get a ride, okay?"

Daniel narrows his eyes. "Are you sure? I want to stay and make sure she doesn't get into trouble."

I nod. "Yeah, I'm sure. You take care of her. You'll come home tonight, though, right?" I'm embarrassed to ask, but I know Mom will stay with Colin, and I don't want to be alone.

For just a second, his face softens. "Yeah, I definitely will be home."

"Okay."

The crowd flows around me as I push through. It bends, but there is no break, even on the stairs. On the main floor, I walk to the deserted kitchen and find the phone on the wall. I pick it up but am unsure who I should call. I have no idea how I'm going to get home, but I'm afraid if Daniel drives me, Leah will leave with that stoned guy and get in an accident.

The phone beeps in my hand, off the hook for too long. I hang it up, then grab it and quickly dial the lodge. As it rings and rings, I look around the kitchen at the empty bottles, the dirty glasses. A cigarette left on the edge of the counter still burns. I reach out and flick the butt into the sink.

Colin picks up.

"Hey, Colin, is my mom there?"

"She is. Where are you, Claire? It's pretty loud."

"Oh, I'm at home. It's the TV. Can I talk to her, please?"

There is mumbling as Colin passes the phone to Mom.

"Claire? What's going on?"

"Nothing. I just wanted to know if you're coming home tonight."

Silence. "Where's Leah?"

Shit. "Oh, I think there was a get-together somewhere. Don't worry, Mom. It's okay. I just wondered –" Calling was a mistake.

"Claire, is there a party at our place?"

"No! It's the TV. I'm sorry. I didn't mean to worry you. Everything's fine."

"Are you sure?"

"Yeah, I just wanted to know if you would be home tomorrow morning, I guess."

Mom is quiet. Then she tells me she's going to stay with Colin, but she'll be there in the morning. And to call if I need anything.

I just did, I think, as I hang up. I should go tell Leah, so she makes sure she gets in before Mom. Instead, I call Jeff.

"Can you come get me?"

Jeff is silent for a long time before he agrees.

"Meet me at the turnoff to the highway. I'll be there in ten."

 Jeff grabs the keys to his dad's truck from his parents' dresser and heads out to the driveway. He doesn't know how much longer it will be before they walk home from the hall, so he has to hurry. He doesn't need a rerun of the fighting that went on before the social.

That's got to be the hardest thing. Acting normal after a massive blowout at home.

Jeff's licence is only a month old, but he's been driving a lot longer than that. He needs to get Claire and have the truck back in its spot as soon as he can. It isn't snowing yet, but Jeff can tell by the weight in the air, by the glow of the street lights against the low clouds that it won't be long.

Jeff races up the highway to the cove turnoff. Claire stands on the side of the highway, hands in her jacket pockets, shoulders hunched against the cold. He cranks the heat as she gets into the cab.

"So?" he asks as he pulls a U-turn on the deserted highway.

"You were right. Booze, drugs and people necking. No puking that I saw." He looks over at her to see if she's joking. Claire looks straight ahead, dead serious. Tiny flakes of ice snap against the windshield.

"Were you drinking?"

"Yeah, a couple bottles of warm beer. I saw Joey there. He tried to kiss me. Daniel is mad at me, and Leah, too. You know what? I don't really want to talk about it. It was a dumb idea."

"Okay."

They don't speak again until they pull into Jeff's driveway. He looks up at the light glowing through the bathroom window and swears under his breath. There's no point in moving the seat back to where he found it, or resetting the heat and the mirror.

"I have to go in, Claire."

"Leah was doing drugs." Claire's hand is on the door handle.

Jeff looks over at her. He needs to get inside, get it over with.

"And she's not coming home tonight."

He can't believe she can't hear the anxiety crashing through his veins. The sound fills his head and pushes everything else out. "Claire, I'm sorry. I have to go. Really. We can talk tomorrow." He opens his door. "I need to go."

"Okay, already." She gets out and slams the door. "Thanks for the ride," she calls back to him.

He trudges up the steps to the house. His mind already on what's to come, he doesn't look back.

The next morning, Jeff shows up at Claire's just after nine. She and Daniel are awake. Leah and Petra are not yet home.

Claire sits on the living room couch, feet up on the middle cushion, reading a book. Daniel is at the piano. Jeff pushes Claire's feet out of the way and sits next to her. She tucks her feet back under his leg.

He tugs down on the sleeves of his sweatshirt. It wasn't as bad as he thought last night, just a few shoves, a few red marks that need to be covered. It could have been worse. At least his mom was in bed, and stayed out of the way.

Think about something else. "What are you playing, Daniel?"

"Beethoven." Daniel sets his hands on his knees. "Any requests?"

Jeff shakes his head.

Daniel looks over at Claire. "Want me to play your song?" His voice is kinder than Jeff has ever heard it.

"Stop sucking up to me." She turns to Jeff. "Daniel didn't get home until almost four. Now he feels guilty."

Jeff touches Claire's knee. "You were by yourself?"

"Yes, and I was totally fine. Go ahead, Daniel, play it."

Daniel begins playing.

Even the song sounds apologetic, Jeff thinks.

"Who is it?" he asks. He knows little about music, only what he learns on his visits here. Daniel often teases him for not recognizing the most famous songs by Mozart or Chopin. Or van Halen for that matter. It doesn't stop Jeff from asking though. He only has to ask once. He knows he hasn't heard this one before.

"Debussy." Daniel's fingers speed up, finding the notes with ease. "Claire's favourite."

"It's not my favourite." Claire slides her toes farther under Jeff's leg.

"Yes, it is, Claire. Now, shush."

Jeff watches Claire as she closes her eyes and lets the music roll over her.

"You do so like it," he whispers, not wanting to break Daniel's concentration.

She opens her eyes. "Yeah, but it's not my favourite. It's called *Clair de Lune*." Daniel just says that it's about me."

"It means moonlight." Daniel starts the song over. Jeff sits and listens as Claire gets up and wanders to the window. She stands looking out until Daniel finishes, then she turns to Jeff.

"Leah's home. She's outside talking with your mom."

He says nothing. He's not sure when Leah decided his mom needed a friend, but he wishes she would stay away from her.

Leah slams into the house.

"Get down here, Claire!"

"I'm right in here, Leah, you don't need to yell."

"What the hell were you thinking, asking Jeff to come get you last night?"

Leah comes into the room. She stops at the sight of him.

Jeff stands as though that can stop whatever else she has to say. "It was fine, Leah. Only took ten minutes."

Claire frowns. "What? I needed a ride."

Leah comes to stand behind Daniel and lays her hand on his back. "Daniel should have brought you home. It wasn't up to Jeff. You shouldn't have been there, Claire."

Claire's face turns red. She doesn't often get angry, but Jeff can see it building.

"And you should have been there? I had to call Jeff. You wouldn't leave. I called Mom and she was busy. Daniel couldn't drive me home because he was worried about you. What was I supposed to do?"

Jeff just wants the conversation to end.

Claire swallows hard. "It's always the same. I'm so tired of you two." Claire takes off up the steps to her room.

Daniel turns and looks up at Leah. "She called Mom? Why would she do that?"

Leah rubs her face with her hand. "It's my fault. I should have just brought her home and then gone back."

Daniel bows his head back to his music. "It's not like you were in any shape to make any decisions, Leah. You were acting like a doped-up sleaze last night. Everyone was watching you."

"Mind your own business, Daniel."

"You are my business. Or you were, until we came here."

Jeff breaks in. "Leah, it's not your decision who Claire calls."

Leah puts her hand on his arm, but he shakes it off. He doesn't know what his mom told her, but he sure as hell doesn't need Leah's pity.

He turns away and takes the stairs two at a time. Claire's door is open, but he knocks on it anyway.

She waves him in from where she sits on the floor. He comes in and settles on the edge of her bed.

"You want to go for a walk or something?"

She looks up at him. "Where to?"

"I don't know. With the snow, the path to the rock will be a mess. Let's walk the main road over to the terminal."

"No, that's okay." She leans her cheek against his knee. He traces a dark tress of her hair that curls across his leg.

Jeff can't believe Claire called her mom. As far as he can tell, she's not the most reliable mother around. "Claire, from now on, call me first. I'll come, I promise."

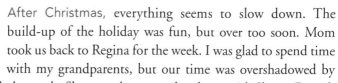 After Christmas, everything seems to slow down. The build-up of the holiday was fun, but over too soon. Mom took us back to Regina for the week. I was glad to spend time with my grandparents, but our time was overshadowed by Leah's dark moods. She spent hours on the phone with Shane. Daniel, in a rare moment of camaraderie, told me she'd sneaked out one night to meet a former boyfriend. He said she came home high as a kite, but I missed it all.

Nothing seemed to come of it though, and once vacation was over, we all settled back into our routines.

It's dark these days when I meet Jeff for our morning walks to the bus stop. The bus trips to and from school seem endless as we travel the icy highway. Even the scene outside the bus is silent. In the fall, I watched as leaves on the aspens and poplars shook, then flew, in the northern wind, creating a landscape in constant motion. Now, the spruce trees stand firm and immovable, their snowy branches silvered with morning moonlight.

But the dark keeps things quiet, on the bus and at the airport. Even on the way home, the deep blue afternoon light seems to dampen the need for loud voices and arguing. It's too dark to do homework, or read, and Jeff and I don't talk about much, content just to sit next to each other.

The part I love best is the walk home from the loop. While the other kids race to get out of the cold, Jeff and I pick our way through the snowy ruts of the front road; sometimes we walk in step along the cleared main street. Every so often, I bump against him, hard enough that I can feel him through his heavy ski jacket.

It's too snowy to go out to our rock, so we keep to the roads at the airport instead. The path to the clearing at the lake is snowed in as well, and we still don't venture down by the pumphouse.

Finally, March arrives, and with it, longer days and my sixteenth birthday, which happens to fall on the same day as the spring concert.

A week earlier, I had a sleepover for a few girls from school. It was fun, until Leah showed up. She was drunk, and brought a bottle of cherry whisky home with her. I sat and watched as my friends got drunker and louder. Leah thought it was funny, but she soon drifted to her room, leaving me with a roomful of passed-out girls. My mom never found out about the booze, but she was mad about the noise. Jeff said his dad was unimpressed, too.

The day before the concert is unspringlike and frigid. The bus is late picking us up from school, and when it does show up, its heater is useless at keeping the cold at bay.

"We need to start getting rides like Leah does," says Jeff.

Leah has been getting rides home with Shane when he's not working. That is, when she bothers to come home at all. I think the fact Shane has his own place is one of the reasons she dates him.

Daniel sits across the aisle from us now, in a seat by himself. I wonder if he wishes he were a little nicer to Shane. Riding in a warm Trans Am with a pothead has to be preferable to riding an icy-cold cheesewagon like this bus.

We're still bundled up in our winter gear when we pull into the loop. There is no drop in temperature from what it was inside the bus as three of us plod back to our place.

As the wind blows across the lake and rattles the north side of the house like a freight train, Jeff and I settle in to listen to Daniel practise his pieces for the spring concert finale. He's also playing all the music for the kids' songs.

After a while, I tire of my homework and ask Jeff if I can watch him sketch Daniel while he plays. To my surprise, he says yes.

I've seen him make sketches on napkins and on my skin and on scraps of paper but never anything like this. My brother appears on the page before my eyes. Before I know it, I'm hunched over Jeff's sketchbook in amazement.

"Claire. I can't move my hand if you're leaning on my arm." Jeff nudges me away.

My face heats up. "Sorry."

He flips back through his sketchbook.

"Here. I want to show you this."

He hands me the book and shows me a sketch of three panels of scenery.

"It's great," I say. "What's it for?"

"It's my sketch for the backdrop I painted for the concert," he says. "Daniel asked me to do it."

"You painted this?"

"Yeah, at the hall."

"When?"

He shrugs. "I've been working on it since Christmas. I work on it at the hall while Daniel practises with the little kids."

It seems the more time Leah spends with Shane, the more Daniel steps into my friendship with Jeff.

I can't believe I didn't notice, but then I've been busy working on my monologue – I'll be reciting "The Highwayman," and it's not an easy poem to perform.

"I painted the coolest moon for your piece."

"Thanks."

I get up and go into the kitchen. I lean against the counter.

Jeff appears, books in hand. "What's wrong?"

I've been waiting for months for him to show me his art. I'd asked to see his paintings once, way back in the summer. He'd said yes, but never invited me over. And yet, Daniel has seen his work.

"Nothing." I want him to ask me again, but he doesn't.

"All right. Well, I'm going to go."

I walk him to the door.

"I'll see you in the morning?" He pulls on his jacket and jams his toque on his head. He gathers his things and puts his hand on the doorknob.

"You bet," I say.

He nods once and he's gone.

Daniel meets me in the kitchen, an empty mug in his hand. "Jeff's dad is a dick."

"This is news?"

He sets the cup in the sink and starts to run the water. "I got the car stuck out front last week, and he just had to come out and give me crap. Like it's my fault. It's his job to clear the roads, not mine." Daniel shakes his head. "He wouldn't even help push me out."

"Jeff and I don't talk about him much."

"I wouldn't either if he were my dad. Aw, shit."

I follow Daniel's gaze to the window. Shane's Trans Am is pulling into the driveway.

"He better not even think about staying for supper," says Daniel.

I pick up the tea towel. "He's not so bad, Daniel." Shane has been pretty nice to me. He gave Jeff and I a ride home once. He'd come by school to pick up Leah, but she was home sick, so he took us instead. He offered to drive Daniel, too, but Daniel said he'd rather take the bus. Leah freaked out on Shane when we walked in, and that was it. No more rides home.

Outside, Shane braves the cold to open Leah's door for her.

"Give me a break."

"Daniel, give the guy credit. He lives in town, and he's willing to drive her all the way back out here. He must really like her."

Leah kisses him goodbye at the car. She's not inviting him in.

Shane comes for my birthday supper, though. Mom asks Leah to have him pick up Chinese food in town and bring it out early, so we can all get to the hall by six. Jeff comes over too, and Colin. There is a sense of ease in the air that I haven't felt before, and I'm grateful for it. Everyone seems content, even Daniel. He ignores Shane, telling Jeff obnoxious stories about me that aren't even true. Leah is quiet, and Jeff is his usual watchful self, but Shane is funny and polite. My mom seems happy to have us all together. Colin brings in a cake that Mom must have baked at the lodge. Right after I make my wish, Daniel leaves. He wants one more practice at the hall.

After cake, my mom shoos Jeff and me away from the table. "Go. Practise with Daniel. Or walk. We'll do this."

We head to the hall. It's been set up and decorated. Jeff's three-panel backdrop is a captivating combination of technique and colour. One entire section is devoted to a night scene, complete with a cloud-covered moon at the top and cobblestones at the bottom. The other two panels depict a pale spring morning and a brighter midday.

I can feel his eyes on me. All I can do is whisper his name.

"Come here, Claire. I have something for you."

Behind one of the panels is a paper bag, its top folded over.

I open it and pull out a small painting of the lake lit by a fiery setting sun.

I can't speak.

"Happy birthday," he says and puts his arms around me.

I hug him for a long time.

"Thank you." My voice cracks. I smile at him.

"If I'd known it would make you this happy, I would have given you one sooner." He steps away. There is a lot to be done before everyone arrives.

I read second last, and as soon as I finish, I leave the stage in the midst of the applause and take my seat next to Jeff. Daniel, ready for a change after playing bouncy spring songs for the kids all night, winks at me and launches into *Moonlight Sonata*. As the familiar melody closes the show, I move my arm so it touches Jeff's. Leah and Shane sit across the aisle from me. I catch Shane's eye and he nods. I feel good.

Back home after the concert, I examine the painting Jeff gave me more closely. The oranges and purples and greens swirl and meld in a stunning representation of what the two of us have seen from the shores of the lake. On the back, he's written, simply: For Claire.

Jeff fills a glass of water at the sink and looks out at the freak spring snowfall. He leans forward and frowns when he sees Shane's car pull in to the Bug Man's driveway.

Leah gets out of the car and stumbles across the street and up toward Jeff's door. He can hear the pause in the soft snap of cards from the dining room where his parents play crib. Jake must have seen her, too. When her knock comes his father is already at the door.

"What do you want?" Jake's gruff words cause Jeff's shoulders to tense.

"Rita." There's a shudder in Leah's voice that Jeff has never heard. He moves next to his father as Rita makes her way through the kitchen.

Leah looks beyond them all, yet focuses on nothing. Her mascara has run, leaving black, smudgy tear-trails down her cheeks. Her lips are so pale they've disappeared. The down jacket she wears is heavy and much too big for her. It hangs open, and as he stares, he can see her neck is red, rubbed raw. There is a slash of blood that has pooled and dried in the very place next to her lips that makes a deep dimple when she smiles. As he looks closer he can see the whirl of a blue bruise forming next to her left eye. He swallows, his mouth dry as straw.

Her legs are bare and streaked with blood and dirt. Her shoes are too big, too. They're someone else's floppy running shoes.

As Jeff stares at her, his mom pushes by his father and holds her arms out. Leah pitches forward, falls to her knees and wraps her arms around Rita's waist. Rita strokes Leah's hair and makes comforting noises.

Jake backs away. Jeff hears his footsteps, heavy, even in socks, on the stairs.

Rita motions with her head for Jeff to go, too.

He does, but not far. Just back to the kitchen, to his place in front of the sink, where he stares out the window. The yellow parking lights of Shane's car glow in the Bug Man's driveway. Jeff's face heats up. If Leah weren't blocking the door, he'd go out there and beat the hell out of Shane.

But Leah starts to talk, and from what he can make out it wasn't Shane. It was someone else, someone at a party. Shane hadn't even been there.

Leah's story comes out in chunks, between sobs and deep breaths. She got herself in over her head, drank too much and was forced into a laundry room at the back of some basement.

Raped.

By Kenny Sparvier, a guy who should have graduated the year

before, but had instead done jail time in Winnipeg. He must have been released.

Then Leah, running, stopping at a gas station, thinking that it was possible to clean herself up.

Jeff listens to the calm timbre of his mother's voice as she questions Leah. Her tone says it will be okay. A lie. No one knows better than he does. His mother can't fix anything.

Jeff can hear most of what Leah says, but he struggles to make sense of the horror of her words. His thoughts go back to that day a few weeks ago when the firefighters at the airport staged a mock airline disaster to practise their emergency response plan. They'd enlisted the senior drama class at the high school to act as victims in the field and Jeff's art class to do the makeup. Jeff's teacher, who'd worked in film down in Winnipeg, had been enthusiastic, helping his students create the wounds and bruising and broken bones that an airplane crash victim might have.

Jeff worked on his plans for weeks, even though he knew Claire was annoyed by the amount of time he put into the gory sketches he worked on during the bus ride.

On the day of the exercise, Leah was assigned to Jeff.

She lifted herself up onto the high table in the art room, flipped her long hair out of her face and flashed that dimpled smile.

"This is great. I'm glad you're doing my makeup. What do I get to have?"

Jeff felt his classmates looking at him, all of the guys disappointed that Leah hadn't been assigned to them.

"I'm giving you some bruises and a wicked head injury." Jeff rearranged his makeup on the table next to her as she pulled her hair into a ponytail. He handed her a pot of heavy face cream. "Put this on. It will help when it's time to take the makeup off."

"You do it. I don't know where I'll need it." Another smile. It made Jeff uneasy. She held his gaze, like she was looking for the answer to some unasked question.

"How have you been, Jeff?" Her voice was low and she leaned in so close he could feel her breath on his face. It smelled sweet, like peppermint. Even now he squirms when he thinks of the intimacy of it.

"Good."

She sighed. "Really?"

His hand shook as he smoothed the cream onto Leah's forehead and left temple. His fingers stumbled over her soft skin as he worked the thick lotion in. He applied the adhesive and pressed the gash he'd created in class just below the hairline. With chunky face paints he created a burgundy-and-black mix of a coagulated blood-like consistency. He pushed the colour into her hair and made blood drip down her chin.

Satisfied with the phony laceration, he brushed a multicoloured bruise onto her left cheekbone. Jeff feels sick now when he remembers how he'd added just enough yellow and green to make it a three-dimensional goose egg. More black and red to create a split lip. Some black under the eyes for good measure.

Now, in his back entrance, Leah still talks. Her voice has turned wooden, the way his mom's does when she makes excuses for Jake's anger. Excuses like it's her own fault.

He hears Leah say the same thing.

Jeff can barely process all that he's heard.

That day in the art room, Leah seemed impressed when he held up the mirror for her. "It's great, Jeff. I look so bad. I love it."

Jeff shrugged, more than a little impressed with himself. It did look good. "Thanks."

She touched his hand. "Are you just as good at covering up your own bruises?"

His head snapped back like she'd slapped him.

"What about your mom? Is she?"

He couldn't think of one thing to say.

"How long are you going to let it go on?" Her voice was so soft.

He mumbled something about getting more tissues and turned away. She was gone when he got back.

He goes to his mom and Leah now, making noise so as not to surprise them. "Mom? What can I do?"

Leah turns her tear-stained face up to him. His mother's white pajama top is covered with makeup and snot and streaks of pale blood. Jeff feels sweaty and lightheaded, like he's going to throw up. He can't meet either woman's eyes.

"Jeff." Leah's voice is ragged and catches on the word. When she tries again, it's stronger. "Jeff."

He drags his gaze to hers.

"Don't tell Claire. Promise."

He nods. "Okay."

"I mean it. I don't want her to know about this."

"I hear you, Leah." His words come out harsher than he intends.

His mom gives him a warning look.

Leah struggles to her feet.

Rita's eyes soften as she turns back to Leah. "Do you want me to call your mom?"

"No. She's not home anyway."

And the real question. "Do you want me to call the police?"

Leah shakes her head. "No."

"Let's get you cleaned up. Jeff, Leah will stay in your room tonight. You can sleep on the couch."

Jeff has no idea where his mother finds this strength. He slides by Leah and reaches for the doorknob. "No problem. I'll be back in a bit."

As he crosses the road, Jeff wonders how Shane could believe that Leah would come back out. He opens the passenger door and slides into the low bucket seat.

Shane's seat is pushed all the way back and he's slumped against the door. The engine growls, and the heater blasts.

"What the fuck is going on?" Shane runs his fingers through his hair. He doesn't wait for an answer. "We had a fight and she took off to this party. She came back late, and rang the bell. The door is always open, she knows that. She just rang and rang it. She had no coat and someone else's shoes. She just kept saying she was sorry."

Jeff stares up at his house. The bathroom light comes on. He can see shadows on the ceiling, his mom's and Leah's. Claire's window next door is dark. She's asleep, unaware of all that's going on. And he can't tell her.

Jeff watches the shadows move. There's no easy way to say it. "Leah was raped, Shane." He looks over.

Shane's face is turned toward the window, but Jeff can see his jaw clench tight.

"Did she say who?" Jeff can barely hear him.

He thinks of all Leah said, and the images come, frame by frame, without end. Leah at the party, alone, dancing and flirting with the wrong person. Shoved down a dark hallway into a laundry room.

And then, the late spring snow falling wet and warm as she ran out.

"Jeff, I need to know." Shane's words are cold and filled with intent.

The part of the story that keeps coming back to Jeff: Leah, in that grimy bathroom at the Esso station, toilet paper wrapped around and around her hand as she tried to scrub herself clean.

He tells Shane who it was.

SEVEN

I want to do something special for Jeff's birthday in May, so I enlist my grandmother in Regina to do some shopping at a real art store for me. She sends a selection of brushes and paints – oils, acrylics and watercolours – as well as some heavy paper.

I have no idea if what my grandma chose is useful, so I'm relieved when Jeff is overjoyed with the art supplies. He examines each package, tube and bottle carefully before opening it. He's especially pleased with the brushes.

"They're perfect."

Shane and Leah are supposed to come to town with us, but Leah changes her mind at the last minute. Shane drives Jeff and me into town anyway, with a promise to pick us up at the café afterwards. I'm a little nervous about driving with Shane, but he assures me that no matter what Leah's doing, he's clean. It seems that as she slips more and more into a fog, he becomes sharper and clearer.

The car is quiet on the way back home. We don't talk about it, but the unspoken hangs heavy between us all. Leah has changed.

At home, when it's clear Shane isn't coming in, Jeff and I thank him and watch him drive away.

"I thought he'd at least say hi to Leah," I say.

Jeff shrugs. "I'm just glad I didn't have to try and borrow my dad's truck. Thanks again for the gift, Claire." He waves and heads for home, while I go into a dark, silent house.

Leah must be in the basement. She barely speaks, now. She rarely stays with Shane, though he still drives her home from school when he's not working. As soon as she walks in, she heads down to her room and won't come out until she's called for dinner. Her silence means Daniel is quiet, too. The twins have grown apart.

One night, about a week after Jeff's birthday, Daniel doesn't come home after school, so it's just Mom, Leah and me for dinner. I jam the pasta I made into my mouth, as fast as I can, eager to get away from the tension.

Leah sits next to me, but doesn't take a bite of her dinner. My mother reads one of her reports at the table, ignoring both of us.

I ask Leah about her day, Shane, her grad dress. She ignores all my questions.

"Leah, did you tell Mom your news?"

The look she sends me is filled with a combination of hatred and the blankness I've become so used to.

Mom looks up, but Leah doesn't say anything.

"She was voted valedictorian."

"Really?" My mom is careful not to show too much excitement. We're all walking on the thinnest of ice around Leah. If Mom seems too excited, or too angry, it can set Leah off into a rant.

"Really." Leah pushes her plate away and stands. "Can I be excused?"

"Clean your spot, Leah."

Leah grabs her plate and takes it into the kitchen. There is a crash as her plate, fork and knife hit the counter.

I stare at my mom. "Clean your spot? That's all you're going to say? How about congratulations?"

Mom sighs. "Everything I say is wrong, Claire. It hardly matters."

I get up too, and clear my dishes. I take my plate into the kitchen and clean up the mess my sister left. Then I go down to Leah's room and knock on the door. There's no answer.

"Leah? It's me."

Nothing.

"Can I come in?"

"Yeah."

Leah sits on her double bed, back against the headboard, holding a pillow.

I sit on the desk chair. "Why are you mad?"

Leah shrugs. "I'm not." She rests her chin on the pillow.

"Why are you fighting with Mom?" I can see tears in her eyes. "Why are you so mad at everyone?"

"Things are just really hard, Claire." Leah doesn't even bother to wipe the tears away.

"Are you sad about leaving Shane?"

Leah starts to laugh, and it scares me a little. Leah is so different from what she used to be. "It's not funny, Leah. You're going to go away to school and he's going to be left behind. I know he'll miss you."

Leah and Daniel are both moving back to Regina for university in the fall. Daniel was accepted into the Fine Arts program on a music scholarship. Leah always planned on going out east to school, but she changed her mind, telling Mom not to make any plans for residence, that she would be sticking with Daniel.

"Oh, Claire." Leah reaches for a Kleenex. "Of course I'll miss him. Shane's a very, very good person. You know that, right? Don't listen to Daniel." Leah blows her nose.

"I know." I fiddle with the makeup on Leah's desk. "You guys probably will be glad to get rid of me, hey? Get out there, be on your own?"

"Claire, it's not that I want to get rid of you."

"Then what? What's going on?"

"I don't want to talk about it."

"Leah, I miss you."

Leah's voice turns hard. "Go upstairs, okay? This has nothing to do with you."

I start to ask her again what's wrong, but Leah just screams at me. "Just go, God damn you!"

I close her door behind me when I leave her room.

Later, I bring a book down to the living room. I don't want to be alone. But my mother has gone out to Colin's and Leah is still in hiding. Daniel comes home a little later, and goes straight up to bed.

Not long after that, I hear Leah come up to the kitchen. It's quiet for a long time, so I go to see what's going on.

Leah stands in front of the open fridge, holding on to the door. The light shines out into the dark kitchen, illuminating her face. Her mouth is turned down and she's been crying. She doesn't seem to be looking at anything.

"Leah?" No response. I place my hand on her shoulder and make my voice as gentle as I can. "Do you want something, Leah? Can I get you something?"

Leah's head doesn't move.

Something's really wrong. I hug her from behind and start to cry.

Leah closes the fridge. "I'm tired. I'm tired of the people here. No one cares about anyone but themselves. Everyone just wants to hurt everyone else." She shakes me off and leaves me standing alone in the kitchen.

For two straight weeks in June, everything centres around the twins. Even though Daniel is graduating too, Leah is valedictorian. She should be putting hours into her speech, but she can't be bothered. Daniel and I cover for her, outlining, then finally putting together, a speech. She contributes very little.

Daniel finally blows up at her. "Leah, it's a choice. You can't say yes to everything I suggest." He tosses the pages at her. "If you didn't want to do it, you should have just said no."

"I couldn't," she says. "People would have asked why."

The old Leah would have accepted without reservation the challenge of writing a speech. I remember how excited Leah was to show me the long, white gown she and Mom bought at Christmas. Now, she can't get excited about anything.

My grandparents come up for the weekend to attend the ceremony. The evening before, everyone but Leah stays at the dinner table for a long time, talking about the fall. My grandparents are happy that both Daniel and Leah will be heading back to Regina to live with them. Leah will start working on her science degree, and Daniel has his music scholarship.

I'll stay with Mom while she finishes out her contract. Things will change, though, because with the twins' departure, the airport manager has already told Mom that we'll need to move to one of the smaller houses across the street. Colin mentioned the possibility of us moving to an old cabin across the back road from the lodge. It was an idea that, when we were alone, my mom turned her nose up at.

The morning of the ceremony my grandmother rolls juice cans into Leah's straight hair. She tries to do the same with mine, but my natural curls don't cooperate, so she pins it all in an elegant up-do that is at odds with the simple pink shift dress I'm going to wear. I don't care. It makes me look older.

When I'm ready, I call Jeff. "Come outside. You have to see this!" I meet him out front.

"Wow, Claire. You look great."

"Great? I look amazing, you jerk." I twirl in front of him.

He reaches out and touches the shoulder strap of my dress. "You look beautiful."

"Come inside, you have to see Daniel. He's been ready for an hour, and he looks so handsome. Leah should be down right away."

Jeff looks toward his place, then agrees. "For a minute."

Shane pulls into the driveway as we walk up the back step, so we wait for him. He wears a black suit with a pearly white tie. His shoes reflect the sunshine as he joins us on the step. He holds a small plastic container.

He looks more handsome than he ever looked in his jeans and leather jacket.

"Can I see the corsage?" Shane had called weeks ago and told me he was looking for something special for Leah. I told him only that her dress was white, and that she would be wearing her special amethyst drop earrings.

Shane opens the container.

There are two flower wrist corsages inside: a white orchid, tinged at the edges with delicate mauve, and a soft pink rose nested into baby's breath and green fern.

"She's going to love it."

Shane reaches in and takes out the rose. "For you, Claire." He passes it to me and reaches for the back door. "Is she ready yet?"

I know I should warn him that my grandparents are there. He'll face the third degree from my grandpa, whom he's never met. I can only hope that Leah has prepared him.

Jeff's fingers brush my palm as he takes the flower from me. "Let me."

He stretches the elastic and slides it over my hand. It's snug on my wrist.

He squeezes my fingers. "You really do look beautiful."

"I wish you could come."

He looks down at his cut-off jeans and faded T-shirt. "Yeah. Me too." He opens the door for me. "Let's go in."

We are just in time for Leah's grand arrival in the living room. When she comes down the stairs, the room goes silent.

Her blonde hair tumbles down her back in a cascade of curls. Her dress is sleeveless, and her skin is smooth. She looks down at us all from three steps up.

Daniel and Shane both step forward to meet her, then with a wary exchange of glances, both take a step back. Leah comes down and slips her arms through both of theirs.

"I'm going to have the best-looking guys at my table tonight."

I agree. "You look like you're getting married."

All eyes turn to me, but Leah just laughs. "I did wonder about the white, but it was such a beautiful dress, I didn't care." She reaches out to touch the flower at my wrist. "Pretty."

For the first time in months, she meets my eyes.

Then she sends Shane a look that's so soft and grateful that I have to look away.

Once the circus that surrounds Daniel and Leah's graduation is over, and school lets out, Jeff invites Claire, Leah and Daniel along on his annual camping trip.

Jeff and Claire are going to take his dirt bike on the paths around to the campground at the east end of the lake. Leah and Daniel will come straight from work at the lodge and meet them in the parking lot, then they'll all hike everything in just far enough that no one will bother them.

When Jeff and Claire arrive, the parking lot is empty. Most campers with kids set up with their trailers back at Pioneer Bay where the beach is sandy, and there's a playground. The few sites here are isolated and rocky and frequented only by the most diehard campers.

Claire and Jeff sit on a picnic table down by the lake and watch the waves roll in while they wait.

At the sound of a car driving into the parking lot, they head back to carry the gear.

Jeff stops so abruptly, Claire almost runs into his back.

"This is not good." He steps to the side of the path so she can see what he sees.

There, pulled in next to Jeff's dirt bike, is a familiar black Trans Am. Shane steps out of it and greets them.

"Oh, no," says Claire under her breath as they hurry to help Shane unload.

Soon after, Leah pulls her Chevette into the parking lot and parks next to Shane. Daniel is out of the car as soon as she stops.

"What the hell are you doing here?" Daniel stalks toward Shane. Leah follows close behind.

"Same as you." Shane puts his arm around Leah.

"So I play chaperone to the kiddies, while you two have a nice romantic weekend?" Daniel glares at Leah. "You never said anything about him coming."

"Daniel, relax. We're all just going to hang out. We don't have much time left all together. It'll be fun." Shane tries. Jeff will give him that.

"I am not staying if he is." Daniel holds out his hand. "Give me the keys. I'll drop your shit, and that's it."

They stare at each other for a long minute, then Leah shrugs and tosses the keys over. "Whatever, Daniel. As usual you're ruining everything."

"He's always around. I've tried to be nice, but this is too much. This is our trip." It's Jeff's trip, but he knows what Daniel means.

Leah shakes her head. "Why can't you just deal with it?"

"Come on, Claire, let's go." Daniel waves her over.

Jeff looks over at Claire's distressed face. He hopes she stays, but it's not often Daniel asks her for anything.

"Daniel, leave her alone." Jeff can hear the anger in Leah's voice. "She wants to stay."

Claire looks between the two of them, then at Jeff, but he just shrugs. Not his decision.

Daniel goes to the car and starts throwing their stuff out onto the gravel. Claire walks over, while the other three wait. Jeff can't hear what Claire says to her brother, but he can see that Daniel is not responding.

Jeff turns to Leah. "Are you going to get in trouble with your mom?" He has to force himself to meet her eyes.

"I'm eighteen, Jeff, what can she do? Anyway, Daniel won't tell. He'll find some place to hide out. Mom will be at the lodge all weekend anyway. Don't worry, we're staying." She walks over and picks up her backpack, the small cooler with their food and a sleeping bag. "Grab your things, Claire. We need to get set up and get lunch ready. See you, Daniel. You're going to miss out on a great weekend."

"Fuck you, Leah." He gets in the car, backs out and peels away in a cloud of dust.

"You should have told him ahead of time that Shane was coming." Claire shakes her head.

"He wouldn't have come at all then. I just hoped he would stay."

"Next time, I guess."

"Yeah. Next time."

Shane unloads his things as Jeff slings his backpack over his shoulders. They each pick up a tent and start off into the bush. Claire follows with the food, and Leah brings up the rear, lugging a cooler. They don't have far to hike, just past the campground to a place near the water, under trees that shade two perfect flat spots for pitching the tents.

Once camp is set up, Leah goes to sit down at the shore to smoke a joint. Leah's head rests on her knees in between puffs.

"I'm so worried about her," Claire says.

Shane nods. "Why don't you two go gather some wood?"

Jeff takes a hatchet out of his pack and sets the pace, Claire close behind. When the path widens a bit, he moves over so she can come up next to him.

"You would have gone with him."

She looks over. "What?"

"If Leah hadn't told you to stay, you would have gone."

Claire shrugs. "They can't be bothered with me unless they have a fight. They argue all the time about Shane. Leah is acting so weird and Daniel is on the outs. He's so jealous. Maybe he needs a girlfriend."

"Claire, Daniel has enough girlfriends. Trust me."

Thoughts of Leah that night two months ago crowd him and he wants to tell Claire that he knows why Leah is acting weird, but he doesn't know how. He promised Leah he wouldn't. Anyway, since telling Shane who it was, he hasn't heard another thing about it.

"Maybe it's a twin thing. I think he really is lost without her." Claire starts pulling chunks of dried wood from around a fallen spruce tree.

Jeff works alongside her, not trusting himself to speak. He's afraid he's going to let something slip, so he changes the subject. "Remember our camping trip last summer?" The mood was a lot different, then.

"Yeah." Claire tosses a log in his direction. "It was so hot that weekend."

Jeff remembers. The two girls shared a tent, while he and Daniel slept outside under a blanket of Muskol and mosquitoes. There hadn't been this undertone of anxiety and sadness. It had been fun.

Claire and Jeff each carry an armload of wood back to the site. Shane has built up a small firepit and laid out bits of wood and twigs as kindling. Jeff lights the fire and throws on a log.

Shane pulls a six-pack of beer from the cooler, hands one to Leah and offers one to Jeff and Claire.

"Not Claire," says Leah as she sits down on the ground in front of the fire. "You don't drink do you, Jeff?" For the first time in a long time, she sends him that fierce assessing look. She scares the shit out of him, all she knows, and all she knows he knows. But the sparks in her gaze die quickly, and despite himself, Jeff is a little sad.

"No, I'm good. Thanks, though."

They all sit and gaze into the flames. As always, the sounds of the crackling fire and the waves hitting the shore lull Jeff and make it impossible to think or worry about anything else. Not his dad, not Leah. Not the fact that they returned from gathering wood to find Leah throwing Claire's sleeping bag into Jeff's tent. He can tell it's eating at Claire, though. She sits quiet beside him, jabbing at the flames with a stick.

They play cards and eat hot dogs cooked over the fire. When Shane and Leah go for a walk, Claire wanders down and sits on the shore. She doesn't seem to want company, so Jeff tucks the cards into his pack and pulls out his sketchbook. He leans back against the log he and Shane dragged over to the fire before supper. He sketches the view of the lake that lies before him. And Claire, as she pulls her curls into a ponytail, her slender arms up, the gentle curve of her neck. He finds it difficult to draw her, especially the expressions on her face. So he draws her from behind.

Shane and Leah return. Shane goes to sit with Claire. Leah comes to stand next to Jeff and looks over his shoulder. She reaches down and takes his sketchbook and flips through it. Jeff makes no move to stop her. He hasn't even shown Claire his drawings of her. He watches Leah's face. She nods slowly and hands his book back.

"You like her."

Jeff closes the sketchbook and places it on the ground by his feet.

Leah opens a beer and takes it to Shane where he sits. She comes back and takes one for herself, then straddles the log.

The sun has just started to set when Leah finishes the last of her beer, stands and calls out to Shane. "Come on, let's go to bed." She turns to Jeff. "You two better keep your hands to yourselves."

Jeff tries to think of something funny to say, but he draws a blank. He waves them on and gets up to add more wood to the fire. The temperature is dropping. They may as well stay warm. Claire walks up.

"Want to go swimming?" she asks. "I don't want to sit here and listen to them in there."

Jeff tries to keep the relief from his voice. "Sure. You change first."

Without the sandbars found in Pioneer Bay, the drop off into deep water is sharp and sudden. The water has calmed, but it's frigid, and as usual, Jeff gets used to it faster than Claire. He swims out toward the fading light, his arms pulling the water back in long, easy strokes. When he stops and wipes his eyes, he sees Claire, over her head but still close to shore, treading water.

"Come out here."

"No. I'm fine."

He swims back in to her, takes her by the hands. "What are you afraid of?"

"I'm not afraid." Her voice shakes. "But it's too dark to see the bottom."

"Relax, just float on your back. Let your feet come up. That's good, now put your head back." His icy fingers touch her warm chin, and she obeys. He pulls her out deeper. "I've got you."

He holds her wrist as they float next to each other in the dark. Clouds scud above them and shred the lingering remnants of light in the sky. When Jeff raises his head and looks over at Claire, he can just make out her face. Her eyes are closed.

They swim back to shore and dry off in the warmth cast by the dying fire. Leah and Shane's tent is quiet. Jeff can't put going to bed off any longer, and it's clear Claire won't make the first move.

He hands her his flashlight and leans against a tree so she can get ready for bed first. He looks out toward the silent lake. There is barely a ripple, the sky perfectly reflected in the calm water.

Claire comes out in sweats and a T-shirt. Her hair is twisted inside her towel.

"Go ahead." She won't look at him.

"Hey." He presses his fingers hard against her shoulder. "You've seen me sleep before."

"I know."

He slides his hand down her arm. She has goosebumps. "Do you have a sweater or something?"

Claire shakes her head. "Just go."

When he's changed, Jeff unrolls both sleeping bags and calls for her to come in. He tosses her his sweatshirt, then watches as she slips it over her head. Once she's settled, he clicks off the flashlight and crawls into his own sleeping bag. For a long time he listens, but her breathing doesn't change.

Finally, she speaks. "I don't know why everything seems wrong. Everyone is angry at everyone else."

Jeff rolls on his side and reaches his hand out. It brushes against her cheek. He doesn't know what to say.

Claire sighs long and loud. "Tell me a ghost story."

Jeff tells her a story, but it's not scary. It's a story his mom used to tell him long ago, when he was young and she still remembered what it meant to be a mother.

Jeff wakes with a start. Grey light filters through nylon, just enough to see that Claire sleeps facing him. Her cheek rests on her arm.

Then, from outside, voices. Whispering. Arguing.

Her eyes open and they stare at each other in the half-light.

"You need help." Shane says this.

"I don't," says Leah. "Just because I don't want you to come with me to Regina doesn't mean there's something wrong with me."

"I'm not talking about that." Shane's voice is getting louder. "And you know it."

"Quiet. They're going to hear you."

"Leah, this is unbearable."

"Unbearable? Try being me!" Leah's voice cracks like a whip through the air.

"That's not what —"

""Fuck you, fuck you, fuck you." Crack. Crack. And the last "fuck you" is muffled. Leah sobs.

Claire sits up and starts crawling for the door. Jeff grabs her ankle. "Stay here."

Claire frowns at him. "She's crying."

"Trust me."

"She's going crazy," Claire whispers. She pulls out of his grasp and reaches for the zipper. By the time she gets out, Jeff is out of his sleeping bag and at her heels.

Shane stands alone by the lake. He watches them walk over, his face blank.

"Hey," Claire says. "I thought I heard Leah out here."

"Yeah. She went for a walk. It's early, Claire. Go back to sleep."

"Shane, tell me what's going on."

Jeff and Shane share a long look, one that leaves Claire with the same empty feeling she gets when Leah and Daniel leave her out.

"Tell me," she says.

Shane nods a slow nod and tells Claire about the rape. Jeff doesn't say a word, just reaches out to steady her as she wavers on her feet.

When Shane's finished talking, he picks up a rock and throws it. It shatters the mirror-calm of the lake. The three of them stand looking out at the rings that ripple out in ever-widening circles.

EIGHT

After Shane's revelations on the trip, our second summer up north seems to float into an interlude of calm. Once Leah knows that I know what happened to her, she is almost her old, responsible self, the way she was back in Regina. Leah and Daniel go back to being friends in that soft way they used to have with each other. Daniel has even made an effort to get along with Shane.

One night in August, Leah comes to my room and asks me to go for a walk. Daniel is out. He hasn't been home for two nights, which leaves me alone with Leah.

We walk to the terminal building, then back around the main road to the highway. We climb up and sit on the back of the concrete base of the wooden sign at the turnoff. A distant street light makes it just possible to see Leah's features.

I listen as Leah talks for a bit about what she remembers from when we were little.

"Mom says I didn't like you from the moment they brought you home." Leah reaches for my hand. "It isn't true though. I always loved playing with you. You'd always let me be the teacher when we played school, or the dentist." I remind her that Daniel, too, let her be the boss.

I know Leah's looking for something, reaching out to me. I am still angry, though, that I had to hear what happened from Shane. I'm still not sure if Daniel knows. No one is talking about it.

"Claire, remember how at night, you'd climb into bed with me when you had a nightmare and I'd rub your back until you fell asleep?"

I nod. "Mom was never home, even then. Just babysitter after babysitter."

"She was working hard at school, Claire, to make things better for us." She removes her hand from mine and reaches into her pocket. "Here. You should have this."

She presses something into my hand. "Your ring?" It's the amethyst ring Mom gave her for grad. I know this means something. Even worse, I should know what she's trying to say. I feel a tremor go through me and I want to throw my arms around her and hug her as tight as I can, but I don't. Instead I pass the ring back to her. "No, it's yours, Leah. I'm sure I'll get my own when it's time."

"I want you to have it, Claire."

"Well, I don't want it."

I'm relieved when I see Jeff walking up the road toward us. I jump down and wave him over.

"Can I have your pocket knife?" I ask. Jeff hands it over and holds the little flashlight from his key chain steady as I scratch my name into the back of the sign. Jeff etches his name above mine. While Leah takes a turn at carving her name, Jeff and I circle around the sign and sit on the ground, backs against the base.

Jeff reaches his arm around me. For a second, I think he's going to kiss me, but instead he points to the sky. I look up in time to see a shooting star. I turn to ask Leah if she saw it, but Jeff squeezes my shoulder.

"Just watch. This is for you."

Another star seems to drop into the lake beyond the trees, then another and another. I want to look at Jeff, but can't. The stellar view holds my attention, but I can't forget the weight of his arm on my shoulders. I count aloud, as Leah walks from behind the sign to see what's going on. Jeff removes his arm from around me but leaves his hand resting on top of mine.

"What is it?" I ask.

"Perseids meteor shower." Jeff presses his thumb against the inside of my wrist. "I noticed it last night."

"I saw twenty-seven shooting stars," I say, trying to keep my voice steady.

"They're not really shooting stars," says Leah as she hoists herself onto the cement. "It's a comet. It's always there, but we can only see it when the earth is perfectly lined up, and we pass through its tail."

We watch the starry sky in silence for a bit longer, but it's over. Every pinpoint of light stays glued in place. No airplanes, no satellites, no meteors.

A car approaches the turnoff to the airport. It's Shane. He pulls over to the side of the road and gets out. I'm surprised to see Daniel get out of the passenger seat.

"I never expected to see those two together," Leah says.

"You haven't talked to Shane? Or Daniel?" I'm used to not knowing what's going on with anyone, but it's odd that Leah doesn't.

Daniel holds his right arm at an odd angle. As he comes closer, I see he has a white plaster cast that reaches from just below his fingertips to his elbow.

Beside me, Jeff sits up straight. "What happened?"

Daniel and Shane look at each other, then away.

"Daniel got in a fight." Shane stumbles a bit over the words. "I called your mom from the hospital last night. She didn't tell you?" He leans in and kisses Leah on the cheek, then hops up on the concrete next to her.

"No."

"Yeah. It was stupid. Over a girl." Daniel is subdued. "Doctor says it's pretty bad."

"How are you?" Shane asks Leah.

She breathes out hard. I know that sound. My sister's annoyed.

"Are you going to ask me that every time you see me? I'm not made of glass you know."

"Check it out." Daniel's voice draws our attention back to the sky. The tricks of the northern lights are played out in green and red and dizzying movement. They remind me of gymnasts, the ones with the ribbons, tiny flicks of the wrist making the ribbon dance and spin. I glance up to see if Leah watches. Shane leans against the sign, Leah rests back against him, hands in her pockets. His arms are around her, his cheek against hers. I think maybe Leah's crying, but it's hard to tell in the dim light, and I don't want to stare.

For a few minutes, we all watch the lights in silence, when the ugly sound of Leah swearing shatters the night.

"What the hell did you guys do?" Leah pushes away from Shane and stands with her fists clenched. "You assholes. You're the same as all the rest."

In the confusion of Leah's anger and the argument that follows, Jeff pulls me away from the group. "Let's go."

"What's going on?"

"Let's just get out of here. It has nothing to do with us."

We are almost back at the Bug Man's driveway when Leah runs by us, sobbing.

It's the last time I see my sister.

I sit backward on the piano bench and watch my mom and Daniel where they huddle in silence on the loveseat. The strain of the days searching for Leah shows. My mother's unwashed hair hangs in limp hanks to her shoulders. She's broken out in a rash around her mouth, and her lips are chapped and peeling from chewing on them. Daniel's dark eyes are puffy and shadowed, darker around one eye than the other, a reminder of the fight he was in just before Leah went missing. The stupid fight that also left Daniel's hand smashed and useless and in a cast.

When it's too dark to continue the search, volunteers start to trickle in through the front door to say goodnight. It bothers me. No one ever uses front doors around here. I think maybe the police started it. Maybe they think ringing the front bell makes their visits more professional.

The searchers speak in low, tired voices and stay just long enough to let my mother know that they'll be back again tomorrow. It's hard to believe that this silent room was the same place that held my mom's raucous birthday party two weeks ago, just days before Leah went missing. All the same people come and go, but now they're bowed by sadness, not drink.

So far nothing's been found, not one clue as to where Leah might be.

Jeff spent the day with a group searching a wooded area southeast of the airport. Now, he sits in the big chair next to the piano, close enough that I could reach out and touch him, if I wanted to. His face is pale. He stares at the floor, avoiding my gaze.

Daniel is on his feet again. He's been like this since he got home. He switches from limp and dazed next to Mom, to agitated and restless. As he paces, he holds his plaster-encased hand close to his body. His other hand makes a fist.

The end of the day is hard for us all.

Enough.

I stand and leave the room. I head past the back door and down the stairs to Leah's bedroom, where I lean against the door frame. The light is on in the furnace room behind me. My shadow carves a black hole into the rectangle of light on Leah's blue carpet.

I step inside and close the door. I feel my way over to Leah's double bed and sit.

As my eyes adjust to the darkness, I become aware of light flashing on and off through the high window. The aerodrome beacon. With every rotation of the light, the room brightens, then fades back to black. I watch the clock and count. Thirty turns a minute.

I close my eyes and listen to the sounds of the house. I hear the wood floor above me creak. Daniel, still pacing. Thumps on the front steps as more people take their leave.

The bedroom door opens. "Claire?" Jeff stands there, hands in pockets. I get up and go to him. He reaches out and pulls me in, arms around my shoulders. I squeeze my eyes closed.

"She's not coming back."

"You don't know that." His mouth brushes against my ear as he speaks.

I breathe in his scent, the cleanliness of soap and lake and the outdoors. I press in closer and his arms tighten.

"I don't want you to find her," I say. That's not what I mean. "I don't want you to be the one."

Jeff pushes the door closed with his elbow, but it doesn't latch. Together, we sit on the bed, his feet flat on the floor, mine hooked into the bed frame. He's grown taller this summer. So many changes.

"Remember the time we broke into the hall?" I ask. I feel him nod. I think of the rainy day when he jimmied the back door of the hall, and how I followed him in. I remember how we played music on the big sound system. How I danced like a maniac while he watched. How we drank huge cups of swampwater pop from the fountain drink machine, then spent the rest of the afternoon playing shuffleboard and running to the bathroom. Things seemed so easy then.

My breath catches in my chest as I think of the time last winter when we snowmobiled out past the dump into the bush. Of the time we climbed through a hole in the fence marked *Accès Interdit* that surrounds the runway. Or when we faced down the Bug Man's empty lot while playing Truth or Dare. Or, even more frightening, enduring the school-bus trip to town, twice a day every weekday. It all feels over, somehow.

Changed.

The only bad thing we ever imagined happening was getting caught. Grounded.

Leah pushed her boundaries, played her own version of Truth or Dare, and now she's gone. *Accès Interdit.*

I haven't cried once since Leah went missing. Now, my thoughts swirling, I put my elbows on my knees and lower my head into my hands. I feel Jeff rest his hand on my back. He keeps it there while I cry. Warm, and heavy, it holds me down. Like a paperweight, it keeps me from flying out of control.

Finally, when all I have left are short, uneven breaths, I wipe my face with my sleeve and lie down, my head on Leah's pillow. The smell of my sister makes my chest ache. Jeff pulls himself over to the other side of the bed. His hand finds mine and I hold on tight.

I roll to face him. His face gains and loses definition with every turn of the beacon. Above us, muffled footsteps continue the parade to the door, the groans of the floor marking their passage. Foreign sounds filter through the vent.

We stay like that, watching each other, then not. After a while, Jeff leans in and touches his lips to mine.

I'm surprised by the kiss. Even before Leah had gone, things had become awkward with Jeff. I thought it was just me. I had never been concerned with what he thought of me. Suddenly, that was all I worried about.

Then Leah left, went missing, and none of it mattered, anyway.

Now, Jeff is kissing me, really kissing me. And there's no one to tell. His mouth is warm and wet and so soft. His kisses are gentle, his tongue just touching mine, promising something – if not release, then relief, from this nightmare. I let go of his hand, put my arm around him and kiss him back, but harder, my desperation driven by the heat that flows through me. I gasp as his hand slides up under my shirt, his fingers roughly stroking the skin of my rib cage, his palm brushing my breast through the fabric of my bra. Jeff makes a sound in the back of his throat and presses me onto my back against the bed. I can feel the hard heat of him right through his jeans. We're both breathing hard, our breaths colliding, tongues touching, making it impossible to get enough air. I arch up against him, trying to get closer. My hands grasp at his shirt. He presses in against my hips; his arms rest on either side of my head.

Then he stops.

He looks down at me. I search his face in the flashes of light. He looks sad.

"Don't stop."

"Claire."

I reach my hands up to frame his face. The thought of Leah bumps up against me, but I push it away. I don't want to think of Leah, of where she might be.

"Kiss me again."

But he doesn't.

With a rough push away, he rolls onto his back. He scrubs his hands through his hair. "I'm sorry."

"It's okay, Jeff. I wanted you to kiss me. For a long time."

"I know."

"I want this. You."

"I know." He takes a deep breath and pulls me to him.

I rest my head on his chest, and he puts his arm around me. I lay my hand under his shirt, flat against his hard stomach. I've seen him without a shirt so many times, but seeing is definitely not the same as touching. My hand burns. That unnamable want courses through me again and forces me closer against his side. I stroke the silky skin of his stomach, trying to get up the courage to go farther. I slide my hand down until my fingers touch the elastic waistband of his underwear.

"Jesus, Claire, stay still." He rests his hand on top of mine. Holds it in place.

I feel like a kite, tethered only by him, by his heat passing through my hand, warming me, lulling me into the first real sleep I've had in weeks.

The light from the runway goes around and around.

Searching.

I wake to the crash of the door hitting the wall. Jeff is already up and moving. In the grey light that filters through the window, I can see Daniel at the door, his face dark.

"You bastard," Daniel says, his voice low. He lashes out with his injured right hand. Jeff throws his arms up and blocks the awkward punch.

I'm on my feet now, pushing Daniel back. "Stop it!"

He turns on me. "What the hell are you doing in here? How could you?" His face is red, and twisted like he's trying not to cry.

My own face is hot with shame.

Jeff puts his hand out. "Daniel, get a grip. Leave her alone. Nothing happened. She's fine."

Daniel shoves me out of the way, and goes after Jeff again. Jeff takes a couple of steps back, but Daniel connects this time, cast to mouth. Jeff still tries to avoid the fight, but when Daniel tries to hit him again, Jeff pushes him back with both hands, hard against the wall. His face is filled with fury.

"Don't start this, Daniel. You will fucking lose."

Jeff hits him, and all of a sudden the fight goes out of Daniel. He doesn't even try to defend himself against Jeff's punches.

"Jeff! Don't!"

As Daniel slides down the wall, crying, Jeff turns to me, his fist still raised. I put my hands up, adrenaline prickling across my scalp. The anger in his face turns to horror and he drops his fist.

"Just stop, Jeff. You've won." My voice shakes.

Jeff wipes the blood from his mouth, backs up to the door. "No one ever wins, Claire."

Daniel mutters something. Jeff stares, a stunned look on his face. I must have – I hope I have – heard wrong.

"What the hell did you say?" Jeff's voice is tight.

Daniel looks right at Jeff and says, "I said, get out of here, you fucking Indian."

"Daniel." I can't believe it.

Jeff stands, clenching and unclenching his hands. For a second I'm afraid he's going to hit Daniel again. But he looks at me, and his shoulders slump. "Heard it a million times, Daniel."

I take a step toward him, but he puts a hand up to stop me. "You. Just stay there." He turns and stalks out, up the stairs. I hear the door slam. Then, a soft thud as his own back door closes on the other side of the duplex.

I turn on my brother. "How could you? Nothing happened, Daniel. We fell asleep." He won't look at me. "He's your friend."

"Not any more."

I've so much more to say, but the sudden noise of yelling interrupts me. It comes from next door, the sound finding its way through the heating ducts. We can hear everything, clear as day. Jeff is in trouble for staying out all night. His father is loud, angry. Cursing. Thuds and crashes. Bumps. Jeff's mom, crying. *Stop, that's enough, you'll kill him.*

No sound from Jeff at all.

I lower myself back onto the bed and grip the rumpled quilt. I think of Leah down here, of the things she heard that no one else did. The things she knew. Daniel sits through it all with his head buried in his arms.

Not soon enough, it quiets.

"Did you know?" I ask. "Did you know it was like that for him?"

"Of course. Everyone knows, Claire." He leans his head back against the wall. "You're the only one living in your perfect world."

In shock, I leave my brother staring at the floor and climb the two flights of stairs to my room on shaky legs. The ache that's lurked in my chest since Leah went missing expands and fills my ears with buzzing.

I want my sister.

I lie down on my bed. It's all I can do not to pound my fist against the wall that separates my room from Jeff's, to signal him, to ask him to come out, to meet me. Instead, I rest my hand against the cool plaster and imagine he's doing the same on the other side.

 Jeff steps through the hall door and eases it closed behind him as he scans the room. The volunteers are focused on the RCMP sergeant doling out grid-search assignments at the front of the room. Petra sits on a wooden chair next to him, her eyes locked on her clasped hands.

And Claire. She leans against the bar between her brother and Shane. She looks tired, Jeff thinks. His gaze slips to Daniel. Jeff feels no satisfaction at the sight of Daniel's swollen nose and the blood that oozes from the cut above his eye. In fact, Jeff doesn't feel much beyond his sore ribs.

Jeff picks his mom out of the crowd. She stands next to his father, their backs a united wall over by the shuffleboard table.

Movement back by the bar. Jeff meets Shane's stare. Shane frowns, no doubt at the sight of him, and nudges Claire.

Jeff knew his face was a mess, but her reaction proves it. Jeff raises his hand to her. The sad softness that slips into her eyes is almost his undoing.

He doesn't want her pity. Or anyone's. He turns and stumbles down the hallway toward the kitchen as the cop finishes up his instructions.

"As always, if you find anything, don't touch it. Let your leader know, and he'll radio us to come take a look. See you back here at six."

Jeff leans against the fridge and waits. He knows she'll come.

It's not long before he hears Claire's voice in the hall. She argues with Daniel.

"Just go. There's nothing you can say, Daniel. Leave him alone."

"Claire, I didn't do that to him."

"I know that." Her voice is furious.

"Should I say something to him?" Daniel asks.

Jeff's hands tighten into fists. *Stay away,* he thinks.

"You can't fix this, Daniel. Not what you did, not what his dad did."

Jeff closes his eyes.

Then she's warm beside him, her fingers gentle against his lip, tentative as they touch the burls on his cheek. "Holy shit, Jeff."

He stands, unyielding. He can feel oily blackness surrounding him, darker and heavier than the deepest waters of the lake. His jaw aches as much from gritting his teeth against letting loose with a string of angry words as from his injuries. He wants to punch something. Hard.

He pushes her away and leans forward on the counter, hands on either side of the sink. Claire comes up behind him and slips her arms around his waist. He flinches at her touch and shoves her hands away.

He turns to face her. "Don't."

Claire looks up at his wrecked face. Her eyes widen as her gaze moves over each wound. A split lip, a cut cheek. Along with the knot on his cheek, a large lump forms near his eye. She reaches out a shaky hand and pulls up his T-shirt. He knows his rib cage is streaked with deep red marks that will no doubt turn into bruises. She can't see it, but they continue around to his back. She traces her fingers against his unmarked stomach. She looks up. He keeps his face still.

"Did he kick you, Jeff?"

He puts his hand on top of hers again, but this time, he pushes it off. "Leave it alone, Claire."

"Don't go today. Stay with me."

"I have to go, Claire."

"Go with a different group, Jeff. Don't go with your dad."

"Stay out of it." He moves toward the hall.

She reaches out and grabs the back of his shirt. "Wait."

He stops.

She leans her head against his back. "I didn't know. I'm sorry. I had no idea it was like that. We could hear –" She's crying now, tears and snot and sobs. *Fuck sakes.*

He turns and takes her by the shoulders. His words hiss between clenched teeth. He shakes her. "Please. Just leave it."

"Jeff." She looks at him like he's a stranger. Just like she looked at him earlier when he almost hit her.

Well, he isn't the same person as the one who held her the night before. That time is done, that guy is gone. She tries again to reach for him, but he holds fast to her shoulders and won't let her near.

"Jesus. Get a hold of yourself, Claire. I need to go."

Later, on the second afternoon break, the young RCMP officer in charge of Jeff's group comes to stand next to him.

"You get in a fight?"

Jeff shrugs.

"Hey, I asked you a question, boy."

Boy? Jeff narrows his eyes. The cop's maybe five years older than him. "Yeah, I got in a fight." He shakes his head. Typical cop, stating the obvious.

"Are you okay? It looks painful."

"Just taking a break. I'm tired."

"Yeah," says the cop. "We're all tired."

The monotony of the grid search, the difficulty of pushing through heavy brush, makes frequent breaks necessary. People switch off, heading back to the clearing to have a drink, to rest. The crowd of volunteers has thinned over the past two days; now it's down to three groups of fifteen or so, all in different areas around the airport. There's a fourth group made up of RCMP officers who are methodically searching the lakeshore. Early on, a bunch of searchers in boats did the best they could on the huge lake, but nothing was found. There's no point dragging the lake. It's too deep. If Leah drowned, they'll have to wait for her body to turn up.

Jeff's body aches. At least one broken rib, he's sure. Walking is painful, but he puts it out of his mind. He puts everything out of his mind.

The constable jumps at a loud squawk coming from his walkie-talkie. He grips it and turns his back to Jeff. He bends his head and listens.

Something has been found.

Jeff eavesdrops a few seconds then turns and runs. The search team is not far from the hall, now making a second pass through the wooded area beyond the curling rink. A ten-minute run to get to Claire.

He pushes through trees and underbrush, twigs and branches pulling at him, slowing him. Every breath rips through his side, and his eyes tear up. Past the dump, up the cutline to the road, then across the dry, brown field where the hospital used to be. His feet slide on the loose gravel on the road in front of the hall, but he rights himself. He grasps the door handle and yanks the door open.

No one even looks up. Petra sits at the front of the room on one of the wooden chairs, her head in her hands, her body folded in on itself. The RCMP sergeant crouches beside her, his hand on her shoulder. Petra already knows.

Rita stands next to the officer, a tablecloth in her hands. She's still, her face frozen in that same mask she wore earlier that morning, the one that she wears whenever his father loses control. She shifts her gaze and looks past him. Her face softens.

Claire. There, coming up behind him from the kitchen. A quick glance at her mother, then her head swivels to Jeff.

"What? What happened?" He can barely hear her voice. He turns to her, takes her again by the shoulders. His grip is gentle this time. He bends over, his face in front of hers, and talks to her, his voice low.

Claire turns her face away from Jeff, as though not looking at him can change things. She looks older than her years, but there is no surprise, and there are no tears.

Jeff reaches his hand up and moves her chin so she's looking at him. He's never seen her eyes so empty. He's done whispering now.

She pulls out of his grip and shoves the door open, pushing past Daniel and Colin on her way out. Jeff lets her go. He knows where to find her.

I lie back on the rock, looking up through my tears at the hole of clear sky that widens and narrows through the swaying trees.

"They found her," Jeff said.

"Amethyst ring on the finger."

"Suicide."

And more, words I just couldn't take in.

"I'm sorry," he said.

God, if I could, I would blast myself through the azure portal above me to a different world.

Someone's coming up the path. I don't even need to look. I know it's Jeff.

He leans against the rock. "Hey."

I wipe my eyes and sit up. I look down at him. "Hey."

His eyes are so blue.

"You make a lot of noise for a fucking Indian." My tongue feels thick, frozen. "That was a joke."

"Yeah." Jeff's face, through all the damage, is serious. "Yeah, I know." He holds my gaze for a moment, then gestures with his head. "Grab the box and come down here. There's no way I can climb up today."

I reach for the box, then slide down the hard face of the rock, landing on my feet next to him. I hand him the silver box and watch him open it. He rummages through our treasures, looking for something.

"Here. Here. And here." He hands me the bolt from the airplane and two rocks. I tuck the bolt into my pocket, then turn the first rock over. *Allegiance.* And then, one in French. *Voler.* "Keep them."

Oh, no. No.

I shake my head. "No."

"Claire, I won't be coming back here." Jeff sets the box on the ground, then closes his hands around my hand that holds the rocks. I pull away and let the rocks fall. "You're leaving."

"I have to go."

"Take me with you." I shake my head back and forth.

He pushes my hair back and holds my face in his hands. "Claire."

"Please. I can't lose her and you, too. Please. Stay."

"Stop it." Jeff drops his hands, his voice cold. "Stop this dramatic shit."

"My sister is dead."

"Don't do that, Claire. Don't fucking make her into an excuse." His voice turns gentle. "I know she's dead. I know. But my leaving isn't about you. You still have a family, Claire. Yes, your mom is a selfish bitch, and Daniel can be an asshole. What do I have?" Jeff reaches down and grabs the bottom of his long-sleeved T-shirt and lifts it up. He feels every one of his stiff muscles and cracked ribs. "This is what I have. I can't stay here one more day, Claire."

"Not even for me."

He just looks at me.

"If not for last night, this would never have happened."

"You think this is the first time? Look at me. No, *at* me." With his free hand, he grasps my chin. I look. His bruised waist narrows into his jeans. The boot marks around his ribs have started to turn black.

He rests his forehead against mine. "Claire, please. Please understand. I am going to kill him if this happens again."

Jeff kisses me before I can answer. He kisses me until my lips feel as swollen as his are. I let him back me right against the rock. He leans into me, just a little, his arms holding most of his weight. This is different than last night. I can feel no gentleness in him, no restraint. His knee pushes between mine, the heat of his thigh coursing right through to my centre. His tongue probes mine, a soft, warm invasion that becomes rougher as I grip the front of his shirt and pull him closer. I hold my breath as his hand slides up

90

under my shirt along the skin of my back. I taste the metallic tang of the split in his lip and sigh, severing the kiss. With gentle fingers, I stroke the back of his neck.

"I'll do anything you want." I look up. He looks back, his eyes stormy. "I trust you."

He knows what I'm talking about. "It won't make anything better, Claire."

"I don't care." I feel sick. Twice now, I've offered, and twice he's said no.

"I do, Claire." He backs away and winces as he touches the split in his lip. I shiver in the cold breeze that comes between us. Pain shoots through my stomach as my mind touches on Leah.

Jeff and I sink down, sit with our backs against the rock. He takes my hand, but I'm still angry.

I trace my finger along the seam of his jeans. "Jeff, you know that song, by Elton John, about the guy that names his son Jesus?"

My thoughts are everywhere, like they're parachuting in from some other planet. I can't hold anything steady in my mind. I feel like I'm trying to get out of a funhouse where the walls are moving, and the floor is rocking, and my exit must be timed perfectly to make it out safe.

"Yeah, I know it." He moves and stifles a moan.

I tell him how it was my dad's favourite song. "He played it on the eight-track all the time." When my father left, I tell him, I cried whenever I heard that song. "Daniel and Leah played it a lot for a while, but only when Mom wasn't home."

Now, I sing it just the way I heard it back then. Even through my tears, I know my voice is true. *"And he shall be leave on, and he shall be a good man. And he shall be leave on."* My voice wavers. "I know it doesn't make any sense. It's just what I thought it said."

I hear Jeff swallow. He leans his head back against the rock. My hand brushes one of the rocks I dropped, and I close my fingers around it. I stroke it with my thumb, its smooth hardness a comfort.

"Don't go."

"Claire," he begins, but his voice is drowned out by the evening flight as it approaches from the direction of the lake. We both look up as the plane passes overhead. It seems to hang above us for a moment, wheels down, landing lights aglow, flaps extended. Then it disappears. Seconds later it lands, wheels shrieking as though in mourning, clamshell reverse thrusters wailing.

"Time to go. They'll be looking for you," he says once the noise has faded away.

My voice is bitter. "I don't think either of us will be missed."

"I think you're wrong." He struggles to his feet.

I stand, too. I reach out and press my palm to his chest. I can feel his heart beat under my hand. "Are you really going to leave me?" My voice breaks on the last word. I won't look at him.

"Claire." His hand grasps my wrist. "I'm sorry about Leah."

I want to scream, to shake him, but I don't. A sharp pain starts in my chest and radiates outward. Everything inside me seems to shatter and fall away from me. I step back out of reach. "Where will you go?"

"I'm going north. To Churchill. I have an uncle there."

"See you around, then."

"Don't be like that."

My voice is calm. "You head on back and get ready for your big trip. I hope you find what you're looking for." My voice gets louder. "But you are going to find out that your *people* are right here." I thump my chest with my hand. I turn and scramble up the rock, where he can't follow. He puts his hands in his pockets and turns to go as I watch him from on high. He starts toward the path.

"Hey, Jeff."

He turns back to me. I cock my arm and let fly the rock I've been holding. He doesn't try to block it or catch it, and it strikes him in the chest, where earlier my hand rested. I watch, my jaw tight, as he reaches down with difficulty and scoops it up. He glances at the word before he shoves it deep into his pocket. Then he's gone.

I let out a scream that's more of a howl.

Then, the words, almost unintelligible. "To hell with *allegiance*, Jeff. To hell with you. Leave on, you bastard, you fucking Indian bastard. Leave on."

Jeff does.

Jeff can't let them worry about her. He walks straight to their place and knocks on the door. Daniel answers. His eyes are red from crying. He listens to the directions Jeff gives him and nods. Daniel grabs a flashlight from the shelf beside the door and calls out to his mom that he knows where Claire is. At the bottom of the driveway, Jeff turns right instead of left toward the runway.

"Aren't you coming?" Daniel asks.

"She needs you, Daniel. Not me." The urge to get away is stronger than the guilt that clutches at him. He has to be waiting at the railway siding down by the lake for the first train north in the morning. He still has packing to do.

Daniel turns and disappears down the path that Jeff and Claire kept secret for so long.

At home, Jeff passes his mom in the kitchen without a word, and as usual, she doesn't try to stop him. His father is in the living room watching TV. He doesn't even look up.

Jeff heads to his room, shoes still on, and stands in front of his window.

He hurts all over, but if he closes his eyes, he can still feel Claire's soft mouth opening under his, the heat of her skin against his hand, the way she pressed herself against him. He leans his head against the glass. He wanted her so bad, and it would have been so easy.

Easy, but not right.

It's full dark when Daniel and Claire come out of the trees. They flicker like wraiths in the slow pass of light from the beacon, then become more solid when they reach the steady phosphorous street light at the end of the road. Daniel's arm is around Claire, guiding her. Claire cradles the box against her chest. She looks up at Jeff's window and stumbles.

Jeff's hand hits the glass, but he can't keep her from skidding to her knees. The contents of the box spill out over the road. Claire scrabbles frantically through all the bits and pieces they've collected over the past year. Daniel crouches next to her and places his good hand on top of hers. Claire stills. Jeff watches as Daniel helps her to her feet, then half-carries her up the driveway. Her feet barely touch the ground. Jeff stays at the window and stares at the empty box in the road until he feels the change in the air that tells him their door has closed.

TEN

At Leah's funeral in Regina, Daniel sits in between my mother and me. I let myself be distracted by the pale flowers, the dark clothing worn by the readers, Daniel's casted hand that rests on the pew. Anything to take my mind off the white casket in front of me.

My grandparents are here; Leah's friends from her old school are here. I know my mom would do anything to erase this past year. It took no time at all to pack up and come back home, moving in with my grandparents like we did so long ago, after my father took off. Mom says as soon as we find a place, our things will be shipped down. Like we were never there at all.

Except.

Leah never came home.

And Daniel isn't coming either.

I was wide awake last night, lying on the old pullout couch in my grandma's basement, when he finally came in from up north.

He didn't say a word, just lay down beside me, trying not to wake me.

It felt strange. Leah and I had always shared the pullout, while Daniel slept on the couch under the window.

I moved closer to him and he grabbed my hand, and for a second I felt like maybe everything was going to be okay. Bearable.

Then he told me he was staying up north. He was going to work for Colin fulltime at the lodge.

"Why?" I had more to say, to ask, but I couldn't get the words out.

"Because I like it. And she's there."

But I'm here. I didn't say it though.

"There's nothing here for me, Claire. With my hand the way it is, there will be no music scholarship. No more piano."

"But you can go to school, do something else."

"Not without her."

I rolled over onto my side. My mind wandered back north, to the lake. It made me think of Jeff, how he's gone, too. Nothing's the same there, either.

When Daniel said my name, I pretended to be asleep.

Very little light passes through the narrow, square panels of stained glass. My eyes rest on Jesus for a while, and then move on. I wish Jeff were here. I wish I didn't have to sit beside the aisle, so close to my sister's body.

I look over my shoulder. The church is so full, people stand against the back wall. Shane sits next to Colin, two rows behind me on the opposite side. Shane meets my gaze with such heavy sadness, I'm surprised I haven't felt his stare sooner. He nods at me without smiling. The acknowledgement, the directness of his look, is too much. I swallow, but can't push down the hard knot in my throat. I face the front.

The priest drones on about forgiveness and despair and eternal damnation. Or maybe it's eternal salvation. I'm not even sure what I'm hearing any more.

I want to tell Daniel I feel sick, but as I look up at his face, I see how white and drawn it is, how wet his eyes are. So I say nothing, just press my fingers to his where they stick out of his cast.

I lean my cheek against his sleeve, and even through the rough fabric of his suit, I feel the warmth and hardness of his arm. I turn and press my forehead against his shoulder, then push hard. I try to move him, but he tenses enough to counterbalance my push, enough to stay still, the same way he used to when we would fight in the back seat of the car when we were little. I'd lean and lean against him, brace myself against the door and shove with all my might, but I could never budge him.

Now, he bends his head to mine, puts his mouth next to my ear. "Almost done. Hang in there." His breath is warm against my cheek.

"Please stand," the priest invites.

I can't. I just can't. The smell of incense wafts down from the altar and my throat closes. I cough and cough and try to catch my breath. Daniel pushes my head to my knees as everyone else gets to their feet.

"Breathe." I feel his forehead against the back of my head, his arm around my shoulder.

I steady myself. Breath in, breath out. "I'm okay, now."

Daniel hauls me to my feet. I grip the wooden railing in front of me and peek at my mom. Her eyes are unfocused. She looks right through me. Nothing new there. My stomach turns and I know if I stay, I'm going to be sick.

I have to get out of here.

I half-run down the aisle, through the narthex and out the main doors of the church. The door shuts with a bang behind me as I skid to my bare knees on the lawn, my breath coming fast as I gulp the hot August air.

I hear someone come out the doors behind me, and even as every part of me hopes it's my mother, I know it won't be.

Shane kneels beside me, pushes a curl behind my ear. He says nothing, just helps me to my feet and leads me to a bench near the doors. We sit, and he hands me a tissue.

"Take me away from here." I pull my dress down over my grass-stained knees.

"Claire, I can't. You need to go back in." His voice is low, but firm.

"No. It's too hard."

"Too hard?"

I look up at the mild annoyance in his voice.

"Claire, who took care of you when you guys were small? Who made sure you had a lunch for school and read to you every night when your mom went to university? Who helped you with your math homework?"

"How do you know all that?"

"How, do you think?"

"What else did she say about me?" My need to know is a burr in my skin.

"That you were a pain in the ass, but funny. A little brat that she needed to look out for." A deep sigh rattles in his chest. "And that she loved you."

I shake my head. "I wasn't a brat. Well, not unless they treated me like one."

"Prove it, then. You need to go back in, Claire. That's why we're here. It's not supposed to be easy."

He lets that sink in a minute, then he stands.

I put my hand in his and he pulls me up.

"Shane."

"Yes?"

"If she thought all those things – how could she?"

He raises his shoulders in a long shrug. "I don't know. Come back in with me, Claire."

"Shane." I look up at him. Even though I know it doesn't matter any more, I have to say it. "Leah lied. She never helped with my math homework. Daniel did."

His sad expression is a mirror of what mine must look like. Together, we head back into the church.

When I return, Daniel steps out of the pew and lets me in. Flanked by him and my mom, with my grandma's hand within reach, I pass the rest of the service in a blur. When it comes time to follow the casket out, I raise my head and step in behind Daniel and Mom. As we pass Shane's row, I reach out and pull him along with me.

Outside the church, I move out of the throng of mourners and stand to the side. I grip Shane's hand to keep him near. I'm afraid if I let him go, he'll disappear. We watch as a line of people forms to speak to Mom and Daniel.

A man who I'm sure is my father approaches my mom and hugs her. It's been a long time since I've seen him. Mom clings to him in what seems to be shared grief, but when he pulls away, I can see that my mother's eyes are dry. She put him to rest a long time ago. We all did. He knows it, too, as he turns to Daniel. There's no question. There will be no father-son embrace. Mom and Daniel join my grandparents in the long, white limousine reserved for family, leaving my father standing alone. He looks around, perhaps searching for me, but I duck my head and hide behind Shane. Soon enough, my father moves on.

Once the back door on the hearse is closed, I pull Shane along to the limo.

"Shane's coming with us," I say. Mom and Daniel sit facing my grandparents. There is a space for me next to my grandmother. There's still plenty of room for Shane.

"No, he's not." Mom's voice is firm. She doesn't seem at all weakened by the fact that she is going to bury her elder daughter.

"I want him to."

"Just get in the car, Claire." Daniel is almost begging me.

Shane sticks his hand out to Daniel and Daniel goes to shake it with his bad hand, then switches to his left and clasps Shane's without hesitation. It's odd to see these two former foes holding hands like this.

"I'm sorry for your loss," Shane says. Like it isn't his loss, too.

Daniel holds Shane's gaze, and a look of kinship passes between them. I'm glad that Daniel sees that Shane holds a piece of Leah too.

Shane steps back. I climb in and glare at my mom as the limo driver closes the door.

"Stop it," Mom says. "He's not family."

"What about our father? You didn't let him in."

Grandma rests her hand on my leg. "Claire."

"He's not family either." Mom's face sags. She looks old. I want to tell her that, to tell her she looks awful and that I'm glad, but something holds me back.

"That's what I thought." I look out the window.

The cemetery isn't far, just a few blocks from the church. We could have walked, but Mom insisted on the limousine. The car is already slowing, pulling to a stop behind the hearse. Soon the whole farce of a ceremony will be done, and I can go home to my grandparents' house. I need some time and space actually to remember my sister.

All this ritual has given me a headache.

I corner Shane at the reception in the church basement after the burial. His eyes are red. I wonder if he's stoned.

"Do you have any pot?" I ask.

He shakes his head. "Sorry, kiddo. Not a great idea right now." He looks down at me. "Anyway, I don't do that any more."

Before I can quiz him on this, he changes the subject. "Did you hear that Jeff left home?"

I feel a jolt at the mention of Jeff's name – the warm feeling I am used to when it comes to him, followed by a searing anger. "Yeah, I know."

"I saw Rita a few days ago at the post office in town. She said he called from Churchill to say he was okay."

"Such a good boy not to worry his mommy." I don't even try to control the bitterness in my voice.

"I thought you were friends, Claire."

"So did I." I look around the room for my mom. There she is, surrounded by mourners at the front of the room. My grandparents sit at a long table with Daniel and Colin. No one is talking; everyone looks lost. I can't even think about my brother right now and his decision to ditch me. "Let's get out of here."

"Okay. Do you want to tell anyone you're going?"

"Were you this much of a worrywart with Leah? God, Shane, you must have driven her crazy." I can see this hurts him. I know I should apologize but I don't. "Come on, if you won't give me any pot, at least you can buy me an ice cream."

I lead him out of the church, out toward Victoria Avenue.

"See how lucky we are that we had her funeral on such a nice day?" I fling my arms out and skip up the street. Shane follows, hands in his pockets.

"Hey, Shane, check it out. Milky Way is open." We cross the street, kitty-corner. A long line of people snakes down the sidewalk, waiting for their turn at the ice-cream shop's order window. "What'll it be today? A milkshake? A cone? They have hard and soft. Oh look, all these people so nicely dressed. They must have come over right after the funeral. What fun. A funeral and ice cream." I blink away the tears in my eyes.

"Claire, don't do this. I'll buy you an ice cream, then we should go back."

I look hard at him. "I'll go for one, but not the other."

"You're being an idiot. Come on."

He buys me a rocky road, Leah's favourite, and we walk back to the church parking lot. His black Trans Am gleams in the sun.

"I don't want to go back in," I say. "Take me for a ride."

Shane drives and I finish my cone. It's strange sitting up front in Leah's place. I direct him past Leah's old high school to the park. We get out of the car and make our way to a picnic table by the ancient goose-shaped slide that we used to play on when we were small.

Shane sits on the bench and faces out toward the lake. I perch on the tabletop next to him. My bare knee rests against his arm.

The stagnant water of the lake gives off the familiar end-of-summer stench of algae and bird shit.

"When are you going back home?"

"Tonight."

"I wish you could stay with us."

"That's okay. My mom needs me at home." His voice is hollow. I can't see his face.

"Leah told me your mom's sick."

"Yeah. MS." He doesn't elaborate.

We sit and watch two geese walk across the grass in front of us.

"You have to be careful around geese, you know," I say. "They're so strong they can break your arm with their beaks if you cross them."

"Really." It's not a question.

My throat is clogged, filled with so many things I want to ask, so many things I need to say to him. The thought of him leaving makes my ears ring and my head ache. The thickness in my throat tastes like blood.

I bend over and rest my head on my knees. "I think I'm going to die."

He slides his hand back and wraps his fingers around my ankle in a tight grip. "Don't say that."

I tell him that Daniel won't be moving back with us. "He's staying at the lodge with Colin."

Shane is quiet.

I feel a rush of anger. "You already knew."

"Yeah."

"You're not even his friend and you knew. All these secrets. No one cares about how I feel." I know I sound like a child.

"I care."

"I have no one to talk to."

"You can talk to me."

So I do. I tell him how my ears hurt and that I think they're filled with unshed tears. I describe the high-pitched whine that's been in my head since Jeff told me Leah had been found.

He nods. "That sound goes away. It was like that when my dad died. Eventually it will fade. You get used to it."

I'm not sure that's a good thing. "I don't want to forget. I'm afraid you'll forget me and someday I'll call you, and you won't remember who I am." *Or who Leah was.*

"Didn't she tell you, Claire? I'm coming back this fall. I was accepted into the RCMP." He turns his head and looks up at me. "I'll be around a lot. You'll be sick of me."

"I don't think so," I say. The chokehold I've been living with for weeks seems to lessen. "Maybe you're right."

We stare out at the water for a few more minutes.

"We should get back," Shane says.

He stands and puts his hand out to help me off the table. With barely a thought, I throw my arms around his waist. He stands frozen for a second, but when I squeeze him tighter, he hugs me back, his arms looped lightly around me.

Jeff keeps the door to his room closed. He knows he's lucky to have a job at the grain terminal and a place to stay, a room rented to him by his foreman. Jeff has no idea what he's going to do when the snow falls. He spends most of his time off wandering the streets of Churchill, staying out of the way of the family that took him.

Not that he gets much time off. The trains come fast and furious, filled with grain that needs to be transferred to ships as soon as possible, to allow the empty ships that wait at anchor in the bay a chance to load up.

He's an errand boy, sweeping floors, cooking meals, cleaning the break room. Sometimes he'll cover for the guys if they need a bathroom break. Mindless work.

There's a commanding knock on his door – it's not the tentative tap that wakes him in the morning. No, this knock is the evening knock. Ted, his boss and his landlord, pokes his head in. "Going to head downtown to the bar. Want to join me?"

Jeff feels he has no choice. It's the third night this week, but it gives him something to do. It's when he has time to think that he feels the despair seep in. It's been disappointment after disappointment since he left home. Best to keep busy.

The trip started out exactly as he'd planned.

It was still dark when Jeff stuffed the small plastic bag that contained his toothpaste and toothbrush, his comb, a bar of soap and a small bottle of shampoo into the huge backpack his father bought him for their hunting trips. Along with his toiletries, he packed underwear, three pairs of jeans, a hooded sweatshirt, five T-shirts, a ball cap and his winter jacket. His sketchbook and charcoal pencils were zipped into the front pocket of the pack along with Claire's copy of *The Pigman* and all the notes she'd ever written him. He couldn't leave those behind to be found.

He left his paintings, his school jacket, his school books. His hockey card collection. The cassettes that Daniel made for him. He left his fishing rod and his rifle. He always hated hunting anyway. Let the old bastard keep it.

Backpack on his shoulders, Jeff turned his back on home, then on the Bug Man's place and set off down the dark street he'd walked almost his whole life.

There were very few lights on. Only the weatherman, Joseph Cameron, was up, getting ready to head to the weather station to release the day's weather balloon.

Jeff felt lighter with every house he passed. He'd watched a lot of people come and go while he waited for his chance to escape.

He figured he'd have a long hike ahead of him to reach the siding where the train would stop, but a guy driving a septic truck stopped to pick him up just past the road to the residential school.

The first inkling Jeff had that things might not be as perfect for fleeing as they seemed was when he saw all the police cars at the turnoff to the caves. Four dark-coloured cars, along with three blue-and-white RCMP cruisers, parked along the edge of the road, with one cop leaning against his car. *Leah.*

The driver dropped him off at the level crossing, where he sat on the rail, waiting for the train to appear around the bend. The eastern sky blazed orange and pink, but he faced west, watching for the train.

Jeff felt the vibration of the tracks underneath him. He stood and pulled his pack onto his back. It was heavy, though it seemed like he'd left so much behind.

Being the end of summer, all the cars were filled with wheat, heading up to the huge grain elevator on Hudson Bay for loading and shipping across the ocean. He hoped there would be an empty boxcar he could ride in, like in autumns past, when his father would take him up the line to go hunting.

The train groaned to a stop, the engine sliding just past where he waited.

"Where are you headed, boy?" The engineer leaned his head out the window. His face was covered in a wide, white beard, and he wore a baseball cap pulled down over his grey hair.

"The end of the line."

The man laughed. "Aren't we all?" He studied Jeff, making him self-conscious of the story his face told. "Who did that to you?"

Jeff didn't even try to lie. "My dad."

The man nodded. "All right, but we're pulling a full load on this run and it's a long, cold trip. Come ride up front with me." He disappeared from the window. He opened the door in the front of the cab, and Jeff climbed the ladder.

"I heard they found that missing girl yesterday." The engineer increased the speed and blew the whistle. Jeff looked behind him as they rounded a curve, but all he saw was the train snaking through the trees. The crossing and the highway were gone.

"Yeah."

"They pulled her out of there late last night, down by the caves at the lake. Everyone in town is talking about it. Looks like she offed herself. Lots of blood."

And with that, all Jeff's lightness turned to stone. The urge to jump from the train and run back home, to help, to be there, was so strong his legs twitched. He'd never been so sure he'd made a mistake in his life.

Too late.

Soon, the rhythm of the train on the tracks lulled him to sleep. His last thought before dropping off was not of Claire, but of his mother, finding his goodbye note.

They'd switched engineers at Gillam. The new guy was more talkative than the first.

He was the one who told Jeff that it wasn't just his uncle who had left, but most of the Dene people. They'd decamped from the deplorable conditions outside of town to make a new start farther north and west of town, in a place accessible only by plane.

He's also the one who talked to Ted about the job at the grain elevator. Jeff is thankful for the kindness of these strangers. With no chance of finding his family, Jeff hopes to make enough money that he can get out of Churchill before the snow flies. Maybe head to Winnipeg. Maybe south will be luckier for him than north.

Jeff finally called his mom this morning, to tell her he was fine. She'd been more upset that he'd come all this way and not found his uncle than that he'd left home. He couldn't bring himself to ask about Claire, but just before he hung up, she'd told him that today was Leah's funeral. He hasn't stopped thinking of Claire all day.

His dreams here are filled with Claire and airplanes and tamarack and spruce. He dreams of the lake and of kissing her.

His reality is a treeless, barren place, where all traces of his mother's family have disappeared, and the closest thing he has to a friend is the waitress at the bar.

Jeff opens the door to the bar for Ted, and they head into smoky clouds of noise and warmth. Ted stops to talk to a man at a table near the front while Jeff makes his way to their usual booth at the back of the room.

A young woman with platinum-blonde hair materializes to his left. She wears a cut-off shirt and a tight skirt.

Jodi.

"Hey, you. The usual?" Her voice is husky. She stands with one hand on the booth behind him, the other rubbing the bottom of her shirt, touching her stomach. She's close enough he can smell her perfume.

Jeff clears his throat. "Yeah, a ginger ale. Please."

"Alrighty."

With a wide smile, she leaves him. He sighs in relief, but there is still a hitch in his sore ribs that cuts his breath off.

Jeff looks around the room, taking in the rough wooden decor, the jukebox in the corner, a small, scuffed hardwood dance floor. A silver disco ball keeps a watchful eye over two men playing pool at one of three billiard tables on the far side of the bar.

The bar itself runs along one wall. Jodi is over there now, laughing with two women who sit on tall stools, drinking beer. He watches her as she places his drink on a tray and heads back to his table.

"How are things going at work?"

He tries to hand her the cash for his drink, but she grabs his hand and pushes it back down on the table.

She doesn't move her hand away. He aches at the warmth of it. He wants to take it and put it against his cheek, but he doesn't.

"Your bruises are fading." She gestures at his face.

Jeff's mouth twists and he pulls his hand away, leaving the money underneath her palm.

Later, when Ted gets up to go to the washroom, Jodi comes by and asks Jeff if he wants a shot of rye in his ginger ale.

He shakes his head. She scares him, like Leah did, but not for the same reason. Leah knew things that had the power to upset his family balance. But even though he worried, he always knew she poked and prodded his dad, or visited and suggested, because she cared about his mom.

Jodi is different. She could upset his whole life.

She stands close to him now. Her hip presses into his shoulder. "Come on. One drink."

"I'm good."

She reaches into her pocket and pulls out a small square of dull foil paper. "Here. In case you want to party later." She leans down. "Come back at closing."

When he arrives, the bar is dark. Jodi comes to the door and pulls him inside.

"Do you still have it?"

He hands the acid-tainted paper back to her. She fumbles with it, then presses it to her tongue, watching him the whole time. She reaches into her pack of cigarettes and pulls out another. She holds it up to his closed lips. He shakes his head once, but he feels that slipping feeling again.

He shouldn't.

He knows it's a bad idea.

He opens his mouth.

Her touch is light on his tongue.

DRAG

It's a short message on the answering machine, and I recognize his voice right away. It's taken five years, but Jeff finally called.

"I'm in town. Let's meet, six o'clock on the steps behind the MacKenzie." The MacKenzie Art Gallery. Jeff says it like a local. It's close to my little house in Lakeview.

Shortly after graduation, my mom came to me and told me she wanted to take a job in Ontario. I refused to go. I'd had enough moving, and anyway, my mom's opportunity in The Pas hadn't worked out so well.

My grandfather, normally so quiet and reticent, surprised me by taking my side. And so now, I live in the small house my mom bought after Leah died.

It was a good move for my mom, though, one that's led to bigger and bigger research posts for the government. When I'm not angry with her, I'm almost proud of her for making something out of the life she has.

Jeff and I exchanged letters, nine or ten in the first few years, but that's dropped off. Today is the first time I've heard his voice since that night at the rock. My hand shakes as I press the Save key on the answering machine.

I sit on the end of my bed and consider whether I'm actually going to show up, but in reality, there is no way I'd miss this chance. I spend a long time getting ready, putting on makeup, taking it off, then putting it on again. Choosing my clothes takes even longer.

Maybe we'll walk down Albert Street to the Clachan for a beer, or we could come back to my place. I have no idea where he is staying. No clue how to get ahold of him. But I will be at the MacKenzie.

The weather is heavy and thick. It's mild for late October, but it starts snowing on my walk over to the art gallery. The light-as-air snowflakes swirl in the glow of the headlights of passing cars; the ten-minute commuters, coming home from downtown. "The shortest commute in Canada," my grandma says. Snow gathers on the ground in puffy drifts, then shifts into whirling wraiths across the sidewalk. The way the city lights reflect off the low clouds above the city, I can tell it's not going to stop snowing soon.

I kick the snow off the steps behind the art gallery to clear a spot to sit. I don't want to wait in the atrium in case I miss him. I sit, tucking the bottom of my long coat underneath me.

I wait for a while. When I check my watch, Jeff is forty minutes late. The gallery closes at seven, twenty minutes to go. Even if he shows up now, we won't be going in. I hug my arms around myself and wish I'd worn a hat. The humid air brings a chill with it.

Fifty minutes, an hour. He's not coming.

Above me, on the second floor of the gallery, the lights go out. A few minutes later, the lights in the atrium dim, and I know there's no point in staying. And there's never any point in crying.

I start walking south. I cut through the mall to warm up, then I'm back outside. The wind picks up.

I know where to go. Shane's place is on the next block. I go up the walk and press the button beside his name. He answers right away.

"It's me." I haven't seen him in a while. We've both been busy, Shane with work, me with my engineering courses at university. "Can I come up?"

The door buzzes and I pull it open. I get on the elevator and unbutton my coat. My jeans are soaked from the knees down. The walls of the elevator are mirrored, and I can't help but look at myself as I unwind the scarf from my neck. My hair is wet with melted snow, and my mascara is running. I scrub under my eyes with my finger.

Fourth floor. I get off the elevator and turn right. Shane leans against the door jamb of his apartment, arms crossed. He seems bigger than the last time I saw him. More solid. I put my arms around his waist and rest my cheek against his soft, black sweater.

"What's new?" he asks.

I burst into tears.

I can feel his deep sigh against me, and it makes me feel worse. I've had such a long run of feeling good, feeling normal. Now here I am, falling apart again. I bet he's thinking the same thing.

I wipe my face with my hand and start to move past him. He stops me. "Go in the kitchen. I'll be right there, okay?"

I can see the blue flicker of the TV from the living room as I slip my boots off and head into the kitchen.

I hear Shane talking to someone in a low voice at the same time as I notice the small table set for two. Understanding lands like a brick in my stomach. I lean against the stove and wipe my eyes again. It's warm, there's something cooking in the oven. My face burns with embarrassment as I try to decide what to do. There is a flash of blonde hair in the hall as Shane walks his guest to the door.

"I owe you a rain check," I hear him say.

His date says something I can't hear, then laughs. I start toward the door to tell Shane I'll go, but stop in the sudden silence where I imagine they're kissing.

I sit down at the table, push the plates away with a loud clank and rest my head in my hands. The door to the hall closes.

"What's going on?"

"Why didn't you tell me? I would have come back. You should have just said you were on a date." I can't even look at him. "Was she mad?"

"It's okay."

"We don't talk for weeks, then I show up when you have your girlfriend here. I am so, so sorry."

He laughs and goes over and shuts off the oven. "Claire, she's not my girlfriend. It was just a date." I watch him pick up a tea towel and pull a pan of lasagna out of the oven.

"Did you eat? I think there'll be a few leftovers."

I can't laugh. I've been on the edge like this before. If I start I won't stop. "What did you tell her?"

"Family emergency."

I feel a sinking inside me. "There's no emergency. There doesn't always have to be a crisis, you know."

He comes and sits across from me. "I know." He reaches across the place settings and takes my hand. "So tell me."

I push my wet hair out of my face and tell him about Jeff's call. About being stood up.

He bites his lip and leans back in his chair. "Maybe he had a good reason. He had no way to get in touch with you."

"He could have called someone at the MacKenzie." I glare at him. "Don't stick up for him."

"Sorry." He rubs his hand over his short, dark cop-hair, making it stand up in front. "You're right. What an asshole. What a complete jerk. He should be strung up." He motions to the living room. "Come sit down where it's comfortable."

The living room is cleaner than I've ever seen it. There are two half-full wineglasses along with a bottle of red on the coffee table. The lights are dim. Alex Trebek is on the small screen.

"Jeopardy, Shane? That's your idea of a date? I'm surprised there aren't girls swarming your door. Maybe it's a good thing I butted in." I try hard to keep my tone light.

"We weren't exactly watching it, Claire." He reaches down and picks up one of the wineglasses and hands it to me. "It's mine. You can have it." His voice is soft. "Let me grab you a towel for your hair. I have some sweats and socks you can borrow."

I swirl the liquid in the glass into a red funnel. I take a few big swallows and set the glass on top of the TV before following him into his room.

He's thrown a towel on the bed for me and is digging through his drawers. He hands me a pair of sweats and leaves me alone to change. I towel dry my hair and wipe the makeup from my eyes. I feel stupid now, for taking the time to put it on. I slip my jeans off and drape them over a wide chair next to where he's laid out his uniform. My jeans look small and insignificant next to his official, yellow-striped RCMP pants.

I pull on the dry socks and shake out the sweats he gave me. The sick feeling in my stomach is back. They fit. Some other girl must have left them. I take a deep breath, surprised that it bothers me. I know he's dated since Leah died. He's had a few girlfriends. He must have. But he's never bothered to introduce them.

Back out in the living room, I grab my wine and sink into the couch next to Shane. The other wineglass is gone, and he's drinking a beer, flipping the cap in his hand.

"Is this couch new?" I rub my hand across the red Ultrasuede.

"Yeah." ·

"And you didn't take me shopping with you?" I tuck one knee under me and try not to sound upset. He used to include me in things like that.

"Why, you don't like it?"

"It's okay. I would have bought leather."

"I didn't want leather."

"Well, you should have bought leather. They say it's easier to keep clean."

He raises his eyebrows. "You see any kids around here? I don't really have to worry about keeping my couch clean, Claire."

I finish my wine. "Seriously, I'm really, really sorry about your date."

Shane picks up the bottle and refills my glass. "Don't be, Claire. Nothing was going to come of it."

"How do you know?" I nudge his leg with my foot.

"Because, I didn't want something to come of it, okay?" Annoyance tinges his voice.

"But you would have slept with her. You kissed her." I'm pushing him, and I don't know why.

"Jesus, Claire. She kissed me, okay? On the cheek."

"Liar."

"Want some lasagna?" He stands.

"Depends. Did you make it?"

"What kind of jerk would kick a woman out after she made dinner? Of course I made it."

"I don't know, Shane. What kind of jerk would kick a woman out because another one showed up at the door?"

He throws the beer cap at me as he goes into the kitchen. I know what he's doing. He always tries to tease me out of these moods. I hate it when I'm like this, such a downer, and I try hard to pull myself out of it, but sometimes it's impossible.

Today seems doubly hard, with Jeff, and now Shane with this new girl.

He comes back into the living room with two plates piled high. He hands me one. "Here. Maybe if your mouth is full, you'll be quiet." He sits, and we eat in silence as we watch *Final Jeopardy*.

"This is pretty good, Shane."

"My mom always says a man should have one dish that can impress a girl."

"I'm impressed." I look over at him. "How is your mom?"

"Not good." His answer makes it clear the subject is closed.

I pour myself more wine and reach for his empty plate. "I'll wash up. It's the least I can do for the one-dish wonder."

I'm wiping down the stove when he comes into the kitchen with my wine. "So are you going to tell me why you came?" He leans against the counter.

I reach over with the cloth and pretend to wipe at a spot on his sweater. He grabs my hand and holds it tight.

"Come on, Claire. Don't do that. Talk to me. He stood you up, and you feel shitty. Is that why you're here?"

"I guess. I just started walking and didn't want to go home. Then I got that weird suffocating feeling and ended up here."

"It's been a long time since you've had a panic attack." He lets my hand go, sips from his beer.

I step back against the still-warm oven door. "I think I just got ahead of myself. I haven't seen Jeff in so long, and I was looking forward to it."

"Too bad you didn't talk to him live; it might have avoided the mix-up." Shane watches me, looks right into me, like he always does.

I pick up my wine and drink it down. "Well, his loss, right?" I set the glass in the sink. I'm a little tipsy.

"Definitely."

"You always know what to say. That's why I came here." I turn to go back into the living room, but he steps forward and puts a hand on my arm.

"You know it's not you, right? Any guy would be happy to have you."

"Oh, they're happy to have me, all right. They just never want to keep me." I laugh.

"Stop it. You know what I mean. Look, I'm glad you came here."

"Even though it wrecked your night?" I lean against him, hook my hands together behind him. I'm warm here. I'm happy.

Shane reaches behind me and flicks off the kitchen light. He starts to pull away but I hold on.

"Shane. That girl?"

"Yeah."

"You think you'll see her again?"

"Not likely, Claire."

My breath catches in my throat.

"Why would you kiss her and not me?"

"Claire."

I keep my gaze steady on his.

Shane sets his empty beer can on the counter. His voice is gentle. "Claire. You don't want my old-man lips rubbing all over you."

"How would I know?"

He tilts my face up. Kisses me a quick one on the side of the mouth. "There, see? Not what you're looking for, babe." I watch him walk back to the living room, anger building up in me. He picks up the remote and sits on the chair, not the couch. Flips channels. I stand, my fists clenched.

Shane's brush-off brings back memories of Leah and Daniel hiding on me, locking me out of their forts. Leaving me out.

I storm over to Shane, lean in and kiss him. Hard. It hurts until he relaxes and kisses me back. I move my lips over his, and his mouth opens and I feel his tongue against mine. For a brief second I think how wrong this is, then I fall down the hole of want. I grip his shoulders and lean into him as his hands slide up under the back of my shirt, around my rib cage.

Then he lifts me away, turns his head.

I sink to the floor at his feet.

"Stop it. We can't." He's breathing hard and his voice is harsh.

I peek at his face to see if he's angry. His eyes are teary, and he looks horrified. Or heartbroken.

I reach for him, but he pushes me back.

"What's wrong with me?"

"Nothing. We just can't, okay? Please. Please don't do this."

"Why not?"

"Because you're upset and angry. Because we're not right for each other."

"How would we know? You won't give me a chance."

"Let me finish, for once. No matter what happened, Claire, no matter how good and perfect it was, I'd wake up in the morning and my first thought would always be that you aren't Leah."

I suck in a breath and sit back on my heels. "Oh."

We're both quiet while this sinks in.

"I'm sorry, Claire, I won't do that to you."

"You've given this a lot of thought."

He shrugs. "Look, Claire, you proved your point with that kiss. But you can't go pouting when you don't get what you want." The sadness in his voice is gone. He gets it under control so easily. It's like that with everything. He just absorbs whatever I dish out, calls me on it, then moves on. He never gets upset. "And let's be honest. None of this is about you, or me. It's about Jeff."

I shrug.

"That little-kid kiss in the kitchen pissed me off." I move over to the couch.

"I could see that. I guess I just wasn't prepared for the fallout." He rubs his fingers across his lips, then puts his arms behind his head. "You'd think after all this time I'd be better at reading you."

He's opening a door, teasing me a little, clearing a wide path back to normal. Acting like it was nothing. It was a big deal to me, but I play along.

"Not tonight, obviously."

He comes to sit next to me. We both stare at the commercials on the screen in front of us.

He starts to laugh. "In some ways, you are so much like your sister."

I smack him, then I start to laugh, too. I like it when he says things like that. It's been a long time since he's said something about Leah. I'm glad he did, because I'm thinking of her, too. My sister is more present tonight than she has been in a long time.

"I'm crazy, I know. You're here, and we get along and I'd do anything for you. But it's never going to be right, and it would end badly. I can't lose you."

I don't know what to say. I aim my eyes at the home-video show that's on, but I don't take any of it in. I wonder where Shane's date ended up. I think about school. I think about Jeff. Anything except what just happened.

When Shane falls asleep beside me, I try to ease myself away, but he wakes.

"Sorry, Claire. It's been a long week. Do you want me to drive you home?"

"Can I stay?"

"If you like."

I go to the bathroom, and by the time I come back, he has his room all set up, covers on his bed turned down. I crawl into bed and look up at him. "Homey. I could get used to this."

He shakes his head in mock disgust. "Just like a woman. One kiss, and she wants to move in." He turns to walk out. I call him back.

"Shane, you can sleep in here. I'll leave you alone."

"I'm okay on the couch. I'm going to watch TV for a while. I work early so I'll try not to wake you. Stay as long as you like." He closes the door behind him.

The street light outside shines upward through the window and forms a pale square of light on the ceiling.

Thoughts of Jeff threaten. Him standing me up hurts as bad as Shane pushing me away.

I stare at the shadows of snowflakes drifting through the frame of light above me for a long while before I even realize I'm crying.

Jeff watches the Regina skyline fade in the passenger mirror. It takes a long time, but finally the buildings turn the colour of ash and fade into the horizon.

He blew it yesterday afternoon. He drank his way through at least a half-dozen beer, countless shots and a chance at an art apprenticeship with Bill Stonefield, artist-in-residence at the MacKenzie.

And he stood Claire up.

He doesn't recall what happened before he got kicked out of the bar at the Plains Hotel yesterday afternoon, but does remember his friend James swearing at the bartender, slamming out the door, fists flying.

Then, stumbling down the cracked and heaved sidewalks of Victoria Avenue as the snow started to fall, back to James' sister's place. Whatever happened, Jeff's just relieved he wasn't arrested again.

Jeff woke this morning to a simmering hangover and James' sister lying in the bed beside him, naked from the waist down, bleach-blonde hair in her face. On the floor, more beer bottles. On the dresser, a faux-leather zip case, syringe resting on top. *Fuck.* He examined his arms for red needle pricks, felt between his fingers for tenderness, but there was nothing to show that he'd used.

Once he'd stumbled out of the shower and dressed, he called Claire, but there was no answer.

James came into the kitchen, anxious to get on the road. There was a ton of snow on the highway, and he wanted to get moving before the RCMP decided to close it.

Jeff, having missed his appointment at the art gallery, having missed Claire, knew there was nothing for him here. He asked James if he could head west with him. Head still spinning, he packed his portfolio and the few clothes he'd worn since arriving in town on Friday, and jumped into James' old Ford.

Now, the thud of the wheels on the ruts of snow on the highway makes it impossible to sleep. A feeling as empty and cold as the snow-covered prairie that surrounds him settles in his stomach.

"Pull over," he says, reaching for the door handle.

"Here?" His friend pulls to the side and turns up Dwight Yoakam full blast while Jeff pukes in the muddy slush that camouflages the McDonald's cups and Coke cans and chip bags on the side of the road. Jeff wipes his mouth and gets back in.

"That music is enough to make anyone sick." He leans his head against the window. "What the hell did we do last night?"

"Jesus, what didn't we do? My sister's friends are nuts."

Jeff closes his eyes. He'd stepped on an empty condom wrapper beside the bed when he got up this morning. He hopes like hell he used it the night before. The first time he got laid in months and he can't even remember it.

His life. One mistake piled on top of another. First, Churchill, where he arrived to find his mother's family gone.

Jeff stayed on until spring, but soon found himself in trouble – too many late nights, too much partying. There was no hope of keeping his job.

After Churchill, he worked hard to make things right. He spent too much time in Thompson, driving a forklift at a transport company, then headed south to the city.

His first week there, he met Marie, a waitress at a downtown Winnipeg bar. Jeff watched as a drunk businessman grabbed her ass when she brought him his beer. Jeff had to go and be all noble, and ended up on the curb out front with a cut lip and a nosebleed. Marie followed him out with a glass of water and a job offer from the owner.

He worked nights pouring drinks and attended classes during the day to get his high-school diploma. After that, Marie let him move in. She pushed him to take art classes at the community college. Things were good for a while, but good never lasts for him.

She got pregnant, and he screwed around. She kicked him out.

She lost the baby.

Jeff didn't even try to get her back.

Jeff spent his days in the college art studio, and his nights either working, or drinking at the bar. One of his college teachers told him about the apprenticeship opportunity in Regina and helped Jeff apply. The interview was set, and once again, Jeff took off.

He'd wanted to see Claire in Regina. The letters he received from her every so often were sad, even if the news was good. She seemed lost. He wrote back long, convoluted missives that spoke of everything except what she needed to hear. He never told her about the mess in Churchill, or living with Marie, or the trouble he got into late nights and weekends. He never told anyone about the baby.

He reaches into his pack and pulls out his sketchbook. He flips through the pages, looks at everything he's done, all his ideas, and he is furious with himself. No chance now for his art. He tears out the sketch he worked on yesterday, rolls down the window and chucks the sketchbook out. He tucks the lone drawing into the front pocket of his pack and pulls out his novel.

"You're going to read? You just puked." James shakes his head. "I don't get you. Six hours ago you were slam-dancing with four girls. Now you're reading? I'd be sleeping."

"I'll drive, you can rest."

James doesn't need to be told twice. They are barely back on the highway and he's asleep, mouth hanging open. Jeff flips the radio station.

That country shit has got to go.

The snow disappears at the border and gives way to rolling hills of long, dry grass that bows in the west wind. For some reason it reminds Jeff of the lake, of the movement of the water on a windy day.

But instead of the bright blue of Clearwater's waves, everything here is rendered in shades of brown and yellow. The only trees are planted in regimented rows on the west side of farmhouses. Even the sky isn't blue, it's white. Goddamn prairie. It's something he would have liked to ask Stonefield at the art gallery. How do you find any inspiration in this dry, barren landscape?

When they stop in Medicine Hat, Jeff refuels the truck, then goes into the gas station to pay. Standing at the counter, he sees a help-wanted sign. Damn. Minimum wage. But it's full time. And it's not at a bar.

And he needs to dry out.

He asks the woman at the till about the job. She gives him the same long look that he gets everywhere. The grocery store. The bus. At school. Here comes the Indian, that look says. Then, sure enough, she notices his eyes and surprise lights her face. It's the same every time. He's not a real Indian after all, so he must be okay. He shakes off the bitterness.

She gives him the job.

He heads out to tell James to carry on without him. He grabs his things.

"You're crazy, Jeff. Hot chicks and lots of money in Calgary. Look me up when you get sick of this dump." James pulls away.

Jeff spends the day shadowing Frances. She's in her forties, a little overweight, but her hair is long and red and it shines. The station is just off the highway, and it's busy. During the lulls, he organizes the shelves and cleans the coolers. Families come in to use the washroom and buy treats for the road. Truckers hang around a little too long and chat Frances up. She flirts with all of them, but shows preference to none, just waves them out.

"My ex-husband mortgaged our house and bought this place right before he left me for his little twinkie. I tried hard to sell it, but no takers. I think it actually saved me. I was too busy to be sad." Frances laughs as she says this.

She eyes his pack and the portfolio that leans against it. "Where are you from?"

"North."

"Long way from home?" She busies herself arranging a small display of lighters.

"Not sure. Still looking." Jeff rests the mop against the door to the back room.

"You have a place to stay?"

"Nope. I have money, though. If I can crash in the back room here, I'll check out some places tomorrow."

Frances chews on the inside of her lip. "There's a cheap motel across the highway that rents by the week."

Jeff raises his eyebrows. "Not by the hour?"

She laughs. "No, they rent to oilfield workers and construction crews. I can call over and see if they have room, if you like."

He starts to say no, he can handle it, when he is hit by a feeling of exhaustion so deep it makes his chest hurt. "Sure. Thanks."

After securing a room for the week, Frances hangs up the phone and puts on her jacket. "If you're okay here, I'm going to head home for a bit. I'll come back to help you close up, okay?"

When she returns, she brings him a plate of roast beef and potatoes.

"Grab yourself a drink from the cooler. I don't usually let my employees do that, but you've worked hard today." She covers the till while he eats, then together they close up and cash out.

"Thanks for dinner." It's been a long time since anyone has cooked for him. Bartending doesn't leave much time for home-cooked meals.

"You come in at three tomorrow, and work until close, okay? Next week we'll switch." She hands him a key to the door. "Enjoy your morning. Snow's coming."

Jeff makes his way across the highway to the motel. He checks in and hands over enough cash for the week. His room is small, and the furnishings are worn, but it seems clean.

He stands for a long time under the hot shower. He dries himself with the flimsy towel and looks at himself in the mirror, something he hasn't done much in the past three months. He rubs his rough beard. He looks old. Scraggly. He can't believe Frances gave him a job, looking like this. He shaves, but without a pair of scissors, there's nothing he can do with his hair.

He pulls on clean boxers and a T-shirt and goes to sit on the edge of the bed with his pack. He pulls out a piece of paper with Claire's number on it.

She picks up on the second ring.

"Hey." His voice sticks in his throat.

She's quiet for a long time. "Jeff."

"Yeah."

"Are you coming to see me?"

"No."

"Are you still here?"

"No, Claire, I'm not." He hears her take a shaky breath and he knows he shouldn't have called. "I just wanted to – I should go."

Silence.

"It doesn't matter why, does it?" He can barely hear her.

"What do you mean?"

"Why you weren't there last night."

He could tell her. He should tell her. "No, it doesn't matter." It doesn't. He let her down. Not much else to say. "I'm sorry."

"Oh, no, it's okay. No big deal. I was late getting to the MacKenzie.

I figured I missed you."

She's lying. He remembers how her voice always got all tight like that when she put on her tough-girl act. He wants to call her on it. She hasn't changed a bit, all the fast-talking, *I'm-fine-Jeff* bullshit. But it's easier to let it go. "Listen, I'm heading west. I'll write you when I'm settled, okay?"

"Sure, Jeff. But I'm pretty busy with university. Exams are coming up." Ice creeps into her voice. "It's my last year and I'm thinking about grad school. It's important. You probably wouldn't get that."

He swallows hard. "No, I understand."

"So, thanks for calling." She's close to crying, he can hear it.

"Claire." He tries to think of something to keep her on the phone. She's going to break, and if she does, he can, and maybe that's what they both need.

"Jeff, I'm going to hang up, now." There is a soft click as she breaks the connection.

The sheets are soft, but he twists and turns through the night. Light is sneaking through the shades when he finally falls asleep. He dreams of deep water and snakepits and airplanes.

And Claire. She's there, too.

When he wakes, he reaches for his sketchbook, and then he remembers.

He tears the back cover from the novel he's carried with him since he left home. *The Pigman.* He puts the paper and a pencil in his pocket along with the motel key and closes the door behind him.

It's not a long walk down the valley to the river. The sky is dark to the west, and the cold wind creeps inside his jacket. The opposite bank of the river is lower, and the prairie stretches away to the north.

Jeff finds a spot to sit and starts to draw. He turns a pencilled outline of Claire's face into the lines of the water in front of him, the angles of the hills, and the curves of the clouds. He shades until Claire's face is indistinguishable from the landscape he recreates on the page. He could do a better job if he had paints.

When finished, Jeff stands and makes his way to the river's edge. The slow, brown water will flow east, then north, past Saskatoon, where the river joins her sister tributary to form the Saskatchewan

River. The same river that flows under the bridge he crossed every day on the way to and from school.

I could canoe home from here.

There would be brutal portages along the way, but he could paddle this river right back to where he came from five long years before.

He folds his sketch into the shape of a boat and crouches down to release it into the lazy current. It takes a while, but once it's out of sight, he turns his back on the river. Soft snowflakes start to fall as he follows the trail back up to the top of the valley.

WEIGHT

I look out the window of the Vancouver hotel room at the city of silver and glass. The sun tries to break though the clouds, but can't quite get there. The screenless window opens wide enough that I could squeeze through, if I wanted to. A straight plummet onto the canopy of the lobby overhang ten storeys below.

After just two nights of jazz bars and late-night dancing, and three days of shopping and Stanley Park with my friend Julia, I'm ready to go home. I want to head back to my little house in Regina and my boyfriend and my routine of work. I do better when I'm in a routine.

I'm tired. Tired of sharing a hotel room with someone else. Tired of decisions made by committee: where to eat, what bar to go to, when to go for a run or shopping.

And I'm tired of waiting for Jeff to call. He's lived in Vancouver for a while now, two years, at least. I wrote him weeks ago to tell him about my trip, where I'd be staying, when I would arrive. He wrote back that he looked forward to seeing me. I haven't heard anything from him since.

This isn't the first time Jeff Carlson has let me down.

It's nearly noon and my friend Julia is still sleeping off the night before. I decide to head out for a walk and grab a tea. I'm quiet as I get ready. Jeans, long-sleeved T-shirt, runners. I pick up the little purse I took with me when we went dancing, then think better of it. I transfer my money and ID from the tiny bag back into my wallet and drop it into my carryall. I sling it over my shoulder and across my chest.

Just as I'm easing the door closed, the phone rings.

In my hurry to answer it, I bang into the table and send Julia's empty waterglass to the carpet. She groans and pulls the covers over her head.

"Hey, Claire."

It's Daniel.

I try to keep the disappointment from my voice as I pull the receiver into the bathroom and close the door on the cord.

"I just called to check in with you. Tell you how Finn and I are doing." Daniel's ex-girlfriend, Sherry, showed up last month with a child – Finn – and a raging drug addiction, knocking my brother off-kilter in a way I haven't seen since Leah died. He seems happy, though, with his new status as a father. Yesterday he called to ask me if I'd come to visit him up north. No way in hell would I go back up there, new nephew or not, and he knows it.

"Everything's good, here, Daniel."

"Really?" He won't ask about Jeff outright, though I know that's why he really called.

"The weather up here is warming up, Claire. You should come see us."

"Not coming, Daniel. If you want me to meet Finn, you need to bring him to Regina." My face in the bathroom mirror is pale. There are dark circles under my eyes. "I've got to go, Dan. I fly home tomorrow. I'll call you when I get there."

"Claire, are you okay?"

I can't keep the exasperation from my voice. "Daniel, Jeff didn't even call. You don't need to worry, okay?"

"I'm not worried, Claire."

It flashes through my mind that maybe the phone calls aren't about me at all. Maybe Daniel is the one who needs something.

Things are always dicey in spring – I know it brings back memories for him, as it does for me. Harder for him, considering he still lives up there.

I don't want to ask, but I do. "How about you, Daniel? Are you all right?"

"Oh, yeah. Just getting to know my kid."

"Good."

He's quiet for a bit. "And thinking about Leah. Eight years this year. You know."

I do.

"I miss her too." But not like him.

"I'll let you go, Claire. If that shithead shows up, punch him in the face for me."

He's kidding. I think. I say goodbye and hang up. The lump that is Julia doesn't budge.

In the lobby, I stand at the door of the hotel. *Which way?* I turn toward Robson. As I pass from beneath the overhang, I hear Julia calling my name. I look up to where her bed-head leans out our window.

"The front desk just called up. They have a message for you."

I turn to head back inside.

And he's there.

Jeff's right there, leaning against one of the huge, round planters at the edge of the hotel driveway.

His lips curl into a slight smile. He keeps his hands in his pockets until I'm in front of him, then he reaches out and pulls me in. I grasp the back of his leather jacket and hold tight. He smells the same as he always did, like trees and outside. My thoughts hurtle from anger to annoyance to happiness. He lifts me a little, and I lean in, my weight against him. I can feel the heat of his thighs slide against mine as he lets me down.

Emotion rises in my throat so strong that I know if I give voice to it, it will come out either as a moan of contentment, or a shriek of fury.

A single sob overwhelms me, and this close, I know he feels it.

"Claire," he says, his voice soft.

I step back, look up at him. That face, those blue eyes that shock. Nothing to say. Too much to say. He reaches out and twists a strand of my hair around his finger.

"Sorry it took so long to catch up to you. I was working." He takes my hand. "It's good to see you." It sounds like something my grandmother would say.

The words echo through the hole that rests at the base of my ribs. They don't even begin to fill the emptiness. I pull my hand away and take a deep breath. I force a smile to my lips.

"Yeah, good to see you, too." My voice almost sounds normal. I adjust my bag on my shoulder. "Where do you want to go?"

"Let's walk for a bit." He turns away from the hotel and starts toward the hospital on the next block. Nothing's changed since we were teenagers. He assumes I'll just fall in line. For a split second I consider not following, turning around and running back up to my room.

But I've waited so long to see him.

I catch up to him before he turns right on Davie.

Down Davie to Denman, then along the seawall into Stanley Park. We stop and watch as a huge container ship moves toward the inlet, pushing a wall of water in front of it as it goes. Jeff leads me into the trees, along a dirt path past the lagoon. I walk as I always did, on his left. He has to slow down for me now. It's been a long time since I walked anywhere more demanding than a mall.

"My mom said you finished your engineering degree."

"Yeah. I work for the government now. Roads and Highways." I bump him by accident. I move to give him more space. "So your mom is living at the lodge, now." I glance up at him. "With Colin. Bet that was a surprise."

Jeff's eyes are narrowed. "Yeah. She says she's better off there." Something tells me the subject is closed. "And your mom?"

"She moved out to Ottawa years ago. She works for the Environment minister."

He's quiet for a minute. If he asks about Leah I'm going to lose it. "Do you talk to Daniel often?"

"Couple times a month. More lately. Do you?"

"I saw him around the time I went back to see my mom, but we didn't really talk. Things didn't exactly end well between us."

I take a deep breath. "Things didn't really end well for any of us, Jeff."

His cheeks redden. "He must be content I guess, working at the lodge."

"He's still doing it." On the far side of the lagoon, I can see a bevy of swans, swimming, it seems, without effort. Two swans approach each other, beak-to-beak. They glide into each other, their long necks curving in the shape of a heart.

"He has a kid, did you know that? He just found out."

"Yeah. My mom keeps me pretty up-to-date on what's going on with you guys."

I feel a flash of anger. To know what was going on with me, all he had to do was call.

"Daniel and my mom are pretty close. I know all about Finn and his mother." His tone is mild.

"How's your dad?"

"Drunk. Alone."

I guess he doesn't want to talk about him, either.

Instead, Jeff tells me about his jobs bartending and landscaping. He fills me in on his night classes at the college, his friends, the mansion they are house-sitting in Kitsilano, how much he loves the city. I don't know what to say. Jeff was never one to release a barrage of information this way, and I'm at a loss. It's as though he's piling story after story into my arms, so many I can barely hold on to them.

Eventually, his voice trails off and we walk in silence.

On a path near Prospect Point, an elderly Chinese woman approaches us. Her back is stooped, her face covered with brown age spots. Her hair is still black though, and shiny. Behind her, just past her shoulder, trail four paper butterflies, each no bigger than the palm of my hand. As the woman gets closer, I see that she is holding a thin thread. The butterflies are attached to it, and it's only the slight breeze generated by the woman's forward movement that keeps the tiny kite aloft.

The butterflies are made of pale rice paper, and are inked with vibrant shades of colour – green, red, blue and yellow. Chinese characters in black line the edge of the paper.

She holds the string out to me. I take it, and as I walk, I watch the butterflies spin out behind me. For a moment, the heaviness in me lifts, but then I catch sight of Jeff, who watches with a serious look on his face.

"I want to run, but it's so fragile." I return the kite to the woman, afraid I'll tear it. "Thank you," I say, bowing a little.

"Ten dollars." The woman nods at me and holds out the kite.

I shake my head. "No, thanks. I can't get it home."

The woman pulls a flat plastic package out of her pocket and holds it out. Another kite. A red-winged dragon gazes up at me.

"Ten dollars."

"Here." Jeff hands the woman a ten and takes the dragon kite. He thanks her and passes the package to me. "A souvenir from Vancouver."

"Thank you." I slip it into my bag and say goodbye to the woman. Time slows after that, and so do our feet as we walk under the palest of green canopies. The late-April sun is watered down, and everything is tinged with grey.

I wish Jeff would talk, but when he does, I want him to be quiet. On the cliffs overlooking Siwash Rock, he reaches for my hand, and I pull away.

"Claire," he says. "I'm sorry."

I pretend not to hear him.

He grabs me by the arm. "I am."

"For what? Leaving? Standing me up at the MacKenzie? My sister dying? Not calling until my last day here?"

He drops my arm and I walk away, tears in my eyes.

Jeff follows as I move down a short path beyond a wooden safety fence. Everything feels caught in the wall of thorns that is my rib cage. I move close to the drop-off and look out at the rock. A tree grows on top, a surprising sign of life sprung from stone.

Jeff stands back and doesn't say a word. A little closer to the edge, my feet dig in as though trying to grip the dirt and rock beneath my feet.

"Claire, stop it. Move back."

But I stay where I am. I throw my arms out to the sides and close my eyes. My body sways and my legs shake. Even with my eyes closed, I can see the space in front of me: clear, empty air. Everything seems to tilt, then his arms go around my waist and he pulls me back against him, back from the edge. He half-drags me to the fence and spins me around.

"What the hell are you doing? Are you out of your mind?" His voice shakes. "Was that some kind of test?"

"I wasn't even thinking about you." Tears burn my eyes at this lie.

"I wasn't thinking of anything." I raise my arms and gesture at the lush greenness around me. "The trees are so thick nothing can get through. My mind is so full, I can't even think."

Jeff pushes me away and stalks off, back up to the main trail. I take my time, but I follow. When I come around a bend, he leans against an enormous stump and waits with his arms crossed.

I say his name.

He just shakes his head. I take his hand as we walk.

"Claire, I'm not much for games."

I tighten my grip, then let go. "The Jeff I knew wouldn't have pulled me back. He would have trusted me."

His jaw is tight when he answers. "So, it was a test, then. I guess I failed."

He has it all wrong.

"Failed, passed, it's all the same, Jeff."

A switch flips inside of me. Angry to sad in the space of a footstep.

The afternoon is fading when we come out of the trees into the noise and traffic across from English Bay. The weak sun dips toward the horizon taking the meagre heat of day with it.

I feel awful about what happened on the cliff, but I can't bring myself to apologize. I walk two steps behind him, giving him space. It's strange, straddling past and present. But neither one of us is the same as we were. Back then, he wouldn't have hugged me like he did outside the hotel, all pressed against me.

And he never would have been this angry with me.

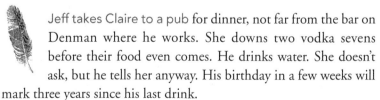 Jeff takes Claire to a pub for dinner, not far from the bar on Denman where he works. She downs two vodka sevens before their food even comes. He drinks water. She doesn't ask, but he tells her anyway. His birthday in a few weeks will mark three years since his last drink.

"But you work in a bar."

He shrugs. "Yeah. I'm not tempted there. I'm more likely to look for a drink when I'm home alone than when I'm out."

"Congratulations, Jeff."

"I am okay with one, but it never seems to end there." He stares down at his hands. "I kind of turn into an asshole after a couple of drinks. After three, I'm through the gateway, looking for something harder."

"You mean drugs?"

"It's been a hell of a long road, Claire."

The food comes then, and he changes the subject. It's a strange dance they're performing, coming close together, and stepping back again. They talk and watch each other, wary of lighting another fuse.

Jeff knows if he'd called her right away, when she first came, things would be easier.

She looks the same, all crazy curly hair and big dark eyes. What's missing though, is that open, expectant look she used to wear every time he saw her. The one that seemed like it was just for him. Like he was the only one who could take her to the places she wanted to go. But she's cautious. Careful.

It's almost dark when they leave the bar and cross to the beach.

They step onto the sand, and the first thing Jeff notices is the strong smell of weed.

"Gotta love it," he says.

"Are you okay?"

"I'm fine."

Jeff guides her to one of the enormous logs placed there for beach-goers. He sits with his back against it and pulls her down next to him.

The lights on the container ships glow brighter as the sky gets darker. The sky is veiled in delicate cloud, and the mountains rise in black jags off to the right.

There is a chill in the air, and the sand beneath him is turning cold. He nudges her leg with his knee. "I missed you."

"I hate you," she says.

Now we're getting somewhere, he thinks. "I don't blame you. If I had known how it would turn out –"

Claire leans into him and he puts his arm around her. They sit like that for a long time. He can feel her breathe out of time with the waves.

"What do you remember about Leah?" she asks him.

Jeff shifts on the hard sand. "She was beautiful. All the guys at school had crushes on her."

"Even you," Claire says.

"Yes, even me." He laughs. "She used to come over and hang out with my mom."

"I didn't know that."

"Yeah. Mostly when my dad had to cover the late shift. Or sometimes after school, she'd help in the garden before he got home. Shane would drop her off when school was done, or after a date, and she would walk over. I'd get home, or come downstairs, and they would be sitting at the table drinking tea. Talking."

"I didn't know any of that. After so long, it's nice to learn something new about her. It makes her more alive." Claire traces her fingers through the sand. "Leah was beautiful, wasn't she? That's why you were so committed when it came to looking for her."

"Claire, everyone wanted to help. It wasn't because she was beautiful." He hugs her closer. "And anyway, it didn't matter. It was always me and you, no?"

If he were to paint the electric quiet that flows between them, he would make it the colour of the lake – a blue both so hot and so cold it would burn.

Claire rests her head on her knees. "I'm so angry." A cloud above them slides away, and the moon shines silver on her.

"I know, Claire." After a while, he stands and reaches out his hand. "It's cold. Let's get going."

She lets him pull her to her feet.

Back on the dark path, as they walk toward Beach Avenue, she apologizes for her craziness on the cliff.

"Sometimes this feeling just comes over me. I can't seem to stop it."

Jeff takes her hand, holds it inside the pocket of his jacket.

Claire stops him under a street light on Denman, right near the Raincity Grill. She shakes her head, clears her throat. "I think, at the end, I was in love with you."

He just looks down at her.

"My big admission." Claire laughs a little. "You knew that."

"Yeah."

"You liked me, too."

"I did. I do."

"You don't even know me."

"I want to, Claire." Jeff thinks back to the first day he met her. Fixing motorbikes and walking through deserted buildings. There is no sign of that bravery now. No stubbornness. She seems broken. And at least a part of that is his fault. "Come home with me, we'll get out of the cold. We can talk." He knows this sounds like a come-on, but it's too late to take it back.

"I want to, but I shouldn't. I'm seeing someone. Oh, I don't know what I want. I don't know anything any more."

He touches her cheek. "I still care, Claire."

"You left me, Jeff."

"I'm here now."

"I don't need you now."

"Maybe that's a good thing."

"I should go back." Claire pulls away.

"I'll walk you." Jeff starts toward the corner where the light has changed.

"Jeff." He stops, but doesn't turn to her. He has no idea what she needs.

"I really should go to the hotel. It's the right thing to do." Claire walks up behind him, puts her arms around him, pushes her face hard against his back.

"Okay."

"But I want to come with you."

"I can't make it right, Claire." He can hear the exhaustion in his own voice.

Her arms are tight around his waist. "You mean now? Or what happened then?"

"Either. Both."

"I'll come."

It's a short bus ride to his place. They sit close, legs and arms touching. Claire looks out the window at the lights of Granville Island as the bus crosses the Burrard Street Bridge. Jeff watches her reflection in the window. She leans forward and her dark hair tumbles forward, cutting off his view.

The two of them, on a bus. Again.

A flourescent light above the seat in front of them flickers with a sizzle. Jeff focuses on it, tries to figure out if the zapping noise comes when it flicks on, or off.

"Jeff." Claire grips his hand. She looks like she's going to cry.

"It's okay, Claire."

Flicker. On, off. There. In between on and off.

Jeff reaches past Claire and pulls the cord.

From the bus stop, they walk together down an uneven sidewalk on a narrow curved street that's overlain by a canopy of cherry trees. The street lights shine through the blossom-laden branches, speckling the road.

He stops and faces her.

A breeze blows up, gentle at first, then he hears it in the trees. Blossoms are torn from their branches, and, borne by the wind, surround them in a pale froth of flowers. They spin and dance like confetti, then float to the ground and skip along the street ahead of them as they walk.

Jeff reaches out and brushes at some petals caught in her hair. "The place I'm house-sitting is just around the corner."

They round a curve and stop in front of a tall, angular house with huge windows and two balconies. The house is lit up. He sees people inside, seated on couches, standing around a massive stone fireplace. Damn.

"This is it?"

"Come on in. Looks like my roommate has friends over, but they won't bother us."

He takes her in through a side door. The house is an open-concept marvel of glass and metal, stone and leather. It's all black and silver, even the kitchen.

"You want anything? A drink?"

Claire shakes her head.

Jeff takes her by the hand and leads her through the crowd in the living room. He introduces her on the fly, but keeps moving.

Jeff leads her up a steel staircase to the top floor. The hall goes a long way in both directions. He turns left.

He pushes a door open and turns on the light. Jeff can't help but see it through her eyes. All this pretentious black and steel. Mirrored closet doors, open to show his piles of dirty work clothes. Canvases against the walls, empty ones facing out, completed paintings facing in. The glass of the balcony doors reflects his neglected easel back at him, as it does every time he comes in here.

Jeff turns away to kill the lights and close the door. Claire crashes into him from behind, hugging him. Her momentum pushes him forward, and he puts his hand up to keep from slamming his face into the wall.

"Easy," he says.

They stand like that for a moment. Her heart pounds so hard he can feel it through the back of his jacket.

"Claire." He turns to her.

She yanks at the layers that cover him. Leather jacket, sweatshirt.

He says her name again.

She presses her fingers to his lips.

He slides his arms out of his sleeves and ducks his head as she pulls his T-shirt off. He kisses her and feels the restraint drain from him. She kisses him harder, now. It's like scratching the aching itch of a three-day-old scab. A scab still too fresh to peel, but healed enough to pull at the healthy skin around it.

She slides her hands up his bare chest and around his neck. "You want me."

"Are you asking, or telling?"

"Yes," she says.

She reaches for the button on his jeans. He reaches down and grabs her hand.

"Claire, wait." This is not what he expected.

"This is going to happen, Jeff."

"Things are just as fucked up as ever," he says as he lets her hand go.

Then they are naked and they are on the bed on top of the blankets and it happens fast. There's no time to think of anything, any more.

Later, in the shower, Jeff makes room for her under the spray. He kisses her, then spins her so she faces away from him. She stands, arms limp as he washes her hair for her. When he's done, he combs his fingers through the curls to make sure all the shampoo is out.

Jeff places his hands on her hips, and holds her, his fingers wrapping around her hip bones, his thumbs pressing in on either side of her spine.

"You have dimples here. Venus dimples, or whatever they're called."

As he turns to shut off the tap, he feels her fingers graze his back, just above his left shoulder blade.

"Oh my God, Jeff."

Shit. His tattoo.

"It's beautiful."

If she didn't run before, she will now.

With a gentle prod, she turns him so she can see it better.

He knows what she sees. A black-and-white loon is inked in three-quarter profile, caught not in serenity, but reared back on indigo waves, its wings opening. The loon's visible eye is bright red. On the plain white of the bird's breast is the simple design of a medicine wheel. Above it all hangs a thin slice of yellow moon. His breath rushes from him as she traces the words written in tight script beneath the water with her fingernail.

"Claire de lune." The words sound viscous in her throat.

Water off, but with his hand still on the tap, Jeff shivers as she presses her nail hard into his skin. His keeps his head bowed, turned away.

"Say something," he says, his voice quiet.

Her voice shakes. "It's spelled wrong, Jeff. You know your French. There shouldn't be an *e* there."

"I designed it, Claire. It's right."

The indelible past. Maybe now she'll see that he carries it with him, too. That he wears her, like he wears his home.

Claire presses her palm hard against his shoulder, like she's blocking out the tattoo, then turns away and gets out of the shower. She grabs a thick black towel from the towel bar and wraps it around herself. He reaches for the other towel, but stands with it in his hand. His head feels thick. His eyes ache.

"You never thought I would see it." Her voice is barely above a whisper.

He shakes his head and wraps the towel around his waist. He doesn't take his eyes off hers, tries to read what she thinks, but a curtain has dropped down.

"Things are just as fucked up as always, hey, Jeff?"

Back in his room, Claire sits in the middle of the bed, wearing the black Joy Division shirt he wore that day.

She slides under the covers.

He turns out the light and gets in next to her, pulls her to him. He keeps his voice light. "I have a Papa Smurf T-shirt, too, if you'd rather wear that one. My friend runs a T-shirt shop on Denman."

"This is fine."

They lie facing each other in the dark, unwilling to talk of the past and unable to talk of the future. He wants to keep this moment, not let it go. He knows that time is almost up, and he feels he holds on to some kind of chance, but he doesn't know what it is.

"Claire, I want to –"

She interrupts. "Me too."

It's not what he was going to say, but he reaches for her anyway. He wants to watch her, to look at her, but he leaves the light off. They start slow this time, and she feels different to him. She is open, softer. Yet, her arms around him are strong, and she holds him steady.

He has to say it. "Claire, you are the only one who ever knew me."

Her tone is sharp. "I never knew you at all, Jeff. Not the important stuff, not about your dad."

"That's just it. That was not who I was, it's not me. You knew me. Everything that mattered, you knew."

Things have flipped somehow, since she saw the tattoo. She seems stronger, shored up, more distant. And he feels more lost.

He wants to explain, to make sure she understands, but she's moving with him now, and he can't think of anything but this.

After, he thinks. *I'll tell her after.*

But after, she lies full against him, and he traces the dimples above her buttocks with his fingers.

After, his palms caress the bumps of her spine and finally, the soft place where her neck meets her shoulder.

After, she dozes, curled into him from behind, arm around his waist.

After, Jeff knows, without a doubt, that she'll be gone in the morning.

TWO

I drive from Regina to The Pas. I could have flown, but somehow, making the trip as I first did – in a car – seems fitting. It gives me hours and hours to think about Jeff, and Vancouver, and that tattoo.

I woke first that morning and lay there, searching out and cataloguing the changes in his face. The new hardness, the lines, the small scars, all softened in slumber. Except for the longer hair, he could have been the same sixteen-year-old boy I met all those years ago.

Not wanting to wake him, I wrapped up in a blanket and stepped out onto his balcony. English Bay lay before me, lazy charcoal waves washing the sand clean, scouring all things left behind, dragging them out with the retreating tide.

On the North Shore, the rising sun lit the windows of the houses and condos that hung from the hills. Thousands of fiery squares reflected the sunrise, the pixels of a new day blinding me. Off to my right, the silver skyline of the city was a cardboard cutout set against a pale, cloudless backdrop.

I knew I couldn't stay.

As I pass through The Pas, my thoughts drift, skipping over my now ex-boyfriend, Luke, and coming to rest on Shane. When I'd made that panicked call to Daniel after leaving Jeff, I didn't think about having to face Shane. When his mother's health deteriorated a few years back, he'd requested a compassionate transfer back to The Pas to look after her, and we'd fallen out of touch. She died last year. Even then, I couldn't bring myself to go back up north for her funeral.

I tried hard over the years to remove him from his self-appointed role as the one who glued me back together whenever I fell apart, which was often in those first years after Leah's death.

He's going to be so disappointed in me. And he's going to be angry that I didn't call him.

There are no longer any signs counting down to Orbit on the highway. The green-and-white airport sign at the 287 turnoff is faded and pitted, but it's still there. I slow and turn east. At the Cove, miles from the airport, I take a left off the highway, then a quick right onto the gravel access road that runs behind the cabins on the lake. I watch for Daniel's place. He's described his renovations to the one-room cabin in detail over the years, so it should be easy to pick out.

I see it now, the peaked roof and cedar siding with green trim, exactly as he said. I pull into the drive and sit in the car for a moment, gazing at the back of the cabin.

I'm not sure what to tell him. I could hear the worry in his voice when I called from Vancouver last week, and again when I called last night.

Now, Daniel's back door opens and Connie, Daniel's huge black Newfie, rushes out. Daniel follows, but it's the small, dark-haired boy bringing up the rear who has my attention. Daniel's son.

Finn.

When Daniel told me about Finn, he'd been furious with Finn's mom, Sherry. She left town nearly five years ago and never told him she was pregnant. Now she's back.

From our phone conversations, I can tell Daniel is thrilled with his son. He is not, however, happy with his ex. Sherry's been in and out of addiction treatment and her mother has custody of Finn. So Finn stays with his *kokum*, his grandma, on the reserve. Daniel gets him two days every week. There will be a custody hearing in the fall. Daniel talks a lot about Finn coming to live with him full time, but he's taking it slow.

I take a deep breath and get out of the car. As I close the door, I'm nearly run down by the dog.

"Connie!" Daniel's voice is sharp. The dog goes to him and sits.

Before I'm ready for it, Daniel steps close and pulls me into an awkward hug. My forehead bumps against his collarbone, and my face is pressed so tight against him I can't breathe. I let him hold me for a second.

I look past Daniel's shoulder to Finn, who waits a few paces behind his father.

There is no doubt he's my brother's son, a black-haired, brown-eyed carbon copy.

I push Daniel away and kneel in front of my nephew. I put out my hand.

"Hello, Finn." The boy takes my hand, but doesn't shake it.

"Auntie," Finn says. "Claire."

"Yes, I'm Auntie Claire." I reach out and put my hands around his slim waist, then let them fall. I want to hug him, but it's too soon. "Will you show me your room?" Kids always love to show off their rooms. This much I remember from babysitting.

Finn nods and turns, looks back to make sure I follow. I stand and wipe the dirt from my knees.

I turn to Daniel. "I love him."

Daniel laughs. "He's pretty great."

Once inside we pass through the small kitchen and turn down a short hallway. Daniel's room is on the right. Straight ahead is the second bedroom. I can tell Finn is proud of his room from the huge grin on his face as he opens the door.

"You must like hockey, hey, Finn?" I ask, as I take in the themed bedspread and poster of Wayne Gretzky on the wall. "Is Gretzky your favourite?"

Finn shakes his head, points at Daniel. "Daniel likes Gretzky."

Hmm. Not Dad yet. "He always did."

"I like Patrick Roy," Finn tells me.

"Good choice, Finn."

"He likes Montreal because no matter what, their games are on every Saturday night. The French channel, the English channel, Finn doesn't care. The announcers talk so fast, he can't catch it in either language." Daniel strokes Finn's straight black hair. My emotions coalesce in my throat as I watch them. It's clear things are going well.

"You're actually going to have Finn's room, Claire. When he comes to stay on the weekend, he's going to share with me. We have a cot from the lodge and a sleeping bag. We're going to camp out, right buddy?"

Finn agrees and slips his hand into Daniel's.

"He doesn't talk much," says Daniel. "He spends most of his time on the reserve. His *kokum* speaks mostly Cree. But we're figuring it out."

I bow my head, hoping he doesn't see the tears in my eyes. I never expected all these feelings. I thought things with Daniel would be the same. But he's so happy.

"Finn, let's go get Auntie's things from the car. Then we'll sit out on the deck and relax for a bit before we have supper."

After I hear the back door close, I wander down the hall to the living room.

I'm drawn to the view of the lake through the wall of tall windows in front of me. Though the lake is still covered in a thick layer of incandescent white-and-green ice, in my mind it remains the perfect blue of the eye on a peacock's tail. I remember Jeff telling me long ago that it didn't matter what the weather was when someone first saw the lake, once they saw it on a sunny day, that first vision is the one that would remain. I rest my forehead and palms against the glass and close my eyes.

I find it hard to believe that in a matter of a few days, and with only a short stop in Regina, I've come from such a verdant coastal spring to this monochromatic, barren north.

"Are you going to clean that window?" Daniel's voice is gentle. I turn. He leans against the wall, arms folded, watching me.

"You have a beautiful home, Daniel."

"It was hard work, but I'm pretty happy with how it turned out."

I gesture toward the piano against the far wall. "You kept it."

"I couldn't bear to get rid of it. Being this close to the lake isn't good for it, though. And it needs a good tuning."

"But you don't play."

Daniel shakes his head and holds up his right hand. "Not often. And never in front of others."

Tears rush to my eyes. "I'm so tired, Daniel." My voice breaks.

Daniel pushes away from the wall, but I wave him off. If he comes over to me now, I'll lose it.

"Well, you can have the afternoon to rest. Then you should spend some time with Finn." He turns to leave the room. "And Claire, you need to call Shane. He's waiting to hear from you."

"You told him?" I follow him into the kitchen.

"When you called so upset, I wasn't sure what to do, so I called him."

Outside the window Finn throws a ball for Connie. Every time the dog brings the ball back, Finn pats her on the nose. Connie is so big, she and Finn see eye to eye. My face feels frozen, the corners of my lips weighted.

Daniel stands next to me. "It's going to be fine."

"Sure," I say. Sure, it will.

I wake late to the sound of the phone ringing. Daniel has gone to town on his day off and Finn isn't coming today, so there's no reason to rush out of bed. Finn's grandmother has been kind about letting him stay for the past few days, but Sherry is back from her latest trip down to Winnipeg and wants to see him. Daniel will get him back on the weekend.

I lie there a long time, gazing at Finn's hockey posters. Nothing has really changed in the week since I arrived. When Finn is here, I feel like I have a purpose, whether it's painting pictures at the scarred kitchen table, building forts out of blankets or walking outside searching for crocus blooms. Finn made up a game that's filled many hours. He collects small, dark rocks that he hands to me to throw out onto the ice as far as I can, then he tries to beat my efforts.

Daniel pushes me to help out at the lodge, but more often I stay here, cocooned in a comforter, hiding from the ever-brightening spring sunlight that streams through the window.

Now, the day yawns empty in front of me. With nothing planned, with no Finn or Daniel, I feel rootless, and all the reasons I came here come washing back over me, trapping me.

The phone rings twice more. Then a third time. Again and again, I let it go. Lunch was hours ago, but I'm not hungry. Tea would be nice, though.

I can't believe how heavy the covers seem as I push them off. The sun shines through the bedroom window, but the north wind skims the ice on the lake and blows strong and hard against the cabin. I dress in jeans and a sweatshirt, and then go to the kitchen to make tea. I lean against the counter and listen to the creaking of the walls as the little house faces the buffeting winds. I take my tea out onto the deck that overlooks the lake.

Far out on the horizon, I see a pale greenish-blue patch of open water where the melting ice shifted during the night. The afternoon slips away as I sit and watch that far-off place where water meets ice, thoughts of Leah and Jeff colliding in my mind.

The snow is gone from the ground. Huge poplars and spruce groan and sway in the wind. Beneath the noise of the trees, there is a tinkling, a shattering sound, like someone pawing through a bin of delicate glass beads. There, then gone, then back again. I sit on the wooden bench outside the door, my empty cup at my feet, and close my eyes. I can't tell where it's coming from, but the sound is perfect for what I feel. A fragile, yet violent, grinding.

I don't know how long I sit like that, but when I open my eyes, Shane stands there, in uniform, one foot on the bottom step of the deck stairs. His left hand grips the railing.

I hold his gaze, aware that I need to say something, but nothing comes to mind.

"Why didn't you call?" He comes up to sit next to me, close enough that his gun presses against my hip. I want to move away, but I can't even summon the will to do that.

"Not sure." I know I've hurt him by not calling. But what could I say? That all the time he spent holding me up, making sure I was okay, was for nothing?

"I couldn't wait any more. I needed to make sure you're okay."

"Sorry."

"Daniel left you alone?"

"He had to get groceries."

I feel his sigh, more than hear it. "Shane, can you hear that noise?" As soon as I ask, I'm terrified that he's going to say no.

He listens. "Yeah. You don't know what that is?" He stands. "Follow me."

He leads the way down toward the lake's edge. As I get closer, I see what I couldn't see from the deck. The wind has forced a huge mass of ice toward the shore. It breaks up as it inches in, the pressure forming piles of thin, glass-like shards that shift and jingle with each push from behind. The slivers of ice glint in the sun and create beautiful, shifting piles of brilliance.

"Pretty." It's more than that, but it's too much effort even to try to find the right words.

"It won't be long now before the ice will be gone."

I imagine all the ice on the lake blowing here, the piles getting bigger and bigger until they are tall enough that I can walk right into them, tiny cold daggers slicing into me as I pass through. Bleeding out through millions of miniscule cuts.

I grip Shane's hand until my fingernails dig into his skin. He doesn't pull away, though, just tightens his own grasp.

"I don't know how to fix this." I barely recognize the sound of my own voice.

"You've had tough times before, Claire."

"Not like this." I return up the stairs, back into the cabin without looking to see if he follows.

I sit on the couch with my head in my hands. I hear his boots drop one at a time, before he comes to crouch in front of me.

"Enough of this. Let's go for a drive."

I raise my head. "I slept with Jeff."

Shane rocks back on his heels. "What?"

"In Vancouver. Then I walked out on him. I went back to Regina, broke up with Luke and took a leave from my job. I thought Daniel would have told you."

"Wait." Shane sits beside me on the couch. "You broke up with Luke?"

"I cheated on him, Shane. It's done. And I just felt like I had to be here, with Daniel." I close my eyes.

Shane clears his throat. "If you could take it back, would you?"

"Sleeping with him?"

"Yeah."

"No."

"So then, what's this all about?"

I don't want to say it. It will hurt him, like it hurts Daniel when I bring it up. "Leah. Being with Jeff seemed to bring it all back. I really thought it would help to be here. But now, I think maybe this is the last place I should have come to get her out of my head."

He doesn't say anything.

I'm disappointed. He still won't talk, won't share how he feels. Daniel, too, steers the conversation away from Leah. The need to say her name, to remember her, is like smoke filling a room. It's been seeping in through the cracks for years, and now, it seems there's no air left to breathe.

"You can't make it better this time, Shane. You can't take this away. No one can."

"I know." I'm glad he doesn't try to tease me out of my mood.

"Claire, are you in love with him?" Shane's voice is gentle.

I can't look at him. "God, Shane, I don't even know him. But I can't stop thinking about him, either. I just want this lost feeling to go away." Finally, I risk a glance at him. He gazes at the floor, his face grave. He takes a deep breath and stands.

"Get your jacket."

He puts on his boots as I gather my things. Before we walk out the door, he puts his hand on my arm.

"Claire. This feeling won't last. I promise." He kisses me on the forehead, something that would usually make me feel like a little kid, but now, it just feels right.

I rest my head against his shoulder for a brief moment. I used to be able to draw such strength from him, but there's nothing there now. I straighten up. "I'm ready." I have no idea what he has in mind, but I do need to get out of here.

I study the array of electronics that lines the dashboard of Shane's police cruiser. All the time he was in Regina, he never took me for a ride in his car. I'm sure if we weren't on a deserted northern highway, he wouldn't let me in the front seat.

I dig deep to say something normal. "You know how to work all this stuff?"

"Yeah. Part of the job."

As we pass the airport, I look away from the empty lots where the houses used to stand. It's been a few years since the government moved the employees into town and sold off the houses to the highest bidders. Daniel says you can find airport houses miles away.

Shane puts his hand on my leg. "Strange, isn't it?"

"It's sad to see all those driveways to nowhere."

"People are still pretty upset."

"I bet." It dawns on me where we're going when he slows at the brown wooden sign that marks the turnoff to the caves. Where Leah was found.

"Shane, no."

"Trust me."

The sun has dipped behind the tall spruce trees that line the narrow gravel road leading to the parking lot. We pull in and Shane backs into a spot. We sit for a long time, not talking.

"Shane, there would be a case file, wouldn't there? When she first went missing, no one thought she killed herself."

"There is."

"You read it."

"Yeah, I did."

"So you know exactly where to go."

"I do." His shoulders slump. "Yes."

Not far from the lot are two paths, two ends of a short horseshoe-shaped trail.

Shane takes my hand and pulls me to the left. It's been a long time since I've been here, and I'm disoriented. When Jeff and I would come here, we only ever took the right fork to where the lookout is perched on top of the cliffs that rise out over the lake. I remember steps, and a catwalk that crosses over the deep fissures below.

Shane stops and gazes into the thick bush.

"There, see?" He pulls me behind him and touches a grimy ribbon tied to a tree a few steps beyond the path. I can't bring myself to ask if he tied the ribbon there. Shane's lived his own story where Leah is concerned, one that had nothing to do with me until after she was dead.

The trees seem to part for us as Shane leads me away from the groomed trail, deeper into the trees. He's left his hat in the car, but following his beige shirt and his yellow-striped pants lends an official feel to this visit.

Soon, he stops. In front of him, the wet, dark earth gives way to bare, golden-white stone. The trees fall away too, opening to a clear view of the sun setting across the lake. A small split in the stone at our feet widens as it approaches the edge of the cliff, forming a deep V-shaped cavern. We are high above the lake.

I step away from Shane and walk along the cracked dolomite. Even at its widest, with a good run, I could jump across the chasm. I look down into the void. Partway down, there is a ledge of rock that stretches almost all the way across. It wouldn't take much to get down there if I put my mind to it. From that ledge, I would have a beautiful view of the sunset. Water laps at the rock and ice at the bottom. I can hear it, but it's too dark to see down there.

I look at Shane.

He nods, his face stony. "She climbed down."

I wonder how Leah even knew of this place, but when I ask Shane he just shrugs.

At that moment, the rays of the setting sun hit the rock at my feet. They turn it a fiery orange and light the shadows in the cavern. A small line of water peeks at the edge of the frozen chunks of blue in the cavern below. The ice refracts the sunlight, sending it spinning and flashing along the stone walls like golden raindrops. The whole area sparkles. The heat of the sun warms the tears on my face. I don't even realize I'm shaking until Shane pulls me back against him. He wraps his arms around me and rests his chin on top of my head. I let him ease me to my knees. I have never cried like this.

"It's okay. You're okay." He lets me cry, doesn't tell me to stop, just sits beside me and rubs my back with his hand. The sun disappears, and the rock seeps cold and damp through my jeans.

"Tell me. Tell me she saw that sun."

"I'm not sure." Shane's takes his hand from my back. "They couldn't say exactly when she came."

I place my palms against the stone underneath me. "She saw it. I know it."

Shane looks out at the lake. "They found her on the ledge. She'd brought four or five blades with her. They found one with her, more in the water below." His voice is tight, like he chokes on the words he says.

In the twilight, his face is as hard as the rock we sit on, and I'm reminded of that day, so long ago, when he told me that Leah had been raped.

Even though he's closed tight when it comes to Leah, he's always been honest with me, when my own family hasn't. He's tried to re-direct me, and rebuild me, teased and jollied and counselled me out of the darkness, without once burdening me with his own pain. He's always been there, telling me the truth when Mom and Daniel and even Leah wouldn't.

"Why did she do it, Shane?"

"Claire, I can tell you how many feet down that ledge is, how far it is from the lake. I can tell you exactly what she looked like when they found her, how many cuts were on her wrists. I can tell you every goddamn detail in that file, but I cannot tell you why she did it."

"You loved her a lot."

"I fucking adored that girl. I wanted to be better because of her, I wanted to be worthy of her love, of her attention. I never had a chance with a girl like that." Shane's voice breaks. I want to take his hand, but I don't. I can't bear it if he cries.

"Tell me something about her, Shane. Something good. Something only you know."

He's quiet for a second. "I used to work the night shift at the mill. I'd get home at 8:30 in the morning, shower and crawl into bed. I'd be out, dead tired. She'd come over at lunch and sneak into bed with me." He looks down at me. "You sure you want to hear this?"

I nod. "If you're sure you want to tell me."

"God, these are the things that I can't get out of my mind. She would get into bed and stick her feet against my legs, press her cold hands on me. And yeah, we'd make love. Jesus, Claire, she was so beautiful. Then I'd fall back asleep and she'd go back to school, or maybe she wouldn't, sometimes she stayed. But before I fell asleep, she would draw on my back with her finger, trace patterns onto my skin, and I felt so safe."

I touch his hand. I thought I was the only one who still ached at all that had gone wrong.

"I've never talked to anyone about any of it. It's all the same. I can't tell you how it feels to miss her any more than I can explain how it felt to love her."

I know exactly what he means. "I wish I knew her like you did. Like Daniel did, or Rita. Even Jeff. It makes me sad that you all have these pieces of her and I don't."

"I guess when someone's gone, that's all we're left with. Pieces. You hold some, too. God, Claire, she loved you so much. One night, right before she went missing, she stayed over and we had such a good night. Even though we never talked about what happened, she seemed better. I was so wrong." He stops here, and again I know he's gone somewhere inside he won't take me, thinking of something he won't tell me. "She talked a lot. She told me how you liked me, how you stuck up for me with Daniel and your mom. She said she wanted me to look out for you when she went away. I thought she meant when she went to school." He takes a deep, ragged breath. "I reminded her I would be in Regina too, for training at Depot. Now I know what she was saying, but then, I had no idea what she was really thinking."

He rubs the heel of his hand against his eyes.

"I didn't see any of it coming. I'm sorry, Claire."

There's no sense telling him it wasn't his fault.

It's almost dark now. We move slowly through the bush back to the path.

"Shane, do you think if she'd loved us more, if we had handled what happened to her better, she wouldn't have done it?"

He stops, grabs my hand. "Claire, it had nothing to do with any of us. It had to do with her, with the pain she was in. And I know she was unhappy here long before the rape. She just got pulled under. The attack was more than she could take. I just wish I'd pushed a little and made her talk about it."

"She was lucky to have you."

At the car, Shane opens my door for me. When he gets in, I hand him a tissue from my purse, then take one for myself. "Coming here helped."

"Me, too."

He starts the car and steers down the gravel road to the highway. His face is serious. "Look, whatever you're going through, if you ever feel like you can't – like you're just finished, please, please call me."

"Shane, I would never do that to you, or to Daniel."

"I bet Leah thought that, too. Just promise you'll get help."

"I'm stronger than that."

Shane looks out the window. "Yeah, well, Leah was the strongest person I've ever known."

At the turnoff to the highway, I put my hand on his arm and wait for him to look at me. "And you're the strongest I've ever known. Thanks for today. I know it wasn't easy."

 Jeff drives all day and night, aiming his truck as straight east as he can on the twisting, roller-coaster roads of the Crowsnest Highway. He feels as though he's a fish on a line being cranked back in, fighting and bucking. Every turn of the reel pulls at the barbed hook buried deep in his chest as it brings him closer to home.

He'd dismissed the first phone call from Daniel just hours after Claire left. Worried after hearing from Claire that morning, Daniel grilled Jeff on what had gone on, but Jeff held his ground, not telling him anything.

But when his mom called and told him that Claire was back up north on a leave from her job, he knew things were bad. He phoned a number of times, but the one time Daniel answered, he stonewalled Jeff pretty much the same way Jeff had done to him.

It took the better part of the week to wrap things up at work before he could load his half-ton and hit the road.

Now, as he comes out of the mountains into the Alberta foothills, he feels like he's shedding the skin he's cultivated since moving to Vancouver.

He drives straight through, only stopping for gas and a few hours of sleep at a roadside motel in Medicine Hat.

By the time he crosses into Manitoba near Madge Lake, he's so hopped up on caffeine that he can barely think straight. He pushes on through the patchwork quilt landscape of the Swan River Valley, then enters the twisting highway that winds through the Porcupine Forest.

It's not long before he rounds a bend and finds himself in the middle of a landscape reminiscent of a war scene. A forest fire has scorched everything, leaving behind denuded, blackened sticks of spruce and tamarack. The new telephone poles stand out, with their sturdy fresh wood. At ground level, spindly, mauve fireweed stretches for miles. He doesn't pass another car until long after he's emerged from the fire zone.

It's dark when he passes the A&W on the outskirts of The Pas. He can't believe it. It's the same. Nothing has changed. Nothing. The one other time he's been home, he flew in and made a point of avoiding town. Now he sees he hasn't missed a thing.

Through town and over the bridge, he drives the homeward bus route. He could do it in his sleep, counting curves and corners until the airport sign appears.

The front of the lodge is dark when he pulls in, but, as he parks next to the hulking building, he can see Colin reading on a couch by the window. A small lamp beside him provides enough light that Jeff can see his mother tucked in close beside him. He takes a deep breath and gets out of his truck.

It's late, and the main door to the lodge is locked. Jeff presses the lit doorbell. Before the buzzer even finishes ringing, his mom opens the door.

They stare at each other for a second, then a smile spreads across her face. He's never seen her look so beautiful.

Wrapped in a plush red robe that suits her dark hair and skin, she looks younger than he remembers. She's cut her hair. He's suddenly aware of how he must look after days in a truck.

"Mom." It seems like years since he's called her that.

Rita pulls him into an awkward hug. She's so small, he feels like a fool in her arms. "Why didn't you tell me you were coming?"

He can't get any words past the lump in his throat. Tears come to his eyes. *It's exhaustion*, he thinks.

All the time, he can feel the comfort of her arms around him as he fights to keep control. Still, he has to wipe his eyes as he steps back.

Colin stands watching. He greets Jeff and holds out his hand. Jeff hesitates only a second before shaking it.

"I've got some reading to do. I'll let you guys catch up." Colin returns to his place on the couch.

"Come in the kitchen. I'll make you something to eat." Rita leads the way, chattering on about the lodge and their bookings for summer. She opens the fridge and starts pulling out what she needs to make him a sandwich.

Jeff's head spins. "Mom."

She turns.

"How's Claire?"

Rita takes a deep breath and goes on making his sandwich. "I don't know. She comes every so often to help out, but she rarely talks. She's stayed for dinner with Daniel, but even then, she was so quiet." She puts his food in front of him and pours him a glass of milk. "She only seems happy when Finn is around."

Neither of them talks as he eats. He stares at the odds and ends stuck to the fridge door. A magnetic notepad with Rita's name on the top lists vegetables, sausage, steak, beans and bleach. Two tiny white-and-green Christmas stocking magnets with the words *joy* and *hope* cross-stitched in red; a glossy photo of a bear cub on the beach at sunset; a ratty old photo of Jeff in junior high; and a handful of plastic magnets shaped like fruit. Glimpses of her life. A life he is no longer a part of.

When he's done eating, Jeff sets his plate in the sink and thanks her. "And how is Dad?"

Rita's face drops. "Okay. He's okay. Jeff, you can stay here as long as you want. We've closed off all the rental rooms upstairs, but the big room on the end is always ready."

He nods. "Mom, I have all my art stuff with me, all my paintings." He brought everything. She probably thinks that means he's going to stay, but he had to get it out of his place. It doesn't mean anything.

"Just find an empty room and unload it. It's no problem."

It occurs to him that she hasn't asked Colin for permission for this. She's making decisions. No wonder she wants to be with him. No wonder she seems at home here.

Jeff moves toward the door. "Well, I better get to it. Thanks for supper."

He has just pulled down the tailgate of his truck when Colin comes out.

"Need a hand?"

"Sure. Thanks."

They're quiet as they work. Jeff thinks about what it would be like to do this with his father. There would be a million questions, suggestions on how best to move the big canvases up the stairs. They'd probably have a big fight about something. It's easy with Colin, and that stirs Jeff's anger.

After the last load, Jeff turns to him. "So. You and my mom."

Colin nods. "She's amazing."

"Yeah. She is." Jeff wants to punch him. "Thanks for your help."

It's a clear dismissal. And Colin takes it.

Jeff knows his father wouldn't.

When Jeff comes in from locking his truck, his mom is waiting in his room with a stack of towels.

"He's a kind man, Jeff. I'm happy."

He can see that. It's just too bad she didn't want to be happy when he was still at home. "I'm going to call Claire in the morning."

"Daniel's off tomorrow. He'll be there." Daniel's obviously told her about the friction between them.

"I don't care. I want to see her."

The next morning, Jeff leaves a message with Daniel for Claire. She's out with Finn.

When she hasn't called back by the time supper is done, he tries again. Daniel says he'll let Claire know he called.

"Did you tell her I called earlier?"

"Didn't really have a chance, Jeff. Nothing personal."

Jeff grabs his keys and heads for his truck. He knows where Daniel lives. He can be there in fifteen minutes, tops.

He makes it in ten.

As he closes the truck door, he hears the creaking of melting ice on the lake. The familiar sounds and the scent of tamarack and spruce calm Jeff's nerves, but only a bit.

He loved this time of year as a kid. He'd go down to the lake to watch the ice break up, feeling like he was straddling a magical line between two worlds. The lake would stretch out before him, majestic in her frozen white mantle, while behind him, the delicate pale green tamarack and aspen announced a new season. A week, ten days and the white would be gone, leaving in its place that liquid turquoise he knew so well.

Jeff's grateful to be away from the lodge. He and Colin spent an uncomfortable afternoon together cleaning out the storage shed while his mom readied all the linens for the rental cabins. The three of them shared dinner, then Colin and Rita slipped away for a walk.

And now here he is.

He heads around the corner of the cabin. Daniel sits on the deck in a lawn chair facing the lake, a beer in his hand. He's bundled up against the wind in a heavy jacket. A large black dog lies at his feet.

Daniel doesn't get up to greet him.

"Jeff." Daniel's face betrays nothing.

"Daniel."

"So, when did you get in?"

"Late last night." Jeff is not surprised by the coldness of Daniel's welcome. "Is she here?"

"She's here. She's sleeping." Daniel takes a long sip of his beer.

"It's early for her to be in bed."

"Yep. She's had a few tough days."

They stare out at the lake, the ice pale against the darkening sky.

"She's been here for a while, Jeff."

Jeff feels his face get warm, but he ignores Daniel's last comment. "My mom says she sleeps a lot. Look, Daniel, I'm not here to cause trouble, I just want to make sure she's okay."

Daniel sighs and gestures at the empty chair beside him. "You might as well have a seat."

Jeff moves the chair so it's at a right angle to Daniel's. "Do you think she'll see me?"

Daniel shrugs. "She hasn't told me what happened. Just that she needed to get away, needed to be alone."

"I think being alone was her problem."

"Jeff, just tell me what happened."

Jeff shuffles the images that come to his mind and chooses only a few to share. Not the kite. Not the cliff. Not the night at his place. None of it seems like it's enough to send her into the tailspin everyone seems to think she's in.

"I don't know. She seemed really, really angry." *And lost*, but he's not going to say that to Daniel.

"She's a lot better now than when she came. She was so out of it, I have no idea how she drove the whole way. My mom's been calling, but it doesn't seem the right time to tell Claire." Daniel frowns out at the horizon. "You're right. She does seem pissed off. Maybe you should wait to see her. Let her decide if she even wants to."

Jeff nods. He doesn't want to upset her.

"Mom says that spending time with your son helps."

"Yeah, Finn's pretty easy to be around. His *kokum* still has custody, but he comes out a few days a week. A couple of days ago, Rita came to get Claire and they drove out to the reserve to pick him up for lunch." Daniel shakes his head. "After that, Claire came back and slept for four hours. So I don't know what to tell you."

Jeff stands up. "Let her know I came by." Daniel just looks at him. "I'm staying at the lodge."

"I know. Look, there are some projects you can work on around there, stuff that we never seem to have time to get to. May as well help out, hey?"

Jeff feels a flash of annoyance that Daniel seems so proprietary, like the lodge is his. "Yeah, that's the plan, Daniel."

Daniel walks with Jeff to his truck.

Jeff opens the door but doesn't get in. He looks back at Daniel's cabin. She's so close.

"Dan, please tell her I came. She needs to know that."

"When she gets up, I'll tell her."

THREE

Supper has long past when I wake, but I feel much better. The afternoon with Shane changed things. After years of shoving thoughts of my sister to the back of a deep, dark closet, pulling them out only on safe days – her birthday, Christmas – I feel like a light has sparked, and I can see more clearly.

Daniel has left chicken and a salad in the fridge for me. As I eat, I listen to him struggling with Leah's old guitar, playing Johnny Cash songs. His hand is just agile enough to hold a pick and strum.

I go into the living room.

"What?" he says, like he used to when I would walk into his room without knocking.

"It sounds good."

He shakes his head and puts the guitar away. "Not good enough."

I go and sit next to him on the couch.

"Claire, what happened in Vancouver?"

"I hung out with my friend, spent some time with Jeff. This shitty feeling has nothing to do with anything he did. Really. I think being with him just made me realize that I was missing something." It's the most I've told him since I came.

"So he didn't hurt you?"

"No, Daniel. I think it was the other way around."

"He was here earlier, while you were sleeping."

All the strength I've felt since waking deserts me.

"He's staying at the lodge with Rita and Colin. He wanted me to tell you."

The look of concern on Daniel's face brings tears to my eyes. I wish I could make all of this go away. I wish we were a normal family. "I wish Leah were here." *There, I said it.*

Daniel blinks. "Claire."

"Did you know that she spent a lot of time with Rita? That she was over there a fair bit?"

"Not until later."

"Did Mom know?"

"Mom knew more than she let on, I think. But I'm not sure. We don't ever talk about Leah."

"Do you talk to Rita about her?"

"No." He stands and looks out the window. I come up beside him and slide my arm through his. He puts his other hand over mine. "I hope you're finding what you need here, Claire."

"I don't know what I need. But I am going to go see Jeff."

"Drive careful," Daniel says. "Be careful."

I have to pass the airport to get to the lodge; there's no way to avoid it. In the dark, I can't see the gaping holes between trees where the houses used to be.

The airport sign at the turnoff is new, though, all silver and blue. It catches me by surprise every time I pass by on my way to the lodge. My chest hurts when I think of the old sign: white-painted letters carved into planks of brown wood, the whole thing mounted on a wide concrete base. I remember that night just before Leah went missing, when we all added our names to graffiti on the back of the sign.

The full moon has risen, turning the night sky that shade of indigo that I have only ever seen here.

The lodge and all the cabins are dark when I pull in. A single bulb illuminates the centre yard. The main door will be locked, so I go to the kitchen door and knock. Rita opens it.

Rita has been so good to me. I've been sporadic with my help, but when I do come, she greets me with a hug and a list of things to keep me busy.

"Sorry to come so late. Daniel told me Jeff's here."

"He went up a while ago. You know which room he's in. Go up the back way, hon."

I can see the worry on her face, but I just wish her good night and go up.

I knock on the closed door. Jeff opens it. He stands shirtless and sockless. He hasn't shaved, and his hair seems longer and messier than when I last saw him. I can only imagine what he sees in me.

"I wasn't sure you'd come," he says.

"You need a haircut." I reach up and brush at his long bangs.

His smile doesn't quite reach his eyes.

"Can I come in?"

He steps aside, and I enter his room. The light from a small black-and-white TV on the pine dresser flickers. The sound is turned down.

Jeff closes the door and reaches for my hand. He hugs me to him, his rough whiskers rubbing my temple. He smells earthy, salty. I press my mouth against the hollow of his throat and tighten my arm around his waist. His heartbeat thuds under my lips; the sound fills my ears. There. Right there. That is the exact place where all the noise in my head stops. For so long, I've lived with the sense that I'm a mistuned radio station; a soft static hums under everything I say or do.

Interference from up the dial.

All quiet now.

"What is this feeling?" I ask. "Sex?"

"I don't know, Claire. I don't think it matters."

"Of course it matters." I pull away and go to the window. The ice on the bay glows, its surface reflecting the brightness of the moon. Jeff comes to stand next to me.

I keep my eyes on the lake. "Can I stay?"

"Of course."

"But do you want me to? If not, I'll go."

"Don't do that, Claire. We're so far beyond that kind of thing." He sounds so weary.

When I finally look at him, his eyes are black in the semi-darkness. He looks wild, with his long hair, his mouth, his bare chest, all lit by the strange blue glow of moonlight. In that moment, I want him. I want to crawl inside him, to wear him like a second skin. But I want him to want me the same way.

He stands motionless.

I try to move away, but he grabs me by the hands, and holds tight.

"Claire, I just want to say, I'm sorry. I'm sorry I left the day they found Leah. The day my dad –" He can't even say it. "I never should have left. It was a mistake."

"It's okay. I don't blame you."

"That day wasn't only about you, Claire." I've seen the exasperated look on his face more than once. He's never held back from telling me when I was out of line. Before I can apologize, he goes on. "You aren't the only one who lost something. I screwed everything up. My whole life is one big fuck-up, and I have no idea what comes next. I don't know how to put it all back together." He turns his face away from me.

What was just a phantom thought to me in Vancouver gains definition now. Jeff, Shane, Daniel. I was never alone in this.

I've been so selfish.

Rita, too. Even my mother.

"We'll figure it out, Jeff."

"Claire, there is no we. I haven't got anything to offer." His laugh is bitter. "God, I need to get outside."

This Jeff, I know. "Sure."

He doesn't look at me as he pulls on a T-shirt. He throws me a sweatshirt. "Here. It's going to be cold."

We head out to the picnic table by the lake. It's in the same place it's always been, under a large sheltering poplar near the white sand beach. I climb up and sit on it, facing the water. Jeff drapes the blanket he brought out around my shoulders and climbs up next to me.

"The wind's changed. It's coming from the south. That'll move some ice." Somewhere in the distance, an owl hoots. "Hunting time," he says.

"Yeah." I'm still not used to the way he tries to make conversation. He never did that before.

Light from the moon kaleidoscopes along the surface of the frozen lake. There is open water at the shore as the wind shifts the solid mass of water back to the north. The movement under the ice's surface makes small waves on the sand, the sound of them loud in the stillness.

"Claire, there's someone else, right?"

"Not any more. Not after what I did in Vancouver."

"It wasn't just you."

"No. But that doesn't really matter to him, does it?"

"Are you sad it's over?"

"Of course." I am sad, but it was already ending. "He was good to me."

"My mom told me he's smart. Some kind of math genius."

"So they say."

"I finished high school at night." I can barely hear him.

"While working two jobs, I heard. That's something." I move a little closer. "What about you? Do you have anyone?"

"Not really." His tone softens. "How long are you going to stay, Claire?"

"Jeff, I can't think past this second. You?"

"I quit my bartending job in Vancouver. My partner in the land-scaping business is fine running things without me. I brought most of my stuff back, so I don't know. I'll work here for a bit, help out, then decide."

I feel a shiver go through his body.

"To be honest, the thought of staying here makes me crazy."

I move to share the blanket with him. He pulls it around his shoulder.

"Because of your dad."

"Because of everything."

I look out at the luminescent ice on the bay. "I forgot how beautiful it is here."

"No matter how hard I try, I can never forget what this place is like. When I first left, I missed it so much. And hated it. Both feelings faded, but never really went away." He steps down from the table. "Are you staying?"

We go in the kitchen door. Colin and Rita are in bed, so we sneak up the back stairs, carrying our shoes. Once in his room, we take off the sweatshirts we wore to keep warm. I go into the bathroom, and when I come out, Jeff is lying on his back on the bed, one arm across his eyes. He still wears his jeans and T-shirt. I stretch out beside him.

The clock radio on the nightstand is old. It's been there for years, at least since I used to help Leah clean these rooms on weekends. Its plastic numbers flip with a snap, marking the passing minutes. The dim orange backlight shows that it's just past midnight.

I roll on my side, turn my back to the clock and lay my hand on Jeff's chest. He shudders. I touch his face. My hand comes away wet. I feel like I did when I first saw his tattoo – out of control, afraid that someone who was always so controlled can lose it.

"Jeff."

"I'm okay."

He is quiet for a bit. "Vancouver was just a big one-night stand."

That hurts.

"I could have been anyone, Claire."

"Me, too, Jeff."

"That's not true."

"You know what, Jeff? That day? The day you say screwed every-thing up? The day they found my sister? That's what makes that time in Vancouver about so much more than sex." I hesitate. "What hap-pened between you and me was different, and you know it."

"You left."

"I had to leave. I kept asking myself those same things. 'What next? What do I do now?' Everything I had made of myself fell apart, and I was that same messed-up girl you walked away from at the rock. I fooled myself into thinking it was okay, that I could take whatever I needed, and no one would get hurt. I figured if you could walk away from me back then, you could never be touched by anything I did, anything I said in Vancouver. Then I saw your goddamn tattoo, and I was lost. I get it, now. But when I left you that morning, I knew exactly how you felt when you left me. There was no other choice. Either time, for either of us."

He says nothing.

"So, when you say you could have been anyone, you're wrong. None of that could have happened with anyone else."

"Sounds like you have it all figured out."

My laugh matches the bitterness in his voice. "God, Jeff. I am so mixed up. I've been running all this through my head since I came here. Now, I'm lying here with you, and whatever this feeling is, whatever that feeling was with you in that godawful black room, is so strong I want to scream, but I can't even name it. Because I'm afraid it all comes from that horrible day, that it will always be between us. And I don't want us to be about that." I hope I haven't said too much. "Jeff, you've always been the one with the answers. Not me." And the fact that he hasn't got any is what scares me.

I brush his hair back from his brow. I lean in and kiss him, hard, on the mouth. "Do you feel that?"

"Yeah."

"I need to know that's about us, not Leah, not your dad, not that day."

He pulls my head back down to his, holds it there and kisses me until I can't breathe and have to pull away.

I lie back down and slip my hand into his. I am so tired of being sad.

Soon, I feel him relax into sleep. I lie awake for a long time, feeling his breath against my hair. The numbers on the clock click, counting the minutes until I, too, sleep.

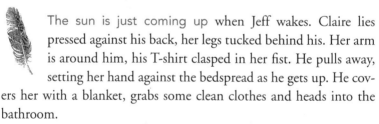 The sun is just coming up when Jeff wakes. Claire lies pressed against his back, her legs tucked behind his. Her arm is around him, his T-shirt clasped in her fist. He pulls away, setting her hand against the bedspread as he gets up. He covers her with a blanket, grabs some clean clothes and heads into the bathroom.

She's still asleep when he's showered and ready. Through the window he can see Daniel's dog sitting by the picnic table, waiting for her master. Shit. He looks down at Claire, but he can't bring himself to wake her. He's going to have to face Daniel on his own.

Jeff passes his mom in the kitchen. "Morning."

She asks if he's hungry, but he just shakes his head and waves on his way out the door. He heads down to the beach and stops to pet Connie.

Just as he thought, the wind pushed the ice far from shore in the night. It's massed in huge chunks in the centre of the bay. Won't be long now. The open water is calm. He can feel the cold coming off it. A few more weeks, and he'll be able to swim.

Daniel comes out of the big lakefront cabin carrying a red tool box. Jeff stands and waits.

Daniel shields his eyes from the sun with his hand and looks at Jeff, his face serious. "I hope you know what the hell you're doing."

"I just wanted you to know she's here. She's okay."

"Would have been nice to know that last night." Daniel pushes by him.

"Don't blame her. She just stayed over, nothing happened." He speaks to Daniel's back as he follows him up the drive to the storage shed.

"Not the first time I've heard that from you. I have no idea what the hell is going on with you two, but I'm pretty sure you're not good for each other. You look like shit, Jeff, and she does, too." Daniel stops and spins to face him. "Why don't you just leave? Make it easy on her? You're not right for her." His face reddens as he looks past Jeff's shoulder. "Sorry, Rita."

Jeff turns to his mom. The conversation brings back his anger and all his unsettled feelings and he snaps at her. "Why are you following me?"

He's sure he hurt her, but she's a pro at hiding it. "You should come eat, Jeff. Maybe it will improve your disposition. Daniel, Colin needs you up at the workshop."

"Claire's awake." Rita and Jeff walk back toward the lodge together. "She has work to do cleaning cabins. You can stain the deck at Cabin Ten. After that, see if she'll help you move your stuff up to my old cabin. It needs a good cleaning, but you'll have your own space. By then I'll have a list of groceries and supplies I need you to pick up in town."

In the kitchen, Claire is rinsing her plate. She looks at him as Rita disappears through the door into the dining room.

"Morning." Her voice is low. She's testing his mood and it pisses him off. It's exactly how his mom used to act. Every goddamn morning.

"Morning."

"Are you okay?

"Great."

She lowers her eyes and turns away. "Okay. Well, I'll see you later then."

"Later."

Jeff is nearly done staining the deck when Claire walks by, a bucket full of cleaning supplies in one hand, a stack of linens in the other.

"I'm going to head up to your mom's old place and start cleaning. Come see me when you're done, then I can help you move your things." She walks away, the pail bumping her leg as she goes.

Rita's cabin is across the back road, away from the water. When she bought the place, she didn't have enough money for a fancy cottage, let alone a waterfront cabin. Colin sold her the small cabin that had been in his family for years. Probably gave her a good deal, too. It's rustic, but it has running water and electricity.

Jeff hurries through the last few feet of deck, then closes the paint can and cleans his brush. He leaves everything next to the front steps at the lodge, and heads across the back road to his mom's.

The cabin is painted brown with yellow trim, and it's hard to see through the trees that surround the place. He steps up onto the small raised deck that serves as a porch and pulls open the wooden screen door.

Claire is in the main room, batting at the corner of the ceiling with a broom. Cobwebs and dust float down around her, and land on the old brown linoleum that covers the entire floor of the cabin.

"Hey," she says, turning to him. "You come do this, you're taller than I am."

He takes the broom from her and runs it around the edge of the ceiling, then sweeps everything that falls into the dustpan and throws it into the garbage can that Claire has pulled from under the sink.

Claire wipes down all the furniture as Jeff takes the cushions off the old, worn green couch and goes outside and bangs the dust out of them. His mother hasn't been here in a while. It eats at him, how he has no sense of home. The house he grew up in is gone, and his mom only lived here for a few years before moving in with Colin. Jeff's grateful that his mom realizes he needs to get out from under Colin's roof. He can work for the man, but he doesn't want to have to live off him, too.

He goes back inside. Claire's swept out all the rooms and is stripping the old bedsheets off. He helps her make the bed in the larger room. He can't meet her eyes as they tuck in the sheets.

He grabs her wrist on her way past him to the door, and she stops. He sees a softening around her eyes as she looks up at him. They've hardly spoken a word since he came up here.

"You're a mess," he says as he brushes cobwebs from her hair.

"True," she says and pulls away. "But so are you. At least we're in it together."

FOUR

In the mornings, I arrive at the lodge with Daniel and go
straight in to have breakfast with Rita and get the cleaning
and cooking schedules sorted out. Along with our own meals,
we have to prepare shore lunches for the guests who, now
that the ice is gone, will be out in the fishing boats all day. Daniel and
Colin spend their days on the boats with clients. Jeff is the one without a set job, so he spends his time catching up on some of the big
projects that need to be done around the place.

By early afternoon, Jeff and I find time for a walk or a paddle
in the canoe before it's time to prepare dinner. I keep my distance,
unsure of what Jeff needs or wants. I never thought he'd seem out of
place at the lake, but he does.

Aside from all that, I don't want to rush whatever is between us.

If Finn is out for the day, Daniel and I sometimes stay to eat.
Colin has been really good though, about letting Daniel have his
Finn-days off.

Shane's been away doing some training at Depot in Regina. If
things were different, we'd be hanging out at my little house there,
catching up. If things hadn't fallen apart the way they did. If I hadn't
fallen apart.

He called one early morning to check in. I know he's talked to
Daniel about me and Jeff, too. It makes me angry, but I realize it's
a consequence of showing up the way I did. I haven't given anyone
much reason to believe I'm okay.

One afternoon, with my work for the day finished, I find Jeff building a new dock for one of the lakefront cabins. He's already moved the
lumber down onto the grass near shore, and he's plugged the electric
saw into a long extension cord that leads back to the cabin. A box of

screws and a drill sit next to the boards.

"Can I help?" I hand him the Coke I'm carrying. It's warm out for the end of May, and he looks hot.

"Thanks," he says and drinks it down.

I squint up at him. The sun reflecting off his white T-shirt blinds me. "You're welcome. Most guys I know would let loose with a big belch."

"Maybe I'm trying to impress you." He turns back to the pile of wood and selects a board.

"Ha. Maybe that would impress me."

He looks over his shoulder at me. I laugh at the expression on his face.

"I'm kidding, Jeff. You're too serious."

He takes a tape measure from his pocket and makes a mark on the board. "Yeah, you've told me that before."

I remember. Back then, I'd chatter at him, tell him my stupid stories about school or home, and he would look at me with that same look, like he didn't understand me at all.

"Cover your ears," he says and fires up the saw. He makes the cut, then moves on to the next board. I watch the way he kneels on each board to hold it steady. He tosses the short pieces into a separate pile. Soon he has a stack of boards that are the right length.

"Do you have another drill? I can help you."

"No, just the one, but you can come over here and hold the boards if you want." I know he doesn't really need my help. I move close anyway and steady each board as he drills the screws through. This is the closest I've been to him in weeks.

When he leans over to drill next to where I hold on, his hair slides forward, leaving the back of his neck bare in front of me.

I press my lips to his warm skin. The noise dies as I feel the drill slip off the screw next to my hand, but I don't flinch.

Jeff doesn't move until I pull back. He looks up at me, a quick glance, then looks away and resets the screw. "That's not really helping."

"Sorry."

"No, you're not." He turns away, grabs more screws, but I can see his eyes are crinkled at the corners. "Let me finish here and we can get the canoe out."

I go to let Rita know we are done for the day.

After that, I bring my own car in the mornings and stay after dinner, long after Daniel goes. I know what he thinks of Jeff. But I can see he's relieved, too, that I've moved beyond rushing home to hide under my covers.

Sometimes Jeff and I play cards with Rita and Colin, or we make a fire on the beach and sit up late, talking. Once or twice, we make our way back up to his place, where we sit on either end of the couch, feet up on the middle cushion, toes touching. We sit there until we fall asleep. Then he asks me to stay and I say no and I close my eyes and he kisses me for ten, fifteen minutes. When I leave, I feel empty and full at the same time.

 Jeff pulls the quad up to the main door and kills the engine. He's already attached the trailer and loaded the chainsaw and an axe. They're going to gather wood for the stoves in the cabins. Even though summer's coming on, the nights and early mornings are still cold.

Claire comes out of the lodge. She looks beautiful today. She wears a button-down checked shirt with the sleeves rolled up and a pair of faded jeans. He throws her a pair of work gloves. She shoves them into her back pocket.

"Move it, Jeff. I'm driving." She puts her hands on her hips.

He slides back on the seat. "It's all yours."

Claire gets on and restarts the engine. Jeff puts his hands on her waist as she accelerates.

"Smooth takeoff," he says, his lips close to her ear.

She speeds up and he tightens his hold. His long legs hug hers, and she steers with one hand as she touches his knee.

They cross the highway, and Claire steers down the cutline. Power poles flash by, then she takes a hard right, and they bounce down a faint trail, long grass whipping at their pant legs. She stops beside a path.

"Colin told me there's a ton of deadfall back here. We'll go in and pull some big stuff out, bring it here and cut it." She pulls on her gloves and heads into the bush while Jeff grabs the chainsaw and follows.

"With two of us, we'll be able to drag out bigger chunks. It won't take us long."

Jeff shakes his head and asks her if her chainsaw skills are as good as her quadding skills. Not waiting for an answer, he pulls the cord, filling the air with noise. They don't speak as Jeff notches the trunk of a tall dead spruce. Together, they push the tree over, and then Claire takes the saw and starts to trim the dead branches as Jeff stacks them by size in three neat piles. The smell of fresh-cut wood envelops them. Claire braces her foot against the trunk of the tree and slices through it. The logs are wide, and she and Jeff move them out to the quad together.

The June air is still and hot. The cool breeze off the lake doesn't reach them, and on their last trip back to the quad, Jeff watches as Claire strips down to a black tank top and twists her hair into a ponytail. He can see the faint dark stubble on her underarm, and he has to look away.

He swallows hard. "What next, boss?"

"Let's hurry up and get back. I'm dying of thirst. Use the axe to cut those chunks in half and I'll load them up."

Jeff splits the wood, then joins Claire as she arranges the logs in neat rows in the trailer. Jeff watches her as they work. She's lost weight in the weeks since he was with her in Vancouver. Her arms are thin; he can see the muscles move beneath her skin. He steps up behind her as she reaches down to load another log. He pulls off his gloves and drops them on the ground. He places his palm against her back, fingers spread wide.

It's been weeks since he touched her. That day, working on the dock, when she kissed him – he almost lost control, took what he wanted right there. He's afraid of hurting her, like he's hurt everyone else who's ever mattered.

Claire straightens up and grabs the side of the trailer, but doesn't face him. She tenses as he moves his hand under the hem of her shirt and traces his fingers up her spine, starting at the indentation above her jeans, damp now with sweat, up over the outward curve at her midback, bump after bump. She is as still as the humid air that surrounds them. His fingers slide under the clasp of her bra and he can feel her start to pull away.

"Jeff."

He pulls his hand out, wraps his arms around her waist, hugs her against him. Still gripping the side of the trailer, she bows her head. He rubs his lips on the back of her neck, kisses it, like she did to him, but he doesn't stop there. He runs his tongue where her shirt meets her shoulder blade. He tastes the pungent sweat on her skin, and, clumsy now, a little rougher than he means to be, he pulls her bra strap out of the way. He presses his mouth to her pale, bare shoulder, drags his teeth against her skin. He feels her jump a little as he nips her shoulder and gently sucks. He feels her body slacken, and her breath leaves her in a rush. He traces the underside of her raised arm with the lightest of touches, from the point of her elbow, along her armpit to the edge of her shirt next to her breast. Her arm falls away as he looks down at the mark he's left on her. His mark. Crimson, with purple specks where the blood vessels have ruptured. A small amount of blood where his teeth broke through her skin.

Satisfied pride overwhelms him. Followed quickly by shame that he hurt her, disbelief that he could even want to.

And she just stood there, not making a sound.

Jeff kisses her shoulder, then arranges her shirt over the spot. Hides the damage. All this, rising from the tenderness he felt at seeing the skin under her arm.

"I'm not sorry," she says, like she knows what he's thinking.

"I am." It's a lie, and that makes it worse. "Did I hurt you?"

"I'm okay, Jeff. Let's get the branches loaded and get going."

He doesn't argue, just picks up the axe and follows her back into the bush. When they're done, Claire lets him drive back to the lodge. She sits close, holds him tight. He can feel the side of her face pressed between his shoulder blades. He wishes he could keep driving, take her to a place where they can be alone, with no one watching. No one judging.

Later, Jeff helps Daniel clean the fish his clients caught. After his first few clumsy attempts with the knife, it comes easy. He still can't believe how quickly it came back. All the things his dad taught him.

Daniel doesn't speak to him as they work, which is fine. Jeff has nothing to say to him either.

Jeff looks up to see an RCMP cruiser pull up to the lodge.

He almost drops his knife into the pile of bloody fish guts. "What the hell?"

Daniel looks up. "It's just Shane." There's a knowing look of satisfaction on his face that makes Jeff want to punch him. "No one told you? We're having a fish fry tonight. I invited Shane to come out and eat with us."

Jeff knew Shane was a cop, but his mom never told him he'd moved back.

Shane mounts the steps to the lodge, but before he can open the door, Claire comes flying through it and throws her arms around him. Shane catches her and hugs her back. Then he kisses her on the cheek and they disappear inside together.

Jeff stands still, knife poised over the fish he's cleaning. He looks over at Daniel, who continues to work, chopping off head and tail, skinning, filleting, grabbing another.

"What did you expect, Jeff? We both abandoned her and did what was best for us. Shane was there for her. She's lucky she had someone to replace us both. You won't break that connection, my friend. They are tight." Daniel's voice is resigned, but there is a note of triumph in it, too.

Jeff helps Daniel clean the benches and dispose of the garbage so bears don't come sniffing around, then heads up to his place for a shower.

His mom, Claire, everyone has moved on. It's not like he expected them to wait around, to stay the same. He's annoyed that no one told him about Shane, but it also pisses him off how his mom, who couldn't get her shit together to make sure her own son was taken care of, can be the den mother here, cooking for everyone, looking after Daniel's kid, keeping watch over Claire.

By the time he gets back down to the lodge, he's in a fury. Shane's changed out of his uniform and sits with Claire on the couch in the living room next to the dining area. Through the floor-to-ceiling windows that overlook the lake, Jeff can see Colin setting up a campfire on grass near the shore.

"Hey, Jeff. I haven't seen you in a long time." Shane stands and puts his hand out. Jeff grits his teeth and shakes it. Shane sits back down.

"Yeah. Hard to believe you're a cop, Shane."

"I've heard that a lot since I came back to town."

"Jeff's been living in Vancouver. He works as a landscaper." As Claire shifts away from Shane, the strap of her shirt slides down, exposing the hickey on her shoulder. Claire doesn't notice, but Shane does. He stares hard at Jeff as she pulls it up.

Shane's voice is cold. "Cutting lawns?"

Jeff nods. "Yeah. Cutting lawns." *Asshole.*

Rita comes in from the kitchen. "Daniel had a good day today. Fish fry tonight. Daniel and Colin are cooking. Jeff, why don't you come get some drinks, then you can all head outside?"

Jeff, glad for the excuse to get away, follows his mother to the kitchen. "You want a beer?" he asks her as he tucks the opener in his pocket.

"No, thanks."

He grabs four beer, then hesitates and grabs another.

"Jeff."

"Mom."

She shakes her head.

"Mom, are Claire and Shane together?"

"They're close. They spent a lot of time together in Regina. Daniel says they're best friends. Shane cares a great deal for her."

Jeff feels like an idiot. Fumbling around, trying to decide how best to approach her, to tell her how he feels. Trying to do the right thing by coming up here. Trying to fix the mess he made when he left.

Fuck it.

He goes back into the family room. Claire and Shane sit with their heads bent close. Shane's whispering something and she's nodding. He catches sight of Jeff and sits back. His gaze is steady, assessing. Jeff gets the same wary feeling he always gets around cops.

He sets the beer down and pops the caps off two bottles. "Here you go. I'll just drop off these others."

Daniel and Colin sit on old aluminum lawn chairs by the fire. Jeff opens their bottles and takes the last one for himself. He drops into an empty chair next to Colin and drains half his beer in one swig. It feels like he's slaking a thirst he's had for a hundred years.

Connie lies, head on paws, at Daniel's feet. She looks up at Jeff, and Jeff stares back at her. He finishes his beer as he listens to Daniel and Colin go on and on with their plans for the summer season. Connie's head perks up when he stands.

"Anyone want another?"

Colin and Daniel both say no.

Inside, he grabs another beer, opens it and drinks it, then with a defiant look at his mother, takes two more from the fridge. Rita says nothing. But then, she wouldn't, would she? That, at least, hasn't changed.

FIVE

At the fire, I take the seat beside Jeff. He sits, sullen, three empty bottles at his feet, a full one in his hand. Shane sits next to Daniel, across the fire from me. Rita and Colin complete the circle, with Rita on Jeff's other side.

I meet Rita's concerned look. We both know this can't be good. I lean over and touch his hand. I keep my voice low. "I'm so glad you're here."

He looks at me through half-closed eyes, then looks at the ground. He jerks his hand away and takes a sip of beer.

I don't know what else I can say.

The fish, fried over the fire, is delicious. As the early evening sun moves closer to the horizon, the lake calms, and it starts to get cool. Rita and Colin head out for a walk. I get up to get my jacket from the lodge.

Jeff catches up to me right outside the kitchen. He pushes me against the dining room wall and tries to kiss me. He smells like beer. I turn my face away.

"Stop it, Jeff. Not now."

"Because Shane's here."

I bump the door frame as I step back. "Because you're drunk. Because we need to get back out there."

"Why? Why can't we stay in here?"

I try to move past him, but he blocks me. "Daniel and Shane know we're in here, Jeff, and I don't want them to worry."

"And they'd be worried because of me."

"Not you. Me. They watch me all the time, Jeff. They're concerned about me." He still won't let me go. "They're afraid I want to slit my wrists."

I put my hand on his chest, take a deep breath and make my voice as gentle as I can. "Why are you so angry today? Your mom is worried about you, Jeff. You're acting just like your dad."

Jeff frowns as he pushes my hand away.

I feel my face flush in anger. "See? Just stop it."

"Fuck you, Claire." He says it with such violence, it feels like he punched me. "You think those guys are so great? Daniel and Shane, all worried about you and your feelings. You think my mom and Daniel and Shane care so much about you?" Jeff's voice is raw. "You think they're family? There's no such thing."

"Come on, Jeff."

"You think they're so good. Couple of lying bastards."

"What do you mean?"

"Go ask your precious Shane what he did. And ask Daniel about his hand."

"What about his hand?"

Realization comes into his face, too late. He grips my arms. "Claire, I shouldn't have –"

"Let her go." Shane stands at the door.

I shrink back from the look of pure fury that crosses Jeff's face. Then he throws his hands up and steps back. He lets Shane pull him away.

"Are you going to arrest me?"

"Don't be stupid, Jeff. Claire, go back outside. I want to talk to him."

I cross my arms. "So talk."

Shane's voice is hard and cold. "Go outside."

I go.

Back at the fire, Daniel sits in silence. I know he must've heard Jeff yelling, maybe not the words, but the noise.

I stand at the edge of the circle of chairs, looking out at the lake. "Daniel, is there something you're not telling me? Jeff said to ask about your hand."

Before he can answer, Shane and Jeff come out of the lodge.

Jeff stands back as Shane clears his throat.

"It's about the guy. The one who hurt Leah."

"Raped her," I say.

"I drove her home that night. She wouldn't tell me anything, not what happened, not who did it. I stayed in the car when she went into Rita's." Shane sounds confused, like it just happened.

"She told you later?"

"I told him." Jeff's voice is low. "I was standing in the hall when she told Mom. I heard it all. What happened, who, everything."

"What?" The ground under me tilts.

He's quiet, thinking of something. "I could see Shane parked at the Bug Man's place, so I went out and talked to him. Shane was the only one I told."

Daniel says the exact words I'm thinking. "You knew who? You knew it all?"

I'm also thinking: *You. You lying bastard. You son of a bitch. You were supposed to be my friend.*

Daniel turns to Shane. "I thought Leah told you."

Shane shakes his head. "Daniel, Leah never said anything to me, ever. If Jeff hadn't told me about Kenny, I never would have known. She and I just tried to carry on like nothing ever happened. She was just holding the line until she got everything in order to end it all. I just didn't know it then."

"Jeff?" I want to hit him.

Jeff raises his shoulders. "Your mom, she wasn't home, Claire. It was late. My mom let her stay."

"In your room?" Right next to mine.

"Yes."

I wonder if I ever really knew anything. "What else? Daniel?" My brother still won't look at me. "What does this have to do with your hand?"

Jeff watches me, his eyes reflecting the firelight. Shane reaches for me but I move away. "There's more. Tell me."

Daniel puts his head in his hands.

A log snaps in the fire, and an explosion of embers flies up. They float down, like stars falling.

I can't put Jeff's words, the accusations he hurled with such anger, out of my mind.

"Please." I kneel next to Daniel and wrap my hand around his wrist. Shane takes a step back and jams his hands in his pockets.

Daniel laces his fingers through mine. "Shane, sit down. We need to tell her the rest."

Shane nods but doesn't sit. He keeps his voice quiet, but it's flat, emotionless. He tells me how he and Daniel planned to pay Kenny Sparvier back. How they finally caught up to Kenny a few days before Leah went missing. He tells me about the beating they laid on him, about almost killing him, leaving him with some kind of brain injury.

He says that Kenny got what was coming to him.

I feel sick. Daniel won't look at me, and Shane won't take his eyes off me.

I stand. "That's the fight that wrecked your hand?"

"Yeah."

"And no one knew?"

Shane shrugs. "People knew."

Jeff breaks in. "They just didn't care."

"I never heard anything."

"It was summer," Daniel says. "The rumour mill shut down once school let out. Once Leah went missing, it was all kind of forgotten."

"The cops didn't care?" I look over at Shane.

"Kenny had a violent history, and the cops didn't really bother to look deeper." Shane shakes his head. "It's not something I'm proud of, Claire."

"Did Leah know what you did?"

Shane sighs. "With Daniel being hurt, it was pretty obvious. It didn't take long for her to figure out that I was involved, too. She was furious."

Daniel's face is sad. "I remember thinking that she should have been happy that Shane and I were finally on the same page about something."

Jeff starts to say something but I wave him off. Just looking at him hurts.

I pull my fingers through my hair. "Was it worth it?"

They answer together. I hear Daniel's soft "I don't know" at the same time as Shane speaks, his eyes hard. "Absolutely."

"And if it had cost you the chance to be a cop, would it be worth it?" I've never seen Shane so cold.

"I'd do it again."

I take a deep breath and turn to Daniel. "How about you?"

"Yeah."

I fight back tears. "Even though you lost your music?"

"Without her, I lost it anyway, Claire."

Finally I look at Jeff. He's stood silent and miserable through it all. "What was your part in this?"

Shane cuts in. "He just told me who it was, Claire. Nothing more." Shane grasps the back of a chair. "I have no regrets. I could have killed him, and I'd still have no regrets. In fact, I wish I had. I can tell you exactly how it felt to kick the hell out of that bastard." Shane's hands clench. "It felt good."

I'm shocked at Shane's absolute lack of remorse.

"Don't judge them, Claire. You weren't there." Jeff sounds a lot more sober than he did ten minutes ago.

I can't believe he's taking their part in this. "I'm not judging, Jeff. I'm trying to understand how two people I thought I knew could do something like that."

"Fuck this." Shane kicks the lawn chair in front of him and it clatters on the ground. "If any of you had been there when she showed up at my house that night, if you'd been there when I opened the door and saw what he did to her, we wouldn't even be talking about this. He beat her, Claire. He held her down and forced her to have sex with him."

"Stop." I can't take any more yelling. I can't hear it this way.

"No, I won't stop. She always knew exactly who she was, what she wanted. And yeah, what she didn't want. Me, for one. Then, all of a sudden she couldn't even decide if she wanted fucking ketchup on her fries."

I get to my feet, but he walks away, back toward the lodge. I'm still standing there when he comes back out. He carries his uniform in one hand, his gun belt in the other.

"Shane, I'll call you tomorrow," I say as he passes by.

"Yeah. Well, I'll be there, won't I, Claire? Like always."

I trail him to his car, watch him put his things on the back seat. He gets in, but I hold the door so he can't close it.

"I don't know what to say, Shane."

He stares at the steering wheel. "Just say you understand."

"I understand part of it."

"I'm sorry you don't like the rest of it, but I'm still the same person. I haven't changed."

"No, but you never told me everything, either."

"Well, now you know." He looks up at me. He looks old.

"I feel like I don't know you."

He shakes his head. "You know me better than anyone, better even than Leah did. I gave you everything I had."

I don't know how to tell him that I don't see that at all, that even with all he did for me, it was one-sided. He rarely let me in. I felt like our time at the caves had finally put us on even ground, as if he finally trusted me to hold that broken part of him.

"Not everything. You never told me about this."

"It doesn't have anything to do with us, our friendship."

I feel my chest tighten with that old familiar anxiety, and I breathe faster. "We can't leave it like this."

"Let go of the door, Claire." He gives me a look of such disgust and anger, I step back, but I don't let go of the door.

"Shane, just listen." I can hear the desperation in my voice. "What you told me that night at the caves. Leah used to draw on my back, too, when we were small." My words come out in a rush. They need to be said before he leaves. "We shared a room and she'd crawl into my bed and rub my back. But it wasn't patterns she drew. It was words. I had to guess them. My name. Her name. And she always wrote I love you. Every single time."

"That was really low, Claire."

He reaches out and wrenches the door from my hand, almost catching my fingers as he slams it shut. The tires of his car spin gravel up at me as he drives away. The tail lights flash red as he turns out of the drive, and he's gone. I stare at the empty road for a moment before turning back to the fire. Jeff stands and watches me, hands in his pockets. Daniel turns away and heads down to the shore to fill a pail with lake water.

"I'm so sorry, Claire."

"Me, too."

"I never wanted this."

I almost believe him. "I know what you wanted, Jeff." I stumble back from the warmth of the fire.

Jeff moves to follow me. "I'll come."

"No. You stay here."

 Jeff sits and watches as Daniel pours water on the fire. Steam rises with a hiss.

"I lost my temper. I said too much." He's created such a mess. Always. He always ruins everything.

Daniel drops the empty pail on the ground.

"Why didn't you tell me who did it to her, Jeff? Why did I have to hear it from Shane?"

"I don't know." Jeff remembers he was confused at the time. He didn't really know Leah, not like he knew Claire. Shane was there that night. He was Leah's boyfriend. Jeff hadn't known what else to do. He didn't know it would turn out the way it did. "I didn't want to hurt Claire."

"So much for that plan."

Jeff ignores the tone in Daniel's voice and comes right to the point. "Daniel, I screwed up tonight, I know. I'll try and make it up to her. To everyone. I wish you would all stop making me feel like I am the worst thing that ever happened to her."

He walks down to the shore, where he kicks off his shoes and pulls his hoodie over his head. He wades into the clear, cold water, until he's wet to the waist, then he dives forward, head under, arms pumping, pulling himself out deeper. He just makes out the ripples of the white sand on the bottom, a black stone here and there, a few large rocks. The freezing water is a shock to his chest, and he can't even breathe out. He stays under as long as he can, and only when his hands hit bottom does he stand. He breathes hard, and his scalp prickles from the icy water.

He is far past the end of the dock, on one of the many shifting sandbars between the beach and the far point. He continues walking out, and goes under again when the bottom drops out from beneath him. It's warmer this time, his body's getting used to it, but he can still feel the blood thudding through his veins as it tries to warm him. He turns and swims back toward the dock, his strokes lazier, his heavy jeans slowing him down. He can't hear a thing except his heart pounding in his ears. He swims for the dock, pulls himself up, breathes deep to slow his chattering teeth. The sun touches the top of the trees at the point. It feels a little like home. He's missed the lake.

The dock shakes as someone walks out to him. Jeff knows it's Daniel even before he speaks.

"You're such an idiot. Here."

Jeff takes the towel Daniel hands him, wipes his face and rubs his hair.

"Move over."

Jeff does, and Daniel sits next to him, not caring that his own jeans get wet. He has two open beer in his hand. He hands one to Jeff.

Jeff sets it beside him on the dock. "I just did my best to sober up."

"Nice tattoo."

"Thanks."

Daniel drinks. "Bet you never thought you'd have to explain that."

"I never thought I'd see her again. Then she showed up in Vancouver."

"Yeah. You're not going to tell me what happened to her, are you?"

"Claire?"

"Leah."

"What do you want, Daniel? Details?" Even now, Jeff can't find the right words. Does he tell him how Leah danced with the guy? How he hit her and choked her? How she spent twenty minutes in a filthy gas station bathroom trying to fix the damage, fix herself up so she could get back to Shane's? How upset she was that she didn't fight back?

Daniel is quiet. "I guess I just need to know that what Shane and I did was justified."

Jeff shivers. He knows part of what happened to Kenny Sparvier.

He knows the outcome. News of the beating did get around, but not like the news of Leah when she went missing. Jeff pulls the towel more tightly around himself. He wishes he'd kept his mouth shut all those years ago, and not told Shane.

"It was bad, Jeff."

"I know. I remember hearing about it."

Daniel drains his beer. Jeff hands his own bottle back to him, and Daniel raises it in a toast to the remnants of pink and red in the sky, then downs most of that one, too.

"We caught up with Kenny and that stupid cousin of his coming out of the Legion." Daniel swallows. "Clayton ran away, the coward, when we jumped Kenny. Kenny knew exactly why we were there, like he'd been waiting for it, like it was some kind of code. He rapes Leah, Leah's boyfriend beats him up, all square."

"Except it didn't work out that way." Jeff doesn't look at Daniel when he says it.

"No." Daniel traces his finger along the palm of his wrecked hand. "Once we started, we couldn't stop. I kept hitting him, even after I broke my hand. I felt it snap and then I felt nothing. I just kept pounding, and Shane was kicking him. God, he was stomping him. We were way out of control." Daniel looks down at the water like he can see it all playing out in front of him. "There was blood everywhere. And teeth." Daniel shakes it off. "I waited to get my hand looked at so the cops wouldn't figure it out, but they did anyway. When they questioned me, they didn't try too hard. I told them we got in a fight over a girl. Kenny couldn't exactly tell them otherwise."

"And Shane?"

"I left him out of it. Even though his dad was a cop, it would have ruined his chances to get into the RCMP. They never knew about him."

"Good thing you beat up an Indian." Jeff can't keep the sarcasm out of his voice. "If he'd been white, they would have nailed you to the wall."

"Jeff, he raped Leah. Being Indian didn't even play into it."

Jeff knows better. "It always plays into it."

Daniel closes his eyes. "I see him sometimes at the mall in town.

Him and his stupid cousin."

Jeff is quiet a long time. Every so often, a chill runs through his body. The sun is down now, and he's cold.

He stands. "You're paying in your own way, aren't you, Daniel?"

Daniel looks at his hand, makes a fist, opens it. "I'm not sure it's a fair trade for his life, though."

"I don't know what to tell you. You lost your sister. Both of them, in a way. You can't play music. He lost the ability to hurt anyone else. I'm not sure what's a fair trade." He stands. "I've got to go change. Build up the fire, I'll grab you another beer."

Daniel calls to him as he walks away. "What would you have done if it had been Claire, Jeff? What would be right then?"

SIX

I wait on the shore with Finn as Daniel gets the boat and the fishing gear ready. The lake is wavy, but not enough to affect our fishing trip. I have a lunch that Rita packed in the cooler beside me, and a book to read while Finn and Daniel fish. It's a quiet day at the lodge, and when Colin suggested we take off for a few hours, Daniel jumped at the chance.

I haven't seen much of Jeff over the past week. He's avoiding me, and as fine with that as I am, I do miss him.

He's been on a mission to prune the dead branches from all the trees on the property. It's kept him busy for days. I can't help but track the progress of the lodge's yellow ladder, as well as the mound of sheared limbs piled by the back road, but I haven't gone out of my way to talk to him about what happened the night of the fish fry. I'm not angry any more. The hurt is taking a little longer to go away.

Rita told me he's been to at least one AA meeting in town.

My calls to Shane have all gone unreturned.

"Auntie, you don't fish?"

"Nope. I'll just read my book and enjoy the sunshine."

"I'll catch you a fish, okay?" Finn holds onto a lure, silver on one side, white and red on the other.

"Thanks, buddy."

Daniel tosses an armful of life jackets into the boat and gets in. I pass him the cooler and he sets it under one of the seats. He reaches his hand out to Finn, but Finn jumps in with ease. Daniel steadies the boat and then helps me in. He looks behind me. I look over my shoulder to see Jeff coming down the dock carrying Finn's Canadiens ball cap.

"My mom sent me down with this."

I reach for the hat and pass it to Finn. "Thanks."

The sun has darkened his skin, and his eyes glow like blue fire as he stares back at me.

Daniel sighs. "Are you getting in, or are you going to just stand there?" He busies himself with the motor. In a minute he's going to pull the cord, and that will end the conversation.

"Please come, Jeff."

I smile, knowing that Finn just tipped the scales.

"Go grab a fishing rod, Jeff. We'll wait." Daniel doesn't even try to hide the exasperation in his voice. Jeff nods and jogs back to the shed.

Once everyone is in and settled, Daniel sets off across the bay. He heads at top speed straight for the midpoint between the north, west and east shores. I haven't been this far out in the middle of the lake for years, and as the boat bounces across the waves, I'm surprised at the sheer amount of water that surrounds me. Finn sits next to me on the middle seat, his grin getting bigger each time the boat hits the trough of a wave, but the movement makes me a little nauseous. I close my eyes in hopes that will help the sick feeling go away.

Finally, Daniel slows the boat and we stop. He doesn't bother to drop the anchor, just lets the boat drift. Daniel helps Finn attach the lure to his line, then Finn goes to stand with Jeff in the bow of the boat while Daniel readies his own hook. Jeff helps Finn cast into the water.

I lean against the gunwale with my book open, watching my brother fumble to attach his hook.

Finn is quiet, but he and Jeff seem to have devised a system. Jeff talks to him in a low voice, coaches him on how to reel his line in, how to cast without losing his hook in his, or someone else's, scalp. Finn listens to everything, a serious look on his face.

I've never been fishing with Jeff, but I know that everything he's showing Finn, he learned from his father. I wonder if his dad was this gentle with Jeff when he taught him to fish.

Daniel fishes off the back of the boat. He uses his left hand, though not naturally.

He catches me looking. "I can cast okay with my right hand, and I can reel it in if I don't have a bite, but if there's a big fish on the line, my right hand is too weak and I have to flip it. The hardest part is attaching the leader, the thing that holds the hook on. It's a bitch to tie." Daniel doesn't look at me while he's talking. Things have been strained between us, too, in the weeks since the fish fry, but he's my brother, and we live together. We've had to work it out.

Book forgotten, I turn my attention back to the bow. Jeff stands, one knee on the front seat, and Finn looks like a pro, his sturdy little legs keeping him balanced as the boat rocks with the waves.

After a while, Daniel and Jeff switch places. Finn is more relaxed with Daniel, jokes around a bit, acts a little silly. I love how easy they are becoming with each other.

Jeff gets his line ready and with an easy flick, casts it into the water not far from the boat. I watch the flashing lure spin and sink out of sight. Jeff fishes with his back to me. I reach out and tug at the hem of his shirt.

He turns his head and looks down at me. "What?"

"Sit down."

He reels in his line, lays the rod along the seats and sits next to me, facing the stern.

I slide closer to him. "I can't stand this. I don't want to fight."

He gives me a quick hug and kisses my cheek. "Same."

"Hey, loverboy. Can you take a time out from sucking my sister's face off and start the engine? We've drifted pretty far. Just move us back to where we started."

Finn laughs. He laughs at everything Daniel says. Jeff gets up and moves the boat. Daniel and Finn hold their lines out of the water until Jeff cuts the engine, then they continue fishing. Jeff moves back beside me and we sit staring out at waves that turn from grey to green to blue as the breeze blows clouds across the sun. We're content just to sit and not talk.

Behind us, Daniel and Finn have a quiet conversation about what hockey players do in the summer.

Then, "I'm hungry, Daddy."

Daddy. I turn just in time to catch Daniel's expression. Unguarded and shocked, he meets my eyes. I have to swallow hard as Daniel places his hand on top of Finn's head, a wide grin on his face. "Take us to shore, Captain Jeff. The boy is hungry."

Rita has packed enough food for all of us. I shake my head. She set the whole thing up – offering to pack lunch, sending Jeff down with Finn's hat. Rita seems mild, but she's a force to be reckoned with when she wants something. And it's obvious she's looking for a way to make Jeff happy.

Jeff sits a little apart from us while we eat lunch. Finn leans against me, his arm on my leg, his hand on my knee.

When we're done, Daniel stands. "Finn and I are going to try again for some fish. We'll come back for you two in a bit." Daniel and Finn make their way back to the boat.

Jeff reaches out and traces the faded yellow of the hickey on my shoulder.

"It's a plot, you know," I say.

"Yeah, I caught on when my mom told me to bring Finn's hat down to you guys. He hasn't even worn it." He releases a long breath. "We need to talk, Claire."

"No, we really don't. Let's just put it behind us."

"I'm sorry for the way I behaved. I was jealous, and I don't always think things through."

"Look, Shane is really important to me. He's picked me up more times than I can count. But none of that has anything to do with the way I feel about you." I hope this is getting through. "But Jeff, I will not put up with your drinking. You can't treat me that way."

"I'm doing the best I can, Claire. I swear."

We watch the waves roll in.

"It's funny. When I would get angry that you never wrote, or that you never showed up when you were supposed to, Shane always stuck up for you. He's been so good to me. It's hard to believe he and Daniel could do what they did."

"I'm sorry it all had to come out like that."

"Me too."

Jeff reaches out and brushes off sand that clings to my thigh. He clears his throat. "Did you ever sleep with him?"

I'm disappointed in the question. "No. But it wasn't for a lack of trying. I would have in a second if he'd wanted me." I look at Daniel and Finn, far out in the boat. "This stuff never used to bother you,

Jeff. You've always been so together. Even in Vancouver."

"No. I was just really good at hiding how together I wasn't." He keeps his eyes downcast. "Especially since I came home."

Home.

I lean into him a little. "Jeff, do you want me to come with you to your dad's when we get back?"

"It's been a good day, Claire. Let's not ruin it. Maybe tomorrow."

I squeeze his hand until he looks at me.

"I want to, Jeff." I say. "No matter what happens."

Daniel drops Jeff and me off at the lodge before he and Finn take the boat back to his place to pick up steaks for dinner.

Jeff heads to the fish-cleaning shack with a cooler full of trout that Finn and Daniel caught, while I take the empty lunch cooler into the kitchen. I'm just unloading the garbage when the sound of a car engine splits the quiet. A horn blares, and the thump-thump of music gets louder. I go look out the back door just as a small, rusted purple car spins around the curve and comes to a stop in a cloud of dust out front of the lodge. Across the road I can see Jeff, standing behind the screen door of the fish-cleaning shack.

A man with long unkempt hair sits in the driver's seat as a woman gets out of the passenger door.

She weaves a bit as she approaches. "I'm here for Finn."

Sherry.

"He's not here, he's with Daniel."

"Where? I want my son." She's wasted on something, and as she gets closer the smell of rye hits me.

"It's Daniel's weekend, Sherry. He'll bring him home tomorrow." I keep my voice calm. Sherry is not allowed to have Finn without her mother around.

"I'm meeting some cousins at the beach. I want them to see my son."

Jeff crosses the drive, filleting knife in hand. The driver's door swings open, but the guy stays behind the wheel.

"Hey, Sherry." Jeff keeps his eyes trained on the guy in the car.

Sherry leans so far over the hood she almost falls. "Hey, I remember you. I haven't seen you in forever. Want to come party with us?"

"No, thanks. We've got work to do today. Look, Finn is out fishing with Daniel. He won't be home for hours." How easily the lie slips from his lips. "Why don't you go meet your cousins, and we'll see if he'll bring Finn by when he gets in. You heading to the beach at Pioneer Bay?"

"Yeah, we're camping there. Finn's inside, isn't he?"

"He's on the lake, Sherry. With Daniel. He'll be in touch okay?"

"No he won't. Daniel hates me."

I don't say anything and neither does Jeff. We watch as Sherry does the careful-drunk walk back to the car. Her friend takes off before she has the door fully closed.

We stand and watch as they drive off. We don't speak until the dust from the departing vehicle starts to settle.

"She is not well at all," says Jeff.

"Daniel's going to be angry."

"Maybe mention it to my mom, too, Claire." Jeff tosses the knife in the air, watches it spin and catches it by the handle.

"Nice," I say. "You're going to cut your fingers off."

He grins. "Doubt it." He starts to walk away, then turns back. "I'd like it if you'd come with me tomorrow."

I wouldn't miss it.

When Jeff arrives at Daniel's to pick Claire up the next morning, she's ready. He's amused by her look of surprise when she sees his haircut.

He rubs his hand across the top of his head. "What? Is it so bad? I went to a meeting in town, then got it done."

"You just look different. Well, the same, actually. You look the same as you used to." She studies him. "I'm more interested in why you did it."

"I don't know. He always used to start in on my hair. I just don't think I can take it today. Anyway, it's time for a change."

Claire goes to grab her bag, then returns to find him standing in front of the piano, running his fingers over the keys.

"I remember how he used to play for us."

"He's teaching Finn the piano, now. I think he's too little, but Daniel thinks he's got natural talent." Claire laughs. "I guess all parents think their kids are amazing."

"Really?" Jeff turns and looks down at her. "Mine don't."

"Your mom does."

"That's what you think."

"You're nervous, aren't you?"

"It's not nerves, Claire."

"You're not a child any more, Jeff. He can't hurt you."

This makes him laugh. "You're right, he can't hurt me."

On the drive to town, Jeff tries to think of something to say to Claire, but anything he comes up with is too charged. They have achieved a delicate balance, and he wants to keep it that way, at least until he's done at his dad's.

In front of a small apartment building, Jeff turns off the truck and sits for a second.

"I'm not sure how he'll be. My mom says he's been dry for a few months, but who knows?"

"Your mom still talks to him?"

"Of course. They're still married, you know. She shops for him, brings him food. They've been through a lot together. She just doesn't love him, I guess."

"Or maybe you weren't the only one who got tired of being hurt."

Jeff never thought of it like that before.

Claire leads the way to the door, but Jeff presses the buzzer and announces their arrival to the gravelly voice that answers.

Jake's apartment is on the main floor, so there is not much time to take in the hallway's dirty carpet and water-stained wallpaper.

Jake opens the door as they approach.

Jeff puts his hand out and says hello. His dad grabs on to his fingers and pulls him into his arms. From the smell of him, Jake's been drinking. Jeff feels his optimism slide away.

"Hey, Dad. You remember Claire?"

His father peers at her. "The dead girl's sister."

It only takes a moment for Claire to compose herself, but Jeff is angry. He pushes past his father. "Her name was Leah, Dad. Jesus, you can be such an asshole."

"Well, he's right. She is dead." Claire's voice is light, but Jeff can hear the quaver in it. He reaches back and grabs her by the hand and leads her to the worn orange-and-brown couch.

Jake sits on the patched vinyl recliner across from them. He tells Jeff there's beer in the fridge, but Jeff just glares at him.

Jake leans forward. "Your hair looks good."

Jeff is pissed off at how good this makes him feel, like he did something right for once. He wishes now he hadn't done it. "I don't know, Dad. Looks like you could use a haircut yourself."

His father's hair is long and grey and greasy, and he hasn't shaved. The stubble on his cheeks is white. His teeth have yellowed. But his blue eyes are still the same.

Claire clears her throat. "Do you need me to do anything? I thought if you wanted some time with Jeff, I could run over to the store, or start a load of laundry or something."

"I'm not an invalid, girl."

"No." Jeff doesn't want her doing anything for his dad. He frowns at her.

Jake turns back to Jeff. "Are you staying here for good now, boy? Are you home?"

Jeff catches Claire looking at him. She's waiting for the answer, too. He feels the familiar tightening in his chest.

"I'll be moving on soon. Just need to decide where I'm headed."

"You could stay. We could go fishing next week, hunting in the fall. Like old times."

Jeff is embarrassed for his father, for his neediness. "Like old times. Sounds like fun."

His father seems to shrink back into his chair at Jeff's sarcasm. Jeff's not falling for it though. Jake was always good at playing the victim. Jeff can feel the look Claire is sending his way. He meets her eyes and raises his chin. She has no idea what the old times were like.

She breaks in. "Jeff has taken my brother's son fishing a few times. He's a good teacher."

Jake waves her words away, waves her away. "You have a job yet, Jeff, or are you still working for that asshole that stole your mother from me?" On the offensive again.

Jeff has to bite back his angry reply. Obviously his parents have spoken since he came. "He makes her happy, Dad. He treats her well." He keeps his voice neutral. "She practically runs the lodge." A small part of him thinks along the same lines as his dad, but he won't give him the satisfaction of knowing it.

"When I first met her, she wasn't the kind of woman who would settle for someone just treating her well. She had spunk, that one."

"You did a good job knocking that out of her, didn't you?" Bitterness rises in Jeff's throat.

His father goes on like he hasn't heard him. He turns to Claire. "I met her when I went up to Churchill to build new houses for her people, the Dene. It was a government program, took a whole summer and more. Rita used to come watch me build, bring me a Coke and then sit and watch me work. It took time, getting to know her. Yeah, she was a little spitfire." Jake's lips are pressed thin. "I came back two summers later to do some other construction work, and there was Jeff, toddling around one of those new houses. He'd just learned to walk."

Jeff narrows his eyes. "And Mom was what, fifteen?"

"Seventeen, by the time I got back up there. There was no doubt you were mine. You were the only blue-eyed Indian up there."

Jeff feels nothing but disgust for this sorry man, so skinny and wasted. "You should have left her up there."

Jeff stands. He can't spend another second here. He looks over at Claire, motions at the door with his head.

"Thanks for the memories, Dad. I'll see you next time I'm in town."

Jake walks with them to the door. "Are you still doing that art thing?"

Jeff hesitates. "Painting? No, not as much."

Jake points to a small oil above his kitchen table. Jeff flushes in anger.

"How did you get that?"

"Your mom brought it to me. She thought I should have it."

"I gave it to her. Not you."

Claire walks over and studies it. It's a painting of a woman and a small dark-haired boy, shown from behind. They sit on a chunk of broken cement looking out at a wide golden field. In the field, there is a small, green wooden building. Off to the left is a baseball diamond, the shale as red as blood. Two people are playing catch, but they are small, too small to recognize.

"You did this?" she asks. "It's really good."

Jeff feels exposed, like it's him hanging from the nail on the wall. "Yeah, it's not done though."

Claire stares at the picture. "It looks finished to me."

"It's not."

Jake grabs Jeff in another hug, and Jeff, startled, hugs him back. "It's good to have a hobby, but you need to get a job, boy."

A hobby. His father always knows just what to say. Jeff pulls away. "We've got to go, Dad." He hears Claire say goodbye behind him, but he doesn't wait.

He gets in the truck and starts the engine. He watches Claire walk toward him. He can't stop himself from checking to see if his father has followed. He hasn't. He's probably inside downing a can of beer.

Jeff turns on the radio, cranks it up. The Cure blasts from the speakers. Claire gets in and he takes her hand. He hopes she can't feel it shaking.

"They never played this music back when it was popular. I don't get how this station can always be years behind." Claire presses his hand between both of hers.

Jeff looks over at her as he pulls away from the curb. "I didn't think it would be that bad."

He can tell she wants to ask something. He watches the road and waits.

"Jeff, why did you get so angry about the painting?"

That's the last question he expected.

"Every so often I ship my work up here – I have nowhere else to store it. When I visited, I saw my mom had taken that one. It bothered me, but I could see why she wanted it. So I let her have it. I never thought she'd give it to him."

"But if it doesn't mean anything to you, who cares?"

"I didn't say it didn't mean anything. I just said it wasn't done."

She looks away, out the window. "I'm just trying to understand, Jeff."

The first turnout he sees, he pulls over and puts the truck in park. He leans in and kisses her. "Understand this, Claire. You're the only thing I'm sure of right now. I'm just hanging on, trying to trust that the rest will come."

SEVEN

I'm just walking out the door at Daniel's when Rita calls.
"Claire, you need to come. Finn's gone."

Daniel is out on the lake. She's called the police, but she needs me to come.

The drive to the lodge passes in a blur. An RCMP cruiser passes me on the way, siren blaring.

At the lodge, two police cars sit at odd angles; the drivers' doors are open and the lights are still flashing. The few guests not out fishing have come out of their cabins onto their decks. Shane looks up from where he stands near the front steps talking to Rita and Colin.

My voice feels tight in my throat. "Where is he? What's going on?"

Shane closes his notebook. "Finn was playing in front of the lodge. Rita went in to get him a snack and when she came out he was gone. The dog is gone, too, so we're pretty sure he didn't go into the lake."

"God, Shane."

Jeff comes out the front door. "I checked every room upstairs. Closets. The basement. He's not inside, Shane."

Shane nods. "He may have wandered off, but Rita said that would be out of character. She told me about Sherry's visit. It's likely that she has him. We have a lot of people looking for them." He turns to Jeff. "I need you to get a boat and find Daniel. Rita says he's out fishing at Jackfish Bay." Jeff starts for the dock.

"No," says Claire. "Jeff knows this area. He needs to help look."

"I'll do whatever you want me to," Jeff says to Shane.

Colin steps up. "I'll go and get Daniel. I'll take the neighbour's ski boat. It'll be faster." Colin takes off for next door at a run.

"Sherry took him." I look at Jeff.

Jeff nods. "She talked about meeting people who were camped at the beach at Pioneer Bay. I can head that way if you want."

Shane relays this information over his walkie-talkie then nods at Jeff. "Okay, go check up the gravel road that leads to the public beach." Jeff takes off at a run.

Turning back to me, Shane says they already have a team looking for Finn at the campground.

Shane doles out duties in a calm, rapid-fire voice. "Corporal Bennett, you head to Pioneer Bay along the highway. Claire, you come with me. We'll check the cabins. Rita, you call the grandmother, see if she's seen or heard from them. Then everyone come back here or find a phone and report to the dispatcher. She'll relay any updates to me. If we don't find him, we'll get more guys out from town and widen the search."

Shane's in complete control, but I'm still filled with a sense of dread. Searching for a little boy in an area like this is futile. He could be anywhere.

The sound of the powerful motorboat from next door fills the air. Colin's on his way. I'm glad I'm not the one who has to bring Daniel back in, no matter how fast the boat is.

It takes no time at all for us to check the ten cabins. No one has seen Finn since earlier that morning. Rita has no luck with Finn's grandmother.

So we wait.

Shane paces the circular driveway, walkie-talkie in hand. Rita and I stand together near Shane's car.

"I feel awful, Claire. I only left him for a minute. I never even thought."

There's nothing I can say.

Another police car turns into the drive. Shane strides over as it comes to a stop.

It's Sherry. No Finn.

A young female constable gets out. "I found her at the picnic area, but the little boy wasn't with her." She opens the back door, and Sherry gets out.

"Didn't he come back here?" Sherry's words are slurred. She can't seem to focus. She rocks back and forth.

"Sherry, where did you take him?" I scream at her, but Shane pulls me back.

"Let me do my job, Claire."

"Where is he?" Shane stands close to Sherry, towers over her.

"He wanted to come to the beach." Sherry's voice is defensive.

Shane talks to her in a low voice, but to no avail. Finn said he was walking back, Sherry tells him. She thought he'd be fine.

I want to scratch her eyes out. "He's not even five, you stupid bitch."

"Claire." Shane sends me the exasperated look I know so well. It's almost my undoing. How on earth is this happening again? I got away from here, and now I'm back, and Finn is missing.

The sound of a boat approaching drowns out whatever Shane says to Sherry, but it's clear she's not talking.

The engine cuts out.

Shane turns back to Sherry. "That's going to be Daniel. You better give me an answer quick. He is going to be very upset."

"I told you, I don't know where he is."

I look down at the dock. Daniel is out of the boat and running. He doesn't stop, heads straight for his ex.

He takes her by the shoulders and shakes her. "Where is he?" Sherry won't look at him. "If anything happens to my son, I will kill you."

Rita steps in and grabs Daniel's arm. "Come on, Danny. This won't help."

Daniel shakes her off and turns to Shane. I can see hope in my brother's face, pinning it all on this man he used to hate. "Tell me where he is, Shane."

"We have a lot of people looking, Daniel. We think Finn's got the dog, too." Shane looks at his watch. "He hasn't been gone long. He can't be far."

Watching Daniel I'm reminded of the days after Leah went missing. He stands alone. Then, I wasn't used to seeing him without his twin. Now, I realize how much a part of my brother Finn has become. All I can do is watch. There is no gesture or word that can help now.

Even Shane seems to have run out of answers. We all stand, staring at the gravel drive, like mourners at a funeral.

With a bark, Connie comes running through the bushes at the edge of the lodge's property. Daniel drops to his knees and buries his face in her black coat. With everyone's attention on the dog, I'm the first to see Jeff, carrying Finn, push his way through the branches.

I'm close to falling to my knees, too.

Daniel is up in a heartbeat, pulling Finn from Jeff's arms.

"I found him huddled on the deck of a summer cabin past the store. He got turned around and ended up heading in the wrong direction. He said he knew the lake was on the wrong side of him so he sat and waited. Connie stayed with him." Jeff rubs the dog's velvety snout. "You're a good girl, aren't you?"

Shane gets on the walkie-talkie and lets his people know that Finn has been found.

Daniel doesn't say anything, just rocks Finn in his arms. Sherry, seeing that Shane is occupied, approaches Daniel.

"Get away from him, Sherry." Daniel turns his back on her.

"He's mine, Daniel."

I'm about to step in, though I'm not sure I could pull Sherry away in the state she's in, when Jeff lays his hand on Sherry's arm. His voice is soft. "Finn and I have a date with the canoe. Maybe you all could work this out once we're gone?"

Gratitude floods through me. Even in all this, he thinks of Finn first.

Jeff eases Finn from Daniel's arms. He sets him on his feet and rubs his hair. "Let's grab a snack before we go, okay?" He nods at Rita, like they've done this a million times – defusing a violent situation, working as a team.

The three of them go inside, Colin following close behind.

Daniel waits until the door closes behind them then turns on Sherry. "You just blew it. You will never get him back!"

"You can't take him away from me." Sherry swears at Daniel. She tries to shove him, but he doesn't budge. She flails at him with her fists, and he grabs them and holds them tight.

I move closer to them. "This has to stop. Finn can't see this."

Daniel's voice is tight and furious. "He could have died, Sherry. You need to get some help. You can't look after him."

"I knew you'd say that. It's not my fault he ran off."

"It's my day, Sherry. You can't take him. It's kidnapping." He looks over at Shane.

Shane and the other cop move in. Shane gently takes her arm. "Let's go, Sherry. I'll take you to your mom's and you can sleep it off."

"Can't you charge her with something?" Daniel asks Shane.

I watch it happen, the silent exchange of pleading and promise between Daniel and Shane. Shane would do it for Daniel, too. The door to the lodge bangs and Jeff comes out alone and leans against the building. His arms are crossed but his expression is unreadable.

"There are a few different ways we can go, Daniel." I don't like the coldness in Shane's voice.

Sherry tries to flee, but Shane tightens his grip. "Just stop, Sherry, it will go a lot easier."

"You're just a fucking Indian hater. Everyone knows it. Everyone knows about you. You don't want me to have my son cause I'm an Indian." Sherry yells "Indian hater" and "white pig" over and over while she tries to twist away from him. Shane's passive expression never changes.

Then, with her free arm, Sherry whacks Shane across the side of the head, and he stumbles. She falls forward in her sudden freedom, and she grabs for him. In her panic, her hand slides down and grasps at Shane's gun belt.

I'm shocked at how fast Shane moves. He throws Sherry to the ground and pins her with a knee to the back and forces her wrists into handcuffs. Sherry screams and fights and curses, but Shane ignores it all.

I look back at Jeff.

He hasn't moved from his casual stance against the wall. When he sees me looking, he stares back. He's not surprised at all.

Shane arrests Sherry for public drunkenness and for assault on a police officer. "All you had to do was get in the car. Now you're in a lot of trouble, Sherry."

He lifts her to her feet. Her chin and lip are bleeding where she hit the gravel, and the side of her cheek is red and peppered with small stones and dirt. The female cop takes her and shoves her into the back of the car. Shane tells her to take Sherry to town, he'll be along soon and they'll get all the paperwork done.

Everyone is silent until the car is out of sight. I approach Shane. He's breathing hard and his eyes are far away.

"Are you okay?"

It takes him a second to focus on me.

"I let my guard down. It was stupid."

"I don't think she meant to go for your gun, Shane."

"Never even thought about it. It's just a reflex." Shane looks at Daniel. "You have shitty taste in girls, my friend."

Daniel's laugh is shaky. "She wasn't always like that."

"Sure." Shane looks up as Finn comes out of the lodge.

Shane crouches in front of him. "You okay?"

"Yes." Finn reaches out and touches the gold on Shane's epaulette. "My mom wanted me to go with her, but I didn't want to. I tried to come back but I got lost."

Jeff breaks in. "If it weren't for Connie, I'm not sure I would have seen him."

"You're a good boy, Finn. If someone asks you to go with them again, you yell really loud, okay? Make lots of noise." Shane straightens up.

Finn nods and goes to Daniel. It hurts to see him put his hands up so Daniel will lift him. He really was scared. Daniel hugs Finn's small body to him.

"I'm proud of you, Finn. You're going to stay with me for a while, okay?" Daniel's voice is muffled against Finn's hair. He lets him down.

Finn nods. He doesn't even ask about Sherry, just turns and waves at Jeff. "Come on. Let's get out on the lake."

We all laugh, a little too hard.

Jeff follows Finn down to the shore.

"What happens now?" I ask, turning back to Shane.

"She'll be formally charged. Daniel, you'll want to call Finn's case-worker and make some kind of custody amendment."

"I need to get him away from here." Daniel leaves no room for argument. "Not sure the judge will let me do that, but I'm sure as hell going to try." He shakes Shane's hand. "Thanks. For everything.

I couldn't have turned him back over to her or her mom tonight." Daniel puts his hands in his pockets and swallows hard. "God, I could see it all rolling out, searching, not finding him."

"Me, too, Daniel." Shane doesn't need to say any more. We're all thinking about Leah. Daniel gives a wave and heads down to the beach.

"I'm sorry about the night at the fire," Shane says to me.

"Me too."

We stop outside his car. "I thought you should know I put in for a transfer a while back and it came through." His voice is soft.

Tears prickle behind my eyes. "Okay."

"I need a new start, away from here."

"Away from me." It's not a question.

His gaze is serious. "Yeah. Probably. Away from Daniel. Away from the people in this town."

In a way, his moving away from here won't affect me; I'm not staying here forever. Still, it hurts that he thinks he needs to get away from me. I'm disappointed but there is no anxiety, no panic. Just a profound sadness at the loss. All the crap I've put him through over the years, and this is what breaks us.

I don't even watch him drive away. It's surprising what a heart can take.

That evening's meal is subdued. Claire has been quiet since Shane left, and Jeff knows even if he asked her to share what they talked about, she won't.

Even Finn is silent. He eats all his supper, then moves onto Daniel's lap and closes his eyes.

"So, Jeff, will you be here to help close up this fall?" The optimistic tone in Colin's voice sets Jeff on edge. He knows Colin is just saying it because it's what his mom wants.

"I don't know how much longer I'll be here, Colin."

Claire doesn't show that she's heard, but Jeff knows she has. She gets up and starts clearing the table.

Daniel and Finn head home soon after the dishes are done. In all the excitement of the day, there are still chores to be done. Jeff follows Colin down to the lake to put the boats away and tidy up the beach.

When the two men are done, they each take a chair and sit on shore to watch the sun set behind a mass of dark clouds building in the west.

"Your mom is hoping you'll stay."

"So is my dad."

"I see," says Colin. "That's a problem, then."

"Yeah, it is."

"Do you remember coming here when you were a child?"

"A teenager? With Claire? Yeah." Things weren't so uncomfortable then. But then, Colin was with Claire's mom, not his own.

"No. When you were little. Four or five. Like Finn."

Jeff shakes his head. "No." And yet. Flashes of memory. His mom, in the kitchen. Long hair, not the short style she wears now. He's not sure it's a real memory.

"Sometimes I see Finn out here, and it reminds me of those days."

"Jesus, Colin. It wasn't that long ago."

Distant thunder rolls long and deep across the lake.

Colin laughs. "Yeah, it was. I used to take you swimming. Like you, and Finn."

Jeff doesn't remember any of this.

"I'd do anything for her, Jeff."

The waves are picking up, crashing stronger into the shore.

"It's nothing to do with you, Colin."

Colin doesn't say anything and Jeff's grateful. How to explain the way he feels? Resentful. He just feels resentful that his mother stayed so long with his father. She should have left long ago. She should have gone, and taken Jeff with her. Things would have been so different.

Colin stands and folds up his chair. "Don't be too hard on your mom, Jeff. Everything she's ever done is because she believed it was best for you. Even if it doesn't seem like it, she thought so."

Alone, now, Jeff stands on the dock and watches the sheet lightning behind the clouds. The wind whips the water into dark foam.

Then the rain starts and he heads in to join the others in a game of crib. As they play, Claire tells them about the time Daniel brought

Sherry to Regina to meet her and their grandparents.

Jeff could listen to Claire talk for hours. He loves the softness of her voice, the smoothness of it. He's surprised when she tells Rita a bit about their visit with Jake.

Rita lays her cards on the table. "It's about time you went to see him, but it's an odd place to take a girl on a date."

Jeff gives Claire a look. "I wouldn't exactly call it a date."

"Sorry," Claire says. "I didn't know it was a secret."

"It's not. There's just nothing to tell."

Rita stands, kisses the top of Jeff's head. Something she never did when he was a child. "There never is with you, my dear. I'm going to watch some TV then head for bed." She says good night, and it's not long before Colin follows. Jeff glares at the door, and Claire kicks him under the table.

"Stop it," she says, laughing. "You're being a baby."

"You're in a good mood."

"You're not?"

"I feel pretty good, actually. I think I'm still on a high from finding Finn." He studies her. She's different tonight. More relaxed.

"Come upstairs with me, Claire. I want to show you something."

He lets her pass by him, and starts up the stairs behind her. She stops and turns, puts her arms around him. Thunder rumbles outside. He presses his face into her neck and breathes her in, content just to hold her.

"I knew you'd find him, Jeff."

"It seemed hopeless at first. I was standing there at the beach, looking out at the water, and it came to me. He just got turned around."

Upstairs, he leads her past the room he stayed in when he first came, to the next closed door. He opens it and flips on the light. Boxes and crates are leaned up against the walls; a large leather portfolio lies on the bed.

"What's all this?" she asks.

"My paintings. My art stuff. Some photos I took. I brought everything when I came." His voice is quiet. "I want to show you why the painting my dad has isn't done." He peels back the cardboard from a large canvas-covered frame.

Jeff sets the painting out against the wall in the hallway, and pulls out another, smaller painting and sets it face in against the wall next to the larger one.

"I don't paint much these days. No time. I did these quite a few years back. Take a look."

Claire steps back and looks at the large painting. Shades of green and yellow hover around the edges, a darker bit lurks at the bottom. Above, deep blue swirls are interrupted by chunks of whitish-grey. She cocks her head.

"I'm really bad at this, Jeff. I know nothing about art. I'd guess trees, and sky?"

"Okay, but you're trying too hard. It doesn't have to be literal. It's about visual sensation. Now look at the smaller one."

He flips it around. She kneels down to see it better.

It's a perfectly rendered painting of the view of the sky above the rock they went to as kids. The opening of the trees overhead is exactly how she remembers it. An airplane is passing above. There are no people in the picture.

Thunder outside. The light above them flickers.

She looks back at the large painting. It's the same scene, fragmented, and the angle is a bit different. She can see what must be the corner of the rock.

"I see. This one is shown from the ground. That one from the perspective of someone on the rock, looking up."

"I never finished the small one."

She looks up at him. "You do the real painting first, then mess it up?"

He smiles a little. He's had art teachers and collectors critique his work, but no one has ever said it was messed up. "The one you call messed up is the real one."

"I didn't mean it like that. Don't most people do a base then do the detail over top?"

"Depends on their vision I guess. This is just the way I do it."

She looks unsure.

He sighs. "When I get an idea, this is the way I see it, Claire. The underpainting is to help get the colours right."

"But what's underneath is the real story."

He laughs. "To you, maybe. It's only a piece of what I see."

"This is what you see?" She motions to the larger painting.

"I see what's actually there, in front of me. Then I see colours and feelings. Textures. They are all part of the painting I make in the end. I can't just do part of it, or it's not done."

"Like the one at your dad's."

"Yeah."

"I want to see things the way you do. The way this one is." She touches the painting. "I love it."

He thinks for a second. He wants her to get it. "I have an idea." He pulls her back into the room and uses a knife to cut open the biggest crate. He slides the painting out.

"Okay, now just look. Don't try to figure out what it is. Just look." He watches the emotions cross her face as she studies the painting. "Now tell me how it makes you feel."

"Cold. Lonely. What's that silver stuff? Tinfoil?"

"Silver leaf."

She meets his eyes. "This one makes me sad. It looks dead."

"It's Churchill. Hudson Bay." He points at the slashes of black and grey. "The lights of town, the grain elevator, a cargo ship."

They stare at each other.

"What's underneath?"

Jeff covers the painting back up. "It's the feeling that matters, Claire. That's the only thing you need to get."

He leans the paintings back against the wall. His back is to her. "Stay with me tonight."

The rain blows hard from the west as they run up the road to his place. She opens the door, but before she can enter, he grabs her and holds her. Thunder and lightning fill the air, and it's cooler. He pushes her through the door into the cabin. The screen door bangs shut behind them. In his room, he pulls off his wet shirt, and she lets him help her out of hers.

He hands her a T-shirt. "Pink Floyd." She laughs.

He flips off the light and presses her back onto the bed. A faint glow comes in through the window from the light near the road. The rain is loud on the roof.

Her voice is soft. "I wish there were some way to unpaint those pictures, so I could see what you see, what's important. Take nail polish remover, or turpentine and just clean and clean until I can see what's underneath."

"You're thinking of Churchill."

"Partly."

He's quiet for a long time. She tucks in against his side, her arm across his chest.

"Churchill was a mistake. It wasn't a good place for me. My mom's family had left. I was angry at them, at my mom and dad. I was stupid and I was cruel to people who tried to help."

"What people?"

"People I stayed with. A family that gave me a job."

"A girl."

"Yes. And her parents."

He hears her swallow. This can't be easy for her.

He tells Claire about Jodi, who made it easy to forget home and his father, with her drugs and booze and body. He tells Claire how his boss caught him, made sure Jeff left town on that floating railroad, evicted across the frozen tundra, exiled back to civilization.

Claire starts to tell him it's okay, that he was young, just a kid, but he cuts her off.

"Don't make excuses for me, okay? Nothing you can say can change anything. I've done so many shitty things. That wasn't even close to the worst."

He puts his hand over hers where it rests on his chest. No sense keeping secrets.

"After Churchill, I worked in Thompson for a bit, then I went down to Winnipeg. I finished high school at night, worked a lot. Painted. I met a woman named Marie and fell crazy in love with her." He stops. Claire lies as still as death against him. She needs to hear it all. He needs to tell it all. He talks about Marie getting pregnant. And, no he didn't leave her. He just made sure he was a big enough asshole that she left him.

"She ended up losing the baby." He turns his head away. "I was so damn relieved."

Claire props herself up on her elbow and he can feel her gaze on him.

"I'm not good at sticking around, Claire." His voice breaks. "But then, I guess you know that."

"Things are different now." She leans in and kisses him, and when he tries to say more, she kisses him harder. "All that's done. All of it."

He pushes her away. "I'm sure Shane's told you I've been arrested, thrown in the drunk tank. I was in a few pretty bad bar fights, too, and there were a couple instances of being in the wrong place at the wrong time." It's all out there, now. He wants her to know how awful he is.

In the other room, the wind bangs the screen door in its frame. Jeff's relieved to get away. He leaves her and goes to close the inner door.

When he turns, she's standing right behind him. He takes a step back, startled.

"Don't run away from me." Her fingers are cool against his arm. She reaches her hands up and holds his face. "You're good. You don't know how good you are." She kisses him.

He has never wanted anyone this much. The memory of their night in Vancouver, these weeks of being near her, touching her but never having her, have built up to this. He kisses her back, hard, pushing her into the small kitchen and up against the counter. As Claire reaches back to steady herself, a stack of dishes he left there this morning crashes into the sink. A glass shatters and before she can get her balance, she cuts her hand on the jagged shards.

He steps away from her. "All I do is hurt people."

He tries to look at her hand, but she pulls it away.

"I'm fine, Jeff. Stop worrying. I'm here." She holds her arms out to the sides. "This is right where I want to be."

EIGHT

 Long before dawn, we lie naked and silent on top of the twisted sheets in Jeff's little cabin. The heavy winds have blown the storms away. All that's left is the lake breeze blowing through the window, cooling us.

I remember how Jeff washed my hair that night in Vancouver, his fingers combing each curl, stroking my neck, my cheek. I think of him the day we cut wood, his teeth in my skin, his mouth sucking, branding me in a way that he knew would fade. There's always going to be this duality in him. With one hand, he'll hold me steady in a careful embrace. With the other, he'll push me, shove me farther into the untried and untouched – the unlived. It's in the way he brushes his thumb across my bottom lip, making me want to cry at his tenderness; it's how he presses me back against the wall, or into the bed, his fingers splayed between my collarbones or tangled in my hair.

If I'd just let go in Vancouver, like I did tonight, he would have held me up. I know he would have cared for all the broken bits of me. I understand, now, why he didn't tell me about Leah, or about what Shane and Daniel did. I don't agree with it, but I accept it.

My hand isn't bleeding any more, but it stings. By the light trickling through the window, I can see my blood on his skin, on the sheets. I think of those women long ago, the stains of their loss hung out for all to see the morning after the wedding. Proof of their purity.

This sheet would have a different story to tell, should I choose to hang it from the window. Blood and sweat. Tears – mine and his. This sheet, our sheet, a symbol of all that is created and held inside, now out in the open to be seen and smelled. Touched. Tasted. Lived.

If only the words we spoke, the stories we shared tonight, were visible, too. It would be an abstract painting only we would share, one we created together.

I shiver.

"Are you cold?"

I reach for the sheet to cover myself. He gets up and retrieves the quilt from where it slipped off the end of the bed. He spreads it over me.

I groan.

He slides in next to me and touches my face. "What is it?"

"I think I'm falling in love with you."

He's quiet for a second. "Just now?"

I don't know how to answer that. "No. Not just. And yes, now."

His mouth on mine feels warm. And right. If he keeps kissing me like this I am never going to leave.

"I should go, Jeff. I don't want Daniel to worry. I'll go home and check in. Then I'll grab some clothes and come back." I close my eyes and let his heat, his scent travel through me for a moment, then I get up.

He watches me dress. When I go to kiss him goodbye, he sits up and wraps his arms around me, rests his cheek against my stomach. I touch his hair.

"You need to grow it out again. I need something to hold on to when I kiss you."

He smiles as he reaches for his boxers. "Let me fix up your hand and then I'll drive you."

My brother is in bed when I get home. I peek into his room. In the light from the hall spilling across his bed, I can see the cot against the wall is empty. Finn sleeps next to his father, covers tight under his chin. Daniel sits up.

I keep my voice low. "I'm grabbing some stuff and heading back, okay?"

"Hang on."

I wait while Daniel, still in his jeans, eases out of the bed and pulls on a T-shirt. We meet in the hall. He closes the bedroom door behind him.

"How's Finn?"

"He's okay. He's probably been through worse with that psycho. I talked to Sherry's mom. She didn't bail Sherry out of jail. Finn will be staying here until I can challenge the custody arrangements through the courts."

"Good."

Daniel follows me into my room and watches while I gather clothes for tomorrow.

I favour my cut hand as I stuff everything I need into a bag. Jeff bandaged it up just before we drove over here, but it's starting to bleed through the gauze. For a second I'm not sure my legs will hold me as I think of him kneeling on the floor in front of me, probing the wound for glass, pulling the shards out with tweezers, then wrapping it up. I had to keep my head on my knees to keep from fainting.

"Claire, why him? Why not Shane?"

I turn to face my brother. I start laughing and can't stop. I sit down on the edge of the bed. "Shane? Are you serious?"

"Why are you laughing? He's not so bad."

"Oh my God, Daniel. You can't see what's so funny? Or is it just that Shane wasn't good enough for Leah, but he'll do for me?"

The look on his face makes me laugh harder.

Finally, he smiles. "I was wrong about Shane." He sits next to me.

"You're wrong about Jeff, too, Daniel. He found Finn. That has to count for something."

"Jeff's not good for you. Look at you. He comes around, you jump. He'll ditch you, I know he will. You'll fall apart. You're all or nothing with him, same as Leah was with Shane." He touches the bandage on my hand. "He's going to hurt you."

I stand and put my bag over my shoulder. "Isn't it all or nothing with Finn, Daniel? There's no sense loving someone halfway." I kiss him on the cheek and walk to the door. "No matter how it ends."

"Don't forget you came here because of him."

I shake my head. "Daniel, stop. I'm here because it all finally caught up to me. You and Shane and Finn have helped. But Jeff has, too. I'm glad he came. Jeff makes me feel better. Stronger." I am firm in this, and I want him to hear me. "Good night, Daniel."

I go back outside to the truck where Jeff waits, but it's empty. I throw my bag in the cab and go looking for him. He's out on Daniel's dock, his hands in his pockets, gazing out at the still lake. I walk out and stand next to him.

The water is as still and dark as ink. It reflects the starlit sky in a shimmering backdrop. The moon, a silver sliver in the west, lights the billowed storm clouds that move off to the east. Everything smells fresh, and the breeze is cool.

I slip my hand into his and lean my head against his arm. We stand like this for a long, long time.

In the distance, the plaintive call of a loon breaks the silence, and Jeff speaks, his voice breaking. "I love this place, but I can't stay here."

I feel a flutter of panic in my chest. I swallow hard and squeeze his hand. I know it has nothing to do with me.

Together we walk back to the truck. The sky brightens in the east; it's that time of day when everything glimmers in the morning-gloaming. Within the hour, the light will spread across the sky, gold from east to west, cloaking the frail moon. No one is around, not on the back road, not on the highway. As we leave the dark western sky behind, Jeff asks if I want to stop by the airport.

I don't, but I know he does. "Okay."

He pulls into the bus loop and turns off the truck. The loop hasn't been gravelled in years, and is slowly returning to hard-packed clay. Beyond, are the empty yards of our old neighbourhood. It's still too dark to see much detail, but I can just make out the rectangular patches on the ground where the nearest houses used to stand.

He shifts in his seat. "Coming home is hard for me. This is the longest I've stayed. It's too easy to be who I was way back then."

"You weren't so bad, Jeff."

"When I come back here, I feel like I am."

Hearing him talk like this, when I always thought he was so together, makes me sad. "You know what I always liked best about you? I liked that you never made me feel like a tagalong. You never had any doubt I could keep up. With you, I always felt like I could do anything."

He closes his eyes for a second, then pulls the key from the ignition. "Let's walk." He gets out and holds the door while I slide past the steering wheel.

We take our time as we make our way down the street. The road is pitted and cracked. In some places the asphalt has heaved, liberating the grass and weeds beneath. All that remains are driveways that go nowhere, cement footings for absent street lights and three fire hydrants.

The sun is over the horizon now. All the cool colours, the blues and greys and purples of the June dawn, are fired with warmer hues of yellow and orange. The sun touches the grass and spruce, still wet from last night's rain, and they glow as if they are brand new.

With every driveway we pass, the sorrow I feel intensifies. On every lot, only a tree remains, along with a slight depression in the ground where a house once rested.

We stop at the foot of Jeff's driveway. I can see my own driveway from here, and the dirt and weed-covered footprint of the duplex.

With no fence to divide the yards, it's easy to cross over to our old place.

"Once the houses were moved, all the basements were just filled in, right?" I ask.

"Probably."

"Then Leah's room is right here. Right underneath us." Finally, the sadness clawing its way from my chest to my throat steals my breath. My gasp comes out as a sob.

"It's okay, Claire."

I don't know if he's talking about Leah, himself or me crying, but I nod through my tears. He puts his arm around me and something eases inside me, and I can breathe. "It is. It is okay. Her room will always be here, no matter what."

We stand for a second, looking at the empty ground, then turn and walk back down the driveway. I look over at the Bug Man's place. It's still surrounded by trees, and the asphalt on the driveway is as pitted and wrecked as it was so long ago.

"It's strange that with everything that's been taken away, the Bug Man's place is the only thing that looks exactly the same as it did the day I met you."

"Yeah." Jeff takes a deep breath. "Do you want to go out to the rock? I'll go if you want to."

I feel the tension between my shoulder blades. "No." I'm done with thinking about what was. I'm tired, and it's still early. "I'd rather just go back to your place."

As we walk back to the truck, Jeff grips my arm and points to the south. A huge white balloon rises over the trees.

"It's the weather balloon, Claire. Remember?"

We stand and watch as the pale balloon rises up, up into the sky. We watch until it disappears, its whiteness disappearing into a sky-field of morning blue.

 Jeff wakes later that morning and starts the day's chores by mowing the lawns in front of the cabins while Claire sleeps. Daniel is out on the lake, guiding, so Finn follows Jeff wherever he goes.

Later, Finn sits and colours while Jeff sorts through some invoices in the office. Jeff watches him for a while and thinks about Colin and his mom. And coming here as a child. Watching Finn, he almost remembers.

The phone rings twice while he's in the office. The first time, the call is from Claire's mother. He chats with Petra briefly and assures her that Claire will call her back.

The second call is from Shane.

"Is Daniel around?"

"No, he's out on the lake."

"What about Claire?"

"She's sleeping." Jeff can't help it. "At my place."

Shane heaves a sigh. "I'm working until seven, then we're all going out for drinks at the Legion. It's kind of a going-away thing for me. Let them know."

Jeff hangs up.

"Auntie Claire is at your house, Jeff?"

Jeff looks over at the boy. "Yeah. She's tired, so she's resting."

"Sometimes my mom rests. She sleeps lots."

Jeff puts his hand on Finn's. "Finn, look at me."

Finn does.

"Your mom is sick. She's probably going to need to rest a lot. So you might not see her for a while."

Finn thinks for a moment. "Okay." He colours for a moment, then stops. "Is Auntie sick?"

"No, buddy, she's fine. In fact, why don't we go and wake her lazy bones up?"

But when they get up to his place, Claire is awake, sitting on the deck with a cup of tea.

Finn settles on her lap and kisses her.

"It's lunch time, Auntie."

"I'm coming, honey. I'm sure Rita's been waiting for me."

Jeff sits next to her. "She's got things under control. As usual. Your mom called again. I don't think you can put it off any more."

Claire waves him off. "I'll call."

"Today, Claire. Just get it over with."

"Every time I start to feel good about something, my mother has to get involved and ruin it."

"Claire, she can only get to you if you let her."

"This, coming from you? Give me a break."

"Yeah, coming from me. I'm kind of an expert. You choose how much you let in, and how much you let go."

"It's like what you said about your dad, Jeff. You go back to being the same scared child when you're around him. When I talk to my mom, it's clear I'm a poor replacement for my sister. And you know what? So is she. We both get frustrated and just end up arguing."

"Give it a chance, okay? All you have to do is call her and tell her you're all right. Five minutes."

"I will."

He hesitates. "I have to go into town for a bit."

She searches his face. "Do you want company?"

"I don't think so. Not this time." What he has to do is better done on his own.

"Okay. Finn and I, we'll hang out here."

He stands. "And Shane called."

"He did?"

"Yeah. Some kind of party for him at the Legion after his shift. He wanted me to tell you and Daniel."

"Okay. I'll tell Daniel. If your mom will keep Finn for a bit, I'll come in with him, then come back out with you."

"Sounds like a plan."

Claire kisses him. "Whatever you're going to town for, I hope it works out."

"Me, too."

Except for two police cruisers, the parking lot at the RCMP detachment is empty. Jeff is the only one in the waiting room. Jeff leans against the wall and watches Shane come toward him. They don't bother to shake hands.

"What can I do for you, Jeff?"

"I want to see Sherry. I know she's still here. Daniel said her mom didn't bail her out."

Shane shakes his head. "What do you want with her?"

Jeff just looks at him.

Shane repeats his question. "I'm not letting you in unless you tell me why you need to see her."

"I want to talk to her about Finn."

Shane laughs. "Good luck getting anything but the words *screw* and *you* out of her." He motions for Jeff to follow him through a locked access door. "You're no stranger to holding cells, are you, Jeff?"

Powerless. Jeff feels completely without power in the face of Shane's words. If he says anything, he'll probably get kicked out before he sees Sherry. If he does what he wants, he'll likely end up in the cell next to her. So he says and does nothing.

"Did you tell Claire yet about those arrests?"

Jeff bites back his reply as they turn down a hallway and pass through another door. It smells like a sewer. The holding cells are on his left. In each, a man watches him walk by. The same dead expression is on each of their faces.

"That's okay, Jeff. I told her the first day I knew you were back."

Didn't do much good though, did it?"

Jeff's surprised. Claire knew long before he told her.

Shane stops in front of Sherry's cell. She sits, back against the wall, on a thin mattress that covers a hard metal bed. Her hair is sweaty and her face is swollen and bruised where she hit the ground the day before.

"You're keeping her in the drunk tank? Jesus, Shane."

Shane has the grace to look ashamed. "The other cells are full. We'll move her once one of the other guys moves on." He opens the door and Jeff walks in. Jeff's shoulders tense as the door closes behind him. Sherry's eyes jump over to him, then away. Her head doesn't move.

He's seen his dad do the same thing. Has done it himself. She must have a hell of a headache.

"Hey, Sherry. Can I sit down?"

She closes her eyes and moves her hand, signalling a place beside her. He perches on the edge. Shane still leans against the bars. There's no point in asking for privacy.

"How are you?" Jeff asks her, his voice low.

"How's my baby?" Now she meets his eyes.

"Honestly, Sherry? He's pretty shaken up. You really scared him."

She brings her knees up and rests her head on them. "I fucked up."

"Yeah."

She sits with her head down for a long time. "You slumming it? Why the hell are you here? You here to tell me what a shitty mother I am?" Tears. He's not sure if they're real. His dad could play the pity card too.

"I want to talk to you about Finn, what's best for him."

"I'm what's best for him." It's a weak argument.

"Sherry, your mom isn't bailing you out. She's ceding custody to Daniel."

Now she really starts to cry.

"So their pet Indian is here to tell me how the whiteys are going to steal my kid, how growing up with his white daddy is going to be better for him?"

Jeff takes a deep breath. He sees her point. "They don't even know

I'm here. But I don't want to talk about Daniel or you or Claire or your mom. The custody stuff can go through the courts. This is about Finn." He glances over at Shane, wishes he would get lost. "I grew up with a drunk."

"I'm not a drunk."

Jeff laughs. "Yeah, my dad said that, too." Jeff lays it all out for her: the weekend alcohol binges that became nightly throw-downs between his parents, until his mom couldn't fight back any more; hiding under his covers as a small child, so his father wouldn't notice him when he was drunk, then walking on the thinnest of ice the next day to avoid a beating for playing with his cars too loud. Spending every moment he could outside, away from the house. The shrinking away from loud noises or any kind of conflict. Avoiding making friends or getting close to his teachers.

"I see it in Finn, Sherry."

She groans. "I'm sick."

He's been there. He's shaken to see it from the outside like this, but he doesn't let on.

"Oh, stop it, you're just drying out. Let Finn go."

"No."

"Get clean, Sherry. Then you will get him back. The courts want kids with their moms."

"Daniel's going to take him away."

"He's afraid you're going to steal him, Sherry. He's doing what my mom should have done for me. He's trying to keep him safe."

She shakes her head. "I don't want my son raised by white fuckers who will make him forget who he is."

"Right now, no matter how good your mom is with him, he's nothing more than the neglected son of a drunken Indian."

She slaps him hard, across the face. Jeff raises his hand to his cheek.

"That's it." Shane opens the door. "Out."

Jeff stands. "Sherry, Finn is always out with Daniel on the lake. He's camping and spending time outdoors. He's learning about his home. Where he comes from. My mom takes him for walks and tells him about her grandmother and how her people trapped and made everything themselves. I know, because she taught me. He has your mom, who teaches him Cree and your family's ways. He has so many people who love him. All he needs is a mother who is sober and he'll be complete. Let him be, Sherry, until you get better."

"You go back and tell Daniel it was a good try, sending you, but when I get out, I'm coming for Finn. He's mine." Sherry turns her face away.

Jeff stares down at her for a minute, then turns and pushes past Shane. He hears the cell door close behind him as he walks down the hall.

Shane follows him out of the building. "You had to try."

"It just makes me sick, all you guys plotting against her. Someone should have given her options." Jeff kicks at the ground. "I think it's bullshit, the way you and Daniel are in cahoots on this thing." He sends Shane a hard look. "She's right about you white bastards."

"Yeah, well, Finn will be safe, won't he?" Shane heaves a sigh. "Look, they're planning to drop the assault charge if she'll agree to go through rehab. Then it becomes a custodial issue. Jeff, even though she was pissed off, I think she was listening to you."

Jeff shrugs. "She won't stop drinking though."

Jeff is halfway to his truck when Shane calls out to him. "I'm getting off early. Want to go for a drink before the party?"

Jeff turns back. "Sure, why not?"

At the Legion, Jeff sips at a ginger ale as Shane downs three quick shots of Jack Daniels. The waitress brought them right away. Shane must be a regular here. He orders a beer when she comes by again, then turns back to Jeff. "You're a watcher, aren't you?"

"What do you mean?"

"You were always like that, quiet and keeping track of what everyone said or did."

"I guess." Jeff shifts, uncomfortable. "I suppose I had to be."

Other cops start to arrive for the party. Jeff has never felt more out of place.

"When do you leave?"

"Looking forward to getting rid of me, hey?" Shane laughs. Jeff's heard that kind of laugh so often, in so many bars. Bitter. "I start in Ottawa next Monday."

Jeff spins his glass on the table. "She's upset you're leaving."

"She's not going to stick around here, anyway. She's got a life to get back to." Shane tips his beer bottle back and drains it. "She's already chosen you, Jeff."

"Maybe she doesn't know you're interested."

"It's not that. She deserves better than me. Than you, too, for that matter."

"You're right."

If Shane's surprised to hear him say that, he doesn't show it. "You better be good to her, Jeff."

Jeff's been waiting for this. How can he promise anything? Anyway, he doesn't owe Shane any promises.

"I worked hard to keep her together. Don't go screwing her up." Shane leans in close. He reeks of booze. "What do you see, watcher?"

Jeff leans back.

"Right now? You're drunk."

"I mean Claire."

Jeff shrugs. "She's better."

"Yeah." Shane takes a long sip of beer. "What about me?"

"Jesus, Shane. I don't know. I'm not a psychic. Or a psychologist." Jeff sees Claire come through the door and he pushes his chair back. "I think you need to deal with this Leah stuff, Shane. It's messing you up. And I think you need to get used to me being around Claire."

Shane laughs. "Likewise, friend. She means the world to me."

Friend. Maybe. Someday.

NINE

I sit on the end of the dock and raise my feet out of the lake. I point my toes and watch the water trickle down toward my ankles.

The lake is calm in the early morning heat. Jeff is still asleep. Daniel and Finn aren't here yet. Colin and Rita sit on shore behind me. She brought me a cup of tea earlier, then retreated, leaving me to my thoughts.

I set my empty cup beside me on the dock. When I hear voices, I look behind me to see Jeff sitting in Colin's place beside his mom. Rita's hand is on his leg. I can't hear what she says, but there is an intensity to the way she leans in to him. Jeff's head is down as he listens to what she says. I don't want to interrupt, so I stay where I am.

I don't have too many mornings left here. I leave on Friday for Ottawa.

I called my mom before heading in to town for Shane's party yesterday. More upset than I've heard her in a long time, she almost begged me to come out east and see her. She'd been trying to get a hold of me since I arrived at the lake, but it seems Daniel's been screening the calls, worried that she might upset me more.

I pick at the bandage on my hand.

I'd wanted to tell Shane last night that I would be in Ottawa when he got there, but he was really drunk and one of the women from town held what little attention he had left. I'd asked him to dance with me. He looked at me for a long time before he said no.

Instead, Jeff pulled me out onto the worn wooden floor.

I'd never slow danced with him before last night. When I said this, he laughed and told me that he was always afraid to get too close to me, that everyone would know how he felt about me.

"And now?"

"As long as you know, who cares?"

I smile at the memory and glance back at the shore. Rita's gone so I walk back to where Jeff sits, alone now.

"Good morning. I wasn't sure if you wanted company."

"Always, if it's you." His eyes are red.

"Everything okay with your mom?"

"Yeah. It's the first time I've really talked to her since I came home." He rubs his eyes. "I told her everything."

I don't say anything.

"You were busy yesterday," he says.

I nod. While he was in town, Finn and I cleaned out the second room in Rita's old cabin. Colin came with the truck and moved the bed down to one of the storage rooms in the loft, then brought Jeff's easel, paints and blank canvases back to the cabin. Finn and I had fun setting up the room.

"Do you like it?"

He nods. "I guess I'd better get started on something, hey?"

"For sure." I look down at his shorts. "Can you swim in those?"

He grins. "I can swim in anything. Or nothing."

My bathing suit is on under my clothes, so I slip out of them. "Come on. Let's go in."

The water is still ice-cold.

"Best thing to do is run, then just dive in," he says.

And so we do.

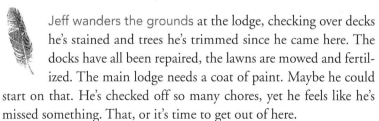

Jeff wanders the grounds at the lodge, checking over decks he's stained and trees he's trimmed since he came here. The docks have all been repaired, the lawns are mowed and fertilized. The main lodge needs a coat of paint. Maybe he could start on that. He's checked off so many chores, yet he feels like he's missed something. That, or it's time to get out of here.

Colin comes out of the lodge and asks for his help putting the big speedboat in the water. A family from Saskatchewan is here and wants a tour of the shoreline. Once Colin and the family are away, Jeff grabs the rake and starts to clean up the dead pine needles and leaves that have washed up on the beach.

Claire comes down with a rake, too, and the two of them work in silence. Jeff attaches the trailer to the quad, and together they clear the piles from the beach. Then they sit on the picnic table, content, until Daniel shows up.

Finn comes rocketing down to the beach, no sign of the tentativeness he's shown since Sherry took him. Daniel follows more slowly.

As usual, it's Jeff that Finn aims for, climbing up and hugging him. "Come on! Let's look for minnows! Please?"

"Sure." Jeff can't say no to the little boy. "Go grab the nets. I'll be right there."

Daniel and Jeff exchange a greeting. Daniel opens a lawn chair and takes a seat, while Finn runs to the shed.

"So, I got a hold of Mom, yesterday," Claire says.

A sheepish look creeps onto Daniel's face. "Oh. Yeah."

"Yeah, Daniel. You could have told me she was looking for me."

He shrugs. "I thought you had enough going on, you wouldn't want to worry about her."

"Daniel." Claire's voice is gentle. "You can't do this any more. You can't keep things from me."

Daniel meets Jeff's eyes, just for a second.

"I was going to tell you. I was just waiting for you to be a little stronger."

"Like talking about Leah? Or what happened with Kenny? Daniel, I have to deal with things on my own." Claire shakes her head. "She wants me to come visit her. I guess you already know that."

"I'm sorry, Claire. You're right. I should have told you."

"Have a little faith in me, Daniel."

Daniel glances at Jeff. "Does he need to be here?"

"Daniel."

"I'm sorry. Look, Claire." His voice shakes and he runs his hands through his hair. "Go see her. Take Finn with you. Get him out of here. This thing with Sherry is just going to get worse."

Jeff tenses. "You can't steal him, Daniel. It's no more legal for you to do it, than Sherry."

Daniel glares at him.

"He's right, Daniel. You need to follow proper channels."

"I'll work it out with Sherry's mom. I know she'll agree to Finn meeting his other grandma. Shane will talk to the judge about what happened. They have to see it's for the best. It won't be illegal."

Daniel has his hands clenched tight.

"Please, Claire. I can't always be worrying that Sherry's going to grab him. Just take Finn with you to Ottawa, then maybe home to Regina. Just until this thing with Sherry is settled."

"Daniel, I'm not sure. That could take months."

"Claire, imagine what that kid saw, living with an addict. I can't let him go back to that."

"You take him, Daniel."

"I can't leave Rita and Colin without a guide. They'll say they won't mind, but it's not fair. I'll come at the end of summer, when the tourist season is over."

"I don't know anything about taking care of a child."

Daniel puts his hand on her arm. "Claire, you'll be fine. And Grandma can help when you get home. Finn loves you. Please, I need you to do this for me. For Finn."

Jeff breaks in. "If you take Finn, it could count against you later on."

Daniel drops his hand and turns to him, defensive. "It's not *taking*, Jeff. He's my son. I'll go to court, I'll do it the right way, I just need him to be safe. I know Sherry, Claire. She won't leave this alone. She'll keep coming for him." He straightens up in his chair. "Jeff, maybe you can go and help Claire until I'm done."

"Stop. There you go, deciding for others again, Daniel."

As the argument between Daniel and Claire heats up, Jeff looks at Finn. He stands in the shallow water, minnow net in hand, and watches them. Jeff can see by his solemn face that this grown-up discussion has him worried.

Jeff puts up his hand. "Just slow down." He looks at Claire and takes a deep breath. "How about this? You and Finn go out east to see your mom. Daniel, you spend the next week or so showing me what you do as a guide, and I'll finish out the summer here. Then, when

Claire and Finn get back to Regina, you head down there. Once the issues with Sherry are resolved, you can come back."

Claire shakes her head. "This is not what we talked about doing."

"It's okay, Claire."

"You'd do that for me?" Daniel's voice breaks.

"I'd do it for Finn." Jeff hasn't taken his eyes off Claire. "But only if Sherry's mom says okay, and only if Claire agrees."

"We had a plan, Jeff," Claire says.

"Well, now we have a new plan."

Finn comes running up behind Daniel and grabs his legs. Daniel turns and touches his son's face.

"Come on, Finn. I'm going to help you find some minnows, and then we'll go for a swim." Daniel looks at Jeff. "I don't even know what to say. Thanks."

Jeff shrugs. "No problem." He watches Daniel and Finn walk away.

Claire hits him in the arm. "You hate it here, Jeff. You told me you had to get away. That you lose who you are."

"It's only a couple more months, Claire. I'll still come to Regina when the season's done. Probably not until fall, but I'll be there. If it keeps Finn safe, it's worth the wait, right?" His face is tight and grim. "I have a few things to work out with my father. This will give me the chance."

"How do I know you'll really come?"

For the first time in a long time, Jeff smiles without forcing it. "Because I said so, didn't I?"

LIFT

The morning I'm to leave for Ottawa, I wake to the touch of Jeff's fingers on my cheek. He sits on the edge of the bed, already dressed. The faint scent of linseed oil lingers in the air, and when I take his hand in mine, I see a smudge of red paint on the knuckle of his thumb.

He holds my gaze for a long moment. "Come on. Let's take the canoe out."

The lodge is silent – all the guests are still sleeping. There is no sign of Rita or Colin. It's just the two of us.

Soon we're paddling our way across the calm lake. I'm stronger now after weeks of activity. The cuts on my hand hurt at first, but the pain is soon numbed by movement of skin against wood.

We make good time out of the bay. The waves pick up a bit once we round the point to the west. We pass the caves, and then the inlet where Leah died. I don't point it out. Some things I need to keep to myself.

Jeff steers us to a small beach. A spit of rocky shore juts out to our right. Once the canoe is stowed, he leads me up a curving path under a canopy of frail aspen. The path turns into a dirt road that skirts a wide, empty clearing. It takes me a minute to orient myself and then it hits me. It's the site of the residential school that Jeff brought me to the very first day we spent together. The graffiti-covered building is gone. No more broken windows or doors ripped from their frames. I remember the mess inside: trash on the floor, stained carpet, broken wallboard. And the stench of urine and rot. It's all gone and in its place is a huge field of grass, waving in the quiet breeze. I had no idea it was this close to the lake.

After a long time, Jeff speaks. "Sometimes change isn't a bad thing."

Later, back down where we stowed the canoe, I sit on one of

the rocks and watch Jeff throw stones into the water. Every single time, he hits the exact line where clear turns azure. The wind is not strong, but somehow the gentle waves are forced onto the tombstone slabs of dolomite in such a way that droplets of water are flung high into the sky, where the sun catches them in a prismatic shower of crystal rainbows.

I close my eyes and tilt my face so that the spray freckles my cheeks. When I open my eyes, Jeff crouches beside me. I reach out and he places a smooth, white rock on my palm. It's blank. He closes my fingers around it and kisses them.

Jeff drives us to the airport in my car so we can all go together. In the back seat, Finn chatters with excitement. He's never been on an airplane and he spends the ride asking Daniel question after question.

"How does the airplane stay up in the air?"

In a low voice, Daniel tries to explain the concept of aerodynamics to him. "Well, see there are these forces, that when they combine in the perfect amounts, they make the plane stay up."

Jeff glances over at me.

I shake my head. "Stick to music, Daniel. Science isn't your strong suit." I turn my face to the window. There's not a whisper of wind in the trees that line the highway. When we left the lodge, the sun came out and ignited the lake, making it glow its deepest blue. We won't catch another glimpse of it before we get to the airport. The spruce and tamarack are too thick.

"Well, you explain it to him, then."

My laugh is quick. "I will, on the plane."

Finn's quiet a moment, then he pipes in. "So, it's magic."

"Yeah," Daniel says. "It's magic."

I start to explain to Finn that it's not magic at all, but definable scientific fact, when Jeff gives me a look.

"It's magic, Claire."

I roll my eyes, still smiling.

Jeff turns at the airport sign. I watch him, but he doesn't look toward the old neighbourhood either. He continues around the bend to the tiny terminal building and parks in the last empty spot out front.

Daniel helps Finn from the back seat.

Jeff squeezes my hand before I get out. "It's going to be okay, Claire."

I focus on Finn's excitement as Daniel talks to the agent at the desk. We check our bags right through to Ottawa, though there will be a layover in Winnipeg.

There is no security line like in the city. The plane sits on the tarmac outside the far window. The big airlines don't fly here any more, only small jets and prop planes. Medevacs. Water bombers.

I hug Daniel. "I'll take care of Finn. I'll make sure Mom spoils him."

"Thanks, Claire." He kisses my cheek. "This means a lot."

"It means you'll be mowing my lawn and making my dinner every day when you get to Regina. I plan on making this work for me." I hug him even tighter, and whisper in his ear. "Be nice. It's Jeff you owe."

"I know."

The desk agent announces the flight to Winnipeg. Finn jumps up from his seat, and Daniel crouches down to hug him. I turn to Jeff and watch him watching Finn.

He catches me looking and holds out an arm. "Come here." Those words from him, always followed by something good – a new path to explore, a kiss.

I step into his embrace and feel that elusive easing of the tightness I carry with me. "I stole one of your T-shirts."

"I know. Joy Division." He tightens his arms around me.

"No, I mean I stole another one." His laugh is warm against my ear.

"It's okay, I left you one of mine."

"That'll look good with a pair of jeans." His face grows serious. "Is Shane going to meet you at the airport?"

I know it's not easy for him to ask about Shane. "No. My mom will be there."

"Are you going to see him?"

I take his face in my hands and kiss him.

They announce the flight again. Jeff kisses me back. I don't want to let go.

"Come on, Auntie. We have places to go." Finn's voice carries, and Daniel laughs, a little too loud.

I step away from Jeff and take Finn by the hand. We turn and wave before we head outside to board the plane. The two men stand apart, Jeff a little in front of Daniel, hands in his pockets. As I watch, Daniel steps up and says something to Jeff. Jeff breaks into an easy smile, and the tangle of emotions in my chest eases a little bit.

On the plane, I give Finn the window seat and buckle him in. While we listen to the flight attendant's spiel, Finn studies the pictures on the safety card, and twists his head around to see if he can find the nearest emergency exit. It's in the row behind us, and he's thrilled when he sees he's figured it out.

We take off to the north, toward the lake. The acceleration of the plane forces me back into my seat. It feels much the same as the heaviness I lived with for so long.

I watch the terminal fly by the window, then the tattered orange windsock that points back the way we came. The weight against me shifts as the plane catches air, and I feel my blood, that bit of life in every cell in my body, pull toward earth.

I lean over Finn to see if I can see the rock where Jeff and I used to hang out, but we're moving too fast, and I can't focus in time. *Allegiance,* I think. *Voler.*

The plane reaches the point where the pull of gravity eases. I feel light with release. We soar over and under the two wide expanses of layered blue that have always held such power over me.

Magic.

We bank right, then another hard right, and we're flying south, back over the water.

"Look, Finn, it's the lodge. You can see the flagpole."

Finn presses his face to the window.

"It's so small, Auntie. It's big up close but from here, it's tiny." He looks at me in wonder.

Finn's right. It's all so small. And so big.

The lake below disappears into endless forest.

I turn away from the view outside the plane and look down at Finn. I take his hand. It's soft and small and brown, and when I close my fingers around its damp warmth, it fits perfectly inside my own.

Acknowledgements

First, last, and always: Trevor Nicol, whose love, support and endless repertoire of homemade soups sustained our family through the craziest of days these past few years. A simple "thank you" will never be enough.

Caelan and Delaney, you are my inspiration. Thank you for sharing me with fictional characters that you're still too young to meet. Rick and Wendy McCullough who supported me in pursuit of this dream. Dustin McCullough and Kelley Rumpel provided the years of sibling rivalry and love that I needed to drive this book forward.

I am forever indebted to my Calgary writing group – Heidi Grogan, reader extraordinaire, knows Claire and Jeff as well as, if not better than, I do. Melanie Bergman kept me grounded and on track. Hal Soby provided a much-needed male perspective.

Up north, Jennifer Dunham was my tireless researcher of facts and locations around The Pas and Clearwater Lake. Without her help, I would have walked the desolate roads of the deserted airport on my own. Kathy and Doug Sangster of Carpenters' Clearwater Lodge provided accommodation and guided fishing trips, answered questions and shared stories.

Clearwater, in its various forms, saw a few summers at the Fernie Writers' Conference. Angie Abdou advised me while I wrote the first draft, and her faith in my work gave me the confidence to carry on to completion. Steven Heighton's encouragement from the start made all the difference. Peter Oliva challenged me to find the obsessions in my work, and to write bravely about the hard stuff.

Thank you to my FWC classmates, especially Carolyn Nikodym, who read an early draft of the novel, and Susan M. Toy, for convincing me to send it out. Jennifer Ellis could be counted on for thoughtful feedback. Mark Kusnir's wonderful wit paled in comparison to his ability to weed out weakness.

To the generous writers who offered advice, easing my journey to publication: Joseph Boyden, Maggie de Vries, Darcie Friesen Hossack, Andrew Gray, Betty Jane Hegerat, Billie Livingston and Katherena Vermette – thank you.

Thank you to Nik Burton at Coteau Books for his boundless patience, wisdom and support. The whole Coteau team has been a pleasure to work with.

And finally, I am grateful to Kathryn Cole, my editor, who worked so hard first to refine the story, then to polish the words.

Thank you all. None of this would be possible without you.

About the Author

Kim McCullough has published reviews and commentary on a number of literary websites. *Clearwater* is her first published book. She is currently working towards her MFA in creative writing at UBC. Originally from Regina, Kim now teaches in Calgary where she leads various writing workshops for students of all ages, including a writing class for women in recovery.